PRAIS]
ELMW

"A dark and compelling mystery, N.T. Morris is an exciting new voice in horror."

DAVID SODERGREN
AUTHOR OF FORGOTTEN ISLAND & MAGGIE'S GRAVE.

"Elmwood is the perfect read for the spooky season, transporting readers to an idyllic small town harbouring some deadly secrets. N.T. Morris cleverly ratchets up the tension, sprinkling clues throughout the story that allow readers to experience the mystery as it unfolds. A blood-soaked tale you won't be able to put down."

PATRICK DELANEY
AUTHOR OF THE HOUSE THAT FELL FROM THE SKY.

"I was hooked from the moment I started reading. Every time I thought I knew what was coming I was wrong… way wrong. So fun and exciting, I'm going to read it again to pick up the things I missed. Highly recommended. Easily top ten of the year."

MIKE SALT
AUTHOR OF THE VALLEY & THE HOUSE ON HARLAN.

ELMWOOD

N. T. MORRIS

Copyright © 2021 N. T. MORRIS

All rights reserved. The use of any part of this publication
reproduced, transmitted in any form or by any means, electronic,
mechanical, photocopying, recording or otherwise, without prior
written consent of the author, constitutes an infringement of the
copyright law.

All characters and events are fictional and any resemblance to real
people or places is coincidental.

ISBN: 978-1-7399622-0-3

For my wife Orla and our son Finn.
Here's to forever.

CHAPTER ONE

Aidan's foot crushed the brake pedal. Tyres squealed as the black Audi skidded down the wet, dark road. He squeezed his eyes shut, shooting forward in his seat. Before his head struck the windscreen, the seatbelt caught him, yanking him back as the car came to a sudden stop. Blood pounded in his ears as adrenaline coursed through his body. It felt like there were a million tiny ants crawling all over his skin. He loosened his white-knuckled grip on the steering wheel and opened his eyes. Everything was blurry at first, but after each startled blink, the world in front of him became clear again. Rain hammered on the roof of the car like a drum roll on a snare. The window wipers were working overtime, moving back and forth in a hypnotic, rhythmic dance with the rain. Without looking, Aidan turned them off and let the rain blur the thing that had almost caused him to swerve off the road. He rubbed at his temples with trembling hands, trying to ease the beginnings of a migraine. His eyes were like two full moons, unable to look away from the thing in the road.

Fuck.

The headlights of the car illuminated something yellow, lying still on the road. It was a beacon of colour in a sea of darkness. There were no streetlights along the old windy roads that lead to Fallbridge City. They were narrow and pothole-ridden, and Aidan hated driving down them, especially at night. But after hearing of the long delays on the motorway, he'd thought he would take his chances. *I should have just sat in traffic*, he told himself.

The pounding of his heart almost drowned out the sound of the rain as he tried to figure out what to do.

Ring! Ring!

Aidan almost jumped out of his skin. *It's just your phone, calm down.* He pulled it out of his pocket. Laura. Probably wondering where he was and what was taking him so long. He sent the call to voicemail, relieved that his wife wasn't here with him as he looked out again at the yellow, rain-blurred thing in the road. *I really don't want to do this*, Aidan thought as he unbuckled his seatbelt and turned on the torch on his phone.

He placed his hand on the door handle, took a deep breath, and pushed the door open.

The pounding rain outside sounded like white noise from an old television. Aidan stepped out of the car and into the blackness of the road. It was darker outside the car than he could've ever imagined. It surrounded him in every direction. Engulfing him. Only the car headlights and the weak torch beam on his phone provided any light. He grimaced, cupping his free hand over his face to shelter himself from the persistent rain. It didn't do much good. Within a couple of seconds, Aidan had soaked to the bone. Wind whistled through the trees swaying on both sides of the road.

He couldn't take his eyes off the yellow thing.

A part of him had known what it was from the beginning, but another – the scared, in-shock part – hadn't wanted to believe it. There was no denying it now. It was a person, lying face down in the middle of the road. The hood of a bright yellow raincoat pulled up over their head.

They weren't moving.

"Hello?" Aidan called, the hiss of the rain drowning out his voice. He took an uneasy step forward, then another, leaving the car door open behind him. He stopped at the front of the car. His feet felt like breeze blocks. *Get back in the car and drive home. This isn't your problem; let the next person who drives by handle it. Just get in your car and go home to Laura.* Aidan shook the thought from his head. There hadn't been another car on this road since he turned onto it half an hour ago, and as badly as he wanted to leave, he just couldn't.

He glanced at the body in the yellow raincoat. The statue-like stillness of it made him think he was already too late.

Finally he got his heavy feet working again, slowly forcing himself forwards.

"Hey, are you okay?" he called out. There was no reply, no movement, only the sound of the rain and the low rumble of the car engine behind him. He shone his torch beam across the raincoat as he approached. From what he could tell, the motionless figure wasn't very tall; maybe five-three or five-four. They were wearing a pair of black converse, covered in thick mud, and a pair of black skinny jeans – equally dirty. The yellow raincoat was clean. Whatever dirt might have covered it was now long washed away.

Aidan grimaced at the unnatural shape of the body's legs and kneeled down beside them. *Someone must have hit them with their car,* he thought. *Hit and run.* Reaching out with a trembling, soaked hand, Aidan gently shook the person. He snapped his hand back as if he had touched something scolding hot. Their body was stiff as a board.

Shit.

Aidan wiped the rain from his eyes. He reached out and gently lifted the top of the hood with two fingers, pulling it back.

Panic shot through his entire body like a lightning bolt.

Aidan jumped backwards. His phone skidded across the tarmac as he scrambled over the soaking road. His back hit the front of the car. "Holy shit. Holy shit. Holy shit."

The car's headlights burned on the body like a spotlight. Aidan clasped his mouth with both hands. He couldn't look away. Not knowing why, and unable to stop himself, he crawled on his hands and knees towards the body, picking up his phone on the way. He shone the torch on the body as he reached out his hand and grabbed the hood again.

What are you doing? Get in your car and get the fuck out of here. This is no hit and run.

With one quick jerk, he pulled the hood the rest of the way down.

There was no head. Dark, soggy flesh hung from the remains of the neck. Quickly, Aidan looked away and threw up the remnants of his dinner. He didn't want to see it again, but he couldn't stop himself from looking back. Something caught his eye. He wiped the vomit from his mouth and shone the light a couple of yards past the body.

He saw it.

His heart pounded in his chest like a trapped dog trying to get out of its cage. It was as if he had no control over his body anymore. He didn't want to move anywhere, but his arms and legs had other plans and they dragged him forward; he was crawling past the body towards the head.

"No, no, no, no," he moaned, trying to will himself to stop. He tried to squeeze his eyes shut, but it was useless. It was like they were glued open, forcing him to see the horror in front of him. Burning the image into his memory forever.

Dark hair clung to a pale, blue face, like washed-up seaweed on a beach. Her mouth hung slack-jawed and her eyes were open just a crack. There was something carved into her forehead: a symbol of some kind.

Seeing her face made the pit of Aidan's stomach twist up.

She was facing away from the road, towards the black abyss of the forest. From what Aidan could tell, she looked to be in her mid-twenties. There was some bruising on the side of her cheek, visible even in the dull light. He reached out, gingerly, brushing clumps of hair away from her face.

Her grey eyes shot open and looked lifelessly up at him. All the air in Aidan's lungs left in an instant.

Dark blood gargled and sputtered from her lips. Aidan's heart was in his throat; he stared at the girl's head in wide-eyed terror. Her discoloured lips wavered. She was trying to say something, but her voice was lost to the hiss of the pounding rain. Every part of Aidan screamed at him as he edged in closer. *No! What are you doing?* he thought, unable to stop himself.

Short, raspy gasps escaped the woman's trembling lips. The smell of rot almost made him gag as he lowered his ear to her mouth.

"Wake up!" she shrieked.

CHAPTER TWO

Laura sat curled up at the edge of the sofa, wearing her comfy sweats and a t-shirt of Aidan's that was at least three sizes too big, browsing the internet in the living room of their one-bedroom apartment in Fallbridge City. A half-finished tub of ice cream slowly melted on the coffee table beside a cold mug of tea. The blue glow of the laptop illuminated her face, reflecting off her glasses as she twiddled the strands of hair sticking out from her messy bun.

It was late in the evening, and Aidan was asleep at the other end of the sofa. Rain drizzled lightly on the window, blending with the sounds of the TV. Max, their golden cocker spaniel, lay sprawled out on the rug, excessively licking at his paws.

Laura looked up from her laptop as she heard a quiet moaning from the other end of the sofa. Aidan's black, sweat-soaked hair stuck to his forehead as he fidgeted in his sleep. Laura sighed. *He's getting worse,* she thought. Ever since he'd found that girl he hadn't been the same; he didn't sleep much anymore. He didn't *want* to sleep. Pacing up and down the apartment all night, drinking excessive amounts of coffee, and going down another rabbit hole on YouTube were just some things he'd do to keep himself awake. And when he finally succumbed to the fine grains of the Sandman, the nightmares would start.

In the two weeks since the accident, he had retreated into himself. He'd become a shell of the man Laura loved, and it killed her to see him like that. She wished she'd been with him that night, so that at least she could understand what he was going through. But he never spoke to her about it; any time she tried to bring it up, he would change the conversation.

The groaning grew louder. It sounded like he was trying to say something, but Laura couldn't make it out. It even startled Max, who jumped up from the rug and started licking the sweat-stained t-shirt that clung to Aidan's body. Laura closed the laptop, set it on the coffee table, and leaned over the sofa.

"Wake up, honey, it's just a bad dream," she said, gently shaking Aidan's chest. His head was clammy with a fever and his breathing was sharp. Worried, she shook him a little harder. "Wake up," she said, louder.

Aidan's eyes burst open. He bolted up on the sofa, trying to catch his breath. The sudden movement sent Max darting into the kitchen at record speed. Aidan's eyes danced around the living room as his brain caught up with his body. His heart pounded in his chest as the nightmare dissolved around him.

"Where is she, where…"

"It was just a nightmare," Laura said, rubbing his arm. "Everything's okay."

Aidan rubbed at his bloodshot eyes as he tried to get control of his breathing. "I'm okay, I'm okay," Aidan said, more to himself than to Laura. His voice was raspy, and he seemed surprised to hear it.

"They're getting worse, Aidan."

"It's fine, don't worry."

Laura sighed, leaned in and kissed his head. "Okay."

"I'm soaked," Aidan said, plucking the wet, cold t-shirt off his skin. He pulled it off and tossed it onto the floor. Max, seeing an opportunity, charged in and dived at the sweaty rag, licking and gnawing it to death. They sat in silence for a moment, watching the spaniel toss his head left and right. The TV caught Aidan's attention.

"...*have discovered the body of another woman on the outskirts of Fallbridge this evening,*" the reporter was saying. "*This, only weeks after a local man found the body of twenty-six-year-old, Emily Pembrook. Police have not yet identified the woman found today; however, it's believed that both cases could be linked. Fallbridge Police have begun to investigate...*"

The TV screen went black. Aidan threw the remote onto the coffee table.

"My God," Laura said, shaking her head. "This city is getting worse."

"I'm going to grab a quick shower." Aidan said, changing the subject. He leaned over and kissed her.

"Everything will be okay."

Aidan gave her a half-smile and headed down the hallway to the bathroom.

When he was inside, he locked the door, turned on the shower, and cried.

He cried so hard he didn't know if he could stop. The last time he had cried like this was when his mother had died. He had only been twelve years old. It was Laura who'd gotten him through that period in his life. They were best friends throughout childhood and it was the time they spent together that brought them closer – then eventually, when they got older, brought them together.

But something was different now. He didn't feel like the same person anymore. The demons inside of him had grabbed hold and weren't letting go. They were trying to drag him down into the pits of himself, and he would not let Laura be dragged down with him.

Finally, the tears stopped. Aidan got out of the shower, dried himself off, and opened up the medicine cabinet. Popping two diazepam and a citalopram into his hand, he tossed the pills into his mouth and washed them down with a mouthful of tap water.

He stared into the mirror for a long time, but he didn't recognise the face of the man staring back at him. He looked like he'd aged a couple of years in the space of a couple of weeks. His eyes had sunken into their sockets and dark purple bags had formed underneath. Even his hair had lost some of its colour and begun to turn grey. In his head, he knew what he had to do. Start eating healthy, start exercising again – hell, even getting a full night's sleep would be a good start – but he couldn't. The emptiness inside him wouldn't allow it, and now all Aidan wanted was to fade away. The only thing stopping him was Laura. She was the one thing he still wanted, still needed in his life. She was the only shining light left in it.

Aidan moved back to the living room. Laura was on the sofa on her laptop with Max curled up, asleep beside her. There was a half-full glass of red wine on the coffee table and a second, full glass beside it.

"I thought you'd like a glass – maybe help you sleep tonight," Laura said.

"Thanks, honey."

Aidan picked up the glass of wine and sunk into the sofa. Lazily, Max lifted his head to see who'd disturbed his nap, huffed a fed-up sigh, and went back to sleep.

"I've been thinking," Laura said, moving the laptop to one side. "I think we should get out of the city for a while. Go somewhere far away from everything."

Aidan took a sip of wine and said nothing.

"I think it would do you good to have a change of scenery. Some fresh air." Laura watched Aidan intently. He just nodded slowly, looking down at the floor.

"How long were you thinking?" Aidan said finally.

"I don't know… a month or two, maybe. We have enough saved up to pay for it, and I think it would do you good to get away from here for a while. Clear your head."

"What about work?"

"What about it? The slow season's coming in. We have nothing booked until mid-December. I checked." Laura was getting excited now, Aidan could hear it in her voice. And she was right; the reason they'd started their own photography business was so they could have the freedom to work and travel wherever – and whenever – they wanted. Over the years, the travelling had become less frequent, and the workload higher.

Aidan looked at his wife; she had a sparkle in her eye that he hadn't seen in a while. She needed this just as much as he did. He thought back to their year travelling around Australia; it had been the best year of his life. It was in Sydney that Aidan had gotten down on one knee and popped the question. A warm feeling crept up inside Aidan, something that felt alien to him. The warmth surprised him, caught him off guard. He missed feeling like that.

"Sure," Aidan said. A smile stretched across his face.

"What… really?" Laura said, shocked. She had expected more resistance.

He nodded and took a drink. Laura reached out and wrapped her arms tightly around him, nearly knocking the wine glass out of his hand. "I found somewhere," she said, setting the laptop between them and scooching closer to Aidan. "It's this little picturesque town, Elmwood. It's right by the ocean, surrounded by a mountain, and forests… It's only a six or seven-hour drive from here. I even found the perfect place to stay."

Laura opened a webpage she'd saved. The screen flickered with a photograph of a massive, Victorian-style three-storey house. The redbrick building had a large chimney and lots of windows with black wooden shutters on either side and a large ornate porch.

"It's called the Lake House. It's surrounded by the forest and has its own private little lake," she laughed. "I guess the name gave that away – look, there's even a little wooden boat we can use. How cute is that?" Laura quickly flicked through the photos, but Aidan wasn't looking at them. He was looking at his wife; he hadn't seen her this happy in some time.

Things between them hadn't been great since the accident. Aidan knew he had been hard to deal with lately, and it was straining their marriage. The trip would be good for the both of them; give them a chance to reconnect, a chance to put the accident behind them and finally move on with their lives.

"It sounds perfect, honey," Aidan said, laying his hand on hers and stopping her mid scroll. "When do we leave?"

CHAPTER THREE

Aidan felt like they'd been driving for an eternity; in reality, they had been on the road for a little over four hours. Still, the tall skyscrapers, pollution and mayhem of Fallbridge were long behind them.

Since the accident, reporters had been harassing Aidan, trying to get any story they could out of him. He couldn't even go to the shop for milk and bread without being hassled. News of the possibility of a serial killer had begun to circulate after the second body was found, and the people in Fallbridge were on edge.

Now, surrounded by the tallest pine trees Aidan had ever seen, he could feel the stress of the city melt away. The air felt cleaner; the sky was a brilliant blue without a single intruding cloud. He glanced over at his wife, who had taken over the wheel an hour ago, and smiled. Her long, brown hair blew gently as the wind came in through the open window in the back. Max's head was out the window, and he sniffed at the forest air and barked at the occasional deer. Aidan glanced over at Laura, feeling lucky to have such an amazing woman to spend the rest of his life with. She was right, of course she was. He needed this time away, time off from his normal life to recharge and get himself into a good headspace again. Time for a reset and for them to reconnect. Their marriage wasn't perfect, despite what their Facebook accounts might suggest.

Since the start of the year, they had been trying to start a family. It was something they'd both wanted for as long as they could remember. They'd talked about it for years and finally decided that this year would be the one. Laura had just turned thirty-five and didn't want to wait any longer to become a mother.

They tried for months with no luck – until April, when everything changed.

The tests came back positive. Aidan and Laura were ecstatic. For the next four months, they felt that their dream was finally coming true. Laura began searching for houses around the Fallbridge area. They would outgrow their one-bedroom apartment in no time and needed to find somewhere more suitable for a new family of three. Meanwhile, Aidan read every baby book for expectant parents that he could get his hands on. Those four months were the happiest of their lives.

And then came the morning of August 15th. That was the worst day of their lives; that was the day the blood came.

***

Aidan grabbed his backpack from between his feet, unzipped it and pulled out his pill bottles. He popped the lids and tipped two of each into his hand.

"Shit." He rattled the pill bottles in front of his eyes.

"What's wrong?" Laura asked without taking her eyes off the road.

"I've only got a few left."

"Why didn't you order more?"

"I thought I had enough. I'll get some when we arrive. I've

got enough to get me through the next couple of days," Aidan said, throwing the pills into his mouth. He grimaced as he washed them down with the last dregs of a bottle of water. "This break will be good for us... after everything, you know..." Aidan crushed the bottle in his hand and dropped it to his feet.

"I know... I know. Everything just piled up – the accident, the sleepless nights, the news reporters, the... the baby. I need a break from it all too. I need the fresh air, the peace and quiet... I want to move forward and I want you to move forward with me. I know how much the accident has affected you – maybe it's everything hitting you all at once, I don't know – but I'm worried about you, Aidan."

Aidan was all too aware. That was why he hadn't told her how bad it truly was. He couldn't close his eyes at night without seeing the woman in the yellow raincoat. Her discoloured face was engraved into his mind. The events of that night replayed over and over in his head like a movie on a loop. He'd even seen her lifeless body lying in his living room one day – and this time he wasn't asleep, he was hallucinating. There was no way he was going to tell Laura about that one. If she knew everything he had seen and felt, she'd have him sanctioned. He had been slipping into the darkness of his mind ever since they lost the baby. But Emily Pembrook was the catalyst that had thrown him headfirst into the abyss.

Aidan had been there before, when his mother had died. It had almost swallowed him whole back then, and he told himself he would never end up in that place again. But here he was, neck-deep in the worst part of his mind, and again Laura was there by his side, trying to keep his head above water.

"I know you are, honey. Don't worry, I'll be fine and we'll get through this," Aidan leaned across and kissed her on the cheek. "I love you."

"I love you too." She changed the subject: "By the way, did you remember to call Will before we left?"

"Yeah, I remembered." Aidan rolled his eyes.

"Did you tell him where we were going?"

Aidan stared at her wide eyed. "Ha! Do you think I'm crazy?"

Laura smiled.

"If I told my brother where we were going, you know as well as I do he'd show up at the front door in a week's time." They both laughed. Laura squeezed her lips together to stop herself. "What? You know it's true." Aidan grinned. "I wouldn't put it past him if he hacked into our emails just to find out where we went."

"I know," she sighed. "I feel bad, though... he's just looking out for you."

"I know he is, and I appreciate it, but he needs to give us some space."

Max started barking and stuck his head between the front seats.

"I guess someone needs to pee," Aidan said, scratching at Max's long, curly-haired ears.

"I wouldn't mind going either," Laura said, then laughed. There was a service station up ahead; the first one they had seen for quite some time.

"Pull in here," Aidan said. "We can grab some snacks, and it beats you peeing against a tree."

Laura cruised slowly off the road. The service station was tiny; an old, rundown place that looked like it had come straight out of the 1950s. It only had one pump, and the store was small and looked abandoned. A flashing, neon *Open* sign – with only the '*O*' still working – buzzed from the store's only window. The only sign of life.

"I think I'd prefer a tree," Laura said, looking out at the

store. Aidan laughed as he got out of the Audi, holding the door open for Max to jump out and do his business. They walked around the side of the store to a small grassy area. Max sniffed the ground frantically, taking in all the unfamiliar scents as Laura headed towards the shop. "You want anything?"

"Sure, grab a couple of waters and some chocolate? Please."

Aidan watched until Laura was inside the shop. He reached into his jacket pocket and pulled out a box of cigarettes, slid one between his lips, and sparked the lighter behind his cupped hands. Laura hated when Aidan smoked. He told her he was trying to quit – which he was – but they helped him relax, which was a hard thing for him to do lately. He took a deep drag, watching as Max finally settled on a spot to take a piss. Turning, Aidan stared out onto the empty road they had been driving down for the last couple of hours. They had only passed two or three cars in that time, but now the road was totally empty.

We really are headed to the middle of nowhere.

***

Laura finished up in the bathroom and hurried out. It was as bad as she'd imagined. The tiny stall stunk of weed, and the floors looked like they hadn't been mopped in quite some time. She walked over to a grease-stained glass refrigerator and lifted out two bottles of water. Fluorescent lights buzzed above her head as she scanned the aisles for snacks. Most of the shelves were empty, as if panic buyers had ravaged them, preparing for some apocalyptic event. She picked up the last packet of Doritos and checked the date. *Still good. That's a plus, I guess.* She tucked the packet under her arm, took two chocolate bars, and headed towards the cashier.

The man behind the counter was leaning back on an old, beat-up garden chair, his legs up on a battered mini-fridge, watching a football game on a square bulky television model that Laura hadn't seen since the nineties. He must have been in his late fifties. The buttons on his food-stained shirt strained under the pressure of a bulging stomach.

"Fuck!" he yelled, slamming his fists on the counter, still glued to the TV.

Laura set the drinks and snacks onto the counter with a purposeful *thump*.

"Jesus Christ, you scared the piss outta me. I didn't hear you come in," the cashier laughed, jumping up out of his seat and brushing the food crumbs off his shirt to the floor. "Sorry about that," he said, slightly out of breath.

"It's fine," Laura laughed. "I'm not easily offended."

"That's what I like to hear. Too many folks these days can't wipe their arses without being offended." The man started scanning the items. "We don't get many stopping here. You're the first person I've seen all day and you'll probably be the last," he chuckled. "What brings a pretty little thing like you out these parts? There isn't much out this way besides the woods."

"My husband and I are going on vacation."

"Husband, huh, where's he at?" the cashier said, looking around the empty store.

"Oh, he's outside in the car."

"Right, right," he nodded. "Where are you going on vacation?"

"We're heading to Elmwood. We came from Fallbridge – we wanted to get away from the hustle and bustle and surround ourselves with nature for a while."

"Uh-huh. Elmwood's a beautiful town. Used to go there a lot as a kid. Beautiful, just beautiful! You say you folks came from Fallbridge?"

"Yeah."

The cashier leaned in closer to Laura, as if he was going to tell her a secret. The smell of weed and body odour radiated off him. *Jesus, I could get high just standing next to this guy.* Laura stepped back, almost unknowingly, but the man didn't notice.

"I heard on the news about those killings up in Fallbridge. Just terrible," he whispered, looking around the empty shop like he was expecting to see someone.

"Yeah, it's horrible."

The cashier leaned back and stared cautiously at Laura. She could almost hear the rusty cogs turning in his head. "You ain't one of those killers, are ya – you and your husband? On the run from the big smoke to the middle of nowhere. We don't want people like you here."

"Wh… wait… what?" Laura said, stunned.

The cashier roared; a deep, booming laugh straight from his gut.

Laura stood frozen, not knowing what to do besides let out a pitiful, awkward laugh of her own.

"I'm just fucking with ya! You should have seen your face," the cashier laughed as he bagged up the water and snacks and set them on top of the counter.

"How much do I owe you?" Laura asked, stumbling through her purse.

"Seven-fifty," he said, still laughing.

Laura slid a ten across the counter. "Keep the change."

"Thank you, enjoy your vacation." He handed Laura the bag, still laughing to himself.

***

Aidan took one last drag of his cigarette and dropped it to the gravel, grinding it with the heel of his shoe. The bell above the shop door rang as Laura came outside. Aidan quickly pulled a packet of gum from his pocket and threw two pieces into his mouth.

"What was so funny in there? I could hear someone laughing."

"It was just the cashier... playing a prank on me," Laura said as she walked towards the car.

"Really?" Aidan asked as he caught up with her.

"Yeah, it was so awkward," Laura laughed. Aidan held the door open and Max leapt into the back seat and curled himself up into a ball.

"This was all I could get," Laura said, tossing the bag across to Aidan in the passenger seat.

"That's all?" Aidan said, disappointed.

"You're lucky we got anything at all. You wouldn't believe how bad it was in there."

***

Over an hour had passed since they'd stopped at the service station. The wrappers of polished-off snacks rattled around at Aidan's feet. He couldn't wait to get out of the car and stretch his legs. Laura leaned over and turned down the music on the radio.

"We're almost there, look." Laura pointed out the windscreen towards a wooden sign at the side of the road.

Elmwood, where the forest stays with you. Population 7,040.

On the sign was a painting of a mountain covered in bright green forest with *Welcome!* painted across the top. They passed the sign, heading towards town. The long, looming shadows of pine trees danced across the windscreen.

"Oh, wow..." Laura said. She pulled the car onto the side of the road and they stepped out. Max bounced to the front seat and watched, whimpering to get out with them.

They stood at the top of a hill overlooking the coastal town of Elmwood.

"It's beautiful," Laura said.

"It is," Aidan agreed, looking at the town spread out in front of him. He wrapped his arm around Laura and pulled her in tight against his chest, kissing her forehead. It was late, and the setting sun cast a beautiful, burning orange glow over the town. "Thank you," Aidan said. Laura squeezed him tightly without saying a word.

After a while they got back into the car. Aidan shuffled Max back into the backseat, and they continued down the hill into the town.

The town of Elmwood lay nestled at the bottom of a forest-covered mountain. Beautiful oak trees, coloured in Autumn reds and oranges, lined the sidewalks. A group of kids rode their bikes down the street, calling out to each other as they raced home before the streetlights came on. Dead leaves scattered from beneath the Audi's tyres as they drove through the town square. Fresh, salty ocean air blew through the window and filled their lungs as they drove past the Elmwood public library. They passed a bank, a small bar called *The Anchor Bar*, and a cute little coffee shop, before reaching the town hall at the end of the square. The entire town had a quaint, vintage feel to it. Neither of them could hide their smiles that stretched from ear to ear. Max had his head stuck out of the back window; his long, curly ears blew in the wind as drool flew off his tongue.

As they left the town square, they passed a small harbour on the right. There were only a handful of small fishing boats docked, and the powerful stench of fish quickly invaded the car. Two fishermen were lifting crates full of fish from their boat and stacking them up on the dock. One man looked up, saw the car passing, and gave them a friendly wave. Laura beeped the horn back at him. Further up from the harbour, atop a steep cliff surrounded by large, jagged rocks, stood the tall, black-and-white Elmwood lighthouse.

Waves crashed on the coast as a bright beam of light shone out to sea.

"This place is so cute, I can't wait to explore it!" Laura said.

"I can't believe we're here for two entire months. I think I'm starting to feel relaxed already," Aidan laughed. The sun quickly dipped behind the tall pines as the streetlights blinked to life.

"Where are we picking the keys up?" Aidan asked.

"The guy online told me he'd leave them in the mailbox for us."

"Here's hoping he remembered. Do you have a number in case we get lost? Or if something happens to the house?"

"No, it was all done through the website. If we have any issues, I guess we can always email."

"Fingers crossed there's WiFi, then," Aidan laughed to himself.

They drove through a neighbourhood filled with identical-looking, Victorian style redbrick houses. Yellow light spilled out the windows onto perfectly cut front lawns, creating spiky, ominous shadows from the white picket fences surrounding each house. Aidan couldn't stop his mind from wandering off, picturing families in each house as they drove by. Kids doing their homework, families sitting down to their dinner. Had they lived here their entire lives? Did their family always live in this little town? Aidan wondered what his life could be like if he lived in a town like this. If he could leave the city behind him for good and settle down somewhere quiet. He imagined a life where he lived in a modest house with Laura and Max and their children. They would have a swing set in the garden and barbecues in the summer. They would have a simple, content life, and he would grow old with his beautiful wife and watch their children grow up.

Laura slowed the car as they approached a red light at the turn for Hawthorne Road, snapping Aidan out of his daydream. It was almost night now. In front of them, a towering, dense mass of pines, oaks and other colourful trees surrounded the entire town.

"It shouldn't be much longer, right? I need to get out of this car soon. I don't think my legs can remember how to walk." Max also looked fed up, curled up on the backseat, uninterested with what was outside now.

"I'm sure you'll live," Laura rolled her eyes. "The directions said Hawthorne Road." She pointed out of the window to the street sign. "That's Hawthorne Road, so I'm guessing we're pretty close."

Aidan pulled his phone from his pocket. No service. It had been like that since before they'd stopped at the service station – just little pockets, here and there, where he'd get a bar or two, and then it would drop again.

"Still no signal… how people drove anywhere before SatNavs were invented is beyond me," Aidan said, stuffing the phone back into his pocket. The light finally turned green, and they started down Hawthorne Road.

"Keep your eyes peeled," Laura said, concentrating on the road. "Apparently you can't miss it."

Aidan shuffled in his seat and sat up straight, as if doing so might help him see better. Night came quickly here; it was almost pitch black outside already. And it didn't help that Hawthorne Road stretched out into the blackness, away from the streetlights of the town. The only light now came from the headlights of the Audi and the silvery blue glow of the moon as they crawled forward at twenty miles an hour.

"There – look, to the right!"

Max bounced to his feet in the backseat, startled by the sudden excitement, then let out a sigh of annoyance. Laura slowed the car and turned into the entrance. Towering, black iron gates stopped them in their path.

"This has to be it," Laura said, looking out the window at the gates. "I haven't seen another property on this road since we turned onto it."

"There's a mailbox, I'll go check." Aidan jumped out of the car and ran to inspect it. A cold autumn breeze whistled through the surrounding forest like a train in the distance as dead leaves scurried up the driveway. Aidan reached into the mailbox and pulled out a packed set of keys, then rattled them at the car.

"Hurry and open the gates!" Laura yelled from the car. Aidan fumbled with the keys in his chilly hands. Finally, he found the key for the gate, and the padlock opened with a satisfying *click*. The hinges screeched as Aidan pulled the gates open. Slowly and carefully, Laura drove through the gates and into the driveway.

"Jeez, it's cold out there now," Aidan said as he got into the car, rubbing his hands together to try and get some heat back into them.

They started up the long, curved driveway towards the Lake House. The drive was only wide enough for one car; trees from the surrounding forest arched over and interlinked like fingers, creating a tunnel around them. The tarmac was a sea of reds, oranges, and browns from all the dead leaves. Eventually, the trees opened up and revealed a vast front yard, with perfectly trimmed hedges leading to the front of the house.

The Lake House was a beautiful, three-storey redbrick building with black painted shutters at every window. The building must have been at least a hundred years old. A black wooden porch stretched around the front of the house; three chimneys stuck out from the roof like old gravestones. A fence at least six feet high separated the front yard from the back and ran right up to the edge of the forest surrounding the entire property.

They parked the car up at the side of the house and got out. Laura lifted her arms towards the sky, giving herself a much-needed stretch. Aidan opened the door for Max, who bounced out and instantly began sniffing out all the fresh smells of his home for the next two months.

"Holy shit, can you believe this place?" Aidan said, looking up at the house.

"Wait till you see this."

Aidan turned and looked at what Laura was staring at. "Wow."

From the Lake House, Aidan and Laura could see the whole town lit up below them like hundreds of tiny stars. After a couple minutes of taking in the view, Max barked, breaking the tranquility of the moment.

Aidan threw the keys to Laura and started lifting their suitcases from the trunk.

"Come on, Max," Laura said, slapping her thigh. Max trotted towards them as they made their way to the front door. "What's that?" Laura asked, pointing to a white shape on the door flapping in the wind.

"Probably a note or something. Left by the owner, I guess."

Laura stopped and held Max by the collar, keeping him close to her. Aidan dropped the suitcases and started up the creaky porch steps.

It was a piece of white paper, folded in half and nailed to the wooden door. It was dirty, and the ink had soaked through. He reached out and pulled it off the nail.

"What is it?" Laura asked.

Aidan opened it up. His eyes flitted back and forth as he read, then he walked back to them. He held it out to Laura and stood quietly for a moment while she read it. It was a poster, decorated with a man's photograph. He wore a black t-shirt, camouflage trousers, and had a rifle resting on his shoulder. He stood proudly beside an elk he had just killed, a triumphant grin across his face.

The poster read, *Missing: John Campbell. Aged forty-three, last seen May 12th in the Elmwood area. If you have seen this man or have any relevant information, please contact the Elmwood Police Department.*

CHAPTER FOUR

Trees swayed in the woods; Aidan thought the rustling leaves sounded like the hiss of white noise. He held the missing persons poster, trying not to think about it too much, while Laura fumbled for the door key. All Aidan wanted to do was get inside, start a fire, and get settled for the night.

"Why the hell are there so many keys? I'm going to be here all night," Laura huffed.

It was a clear, crisp night. Aidan looked up and couldn't believe the cosmic light show above his head. Bright, twinkling stars littered the night sky – more than he'd seen in his entire life. Growing up in the city had its advantages, but the brilliance of the night sky, usually hidden beyond all the light pollution, was something he now realised he'd been missing out on.

"Laura, look up," Aidan said.

"Yes!" Laura said triumphantly as she pushed the front door open. She turned to Aidan and said, "What is it?"

She followed his gaze and looked up at the night sky.

"Wow, it's beautiful! Have you ever seen so many before?"

"No, never."

The vastness of space made Aidan feel insignificant. All his problems seemed minuscule and pointless compared to the greatness of the universe. The feeling surprised him. He liked it, even if it only remained for a fleeting second.

"Right, that's enough star gazing for one night. It's getting cold, lets get inside."

Aidan pulled his gaze away from the stars, picked up the two suitcases and started up the porch steps. The entire house was bathed in complete darkness. Max rushed past them, almost knocking Laura over, and ran straight into the house, disappearing into the shadows.

"Max!" Laura yelled.

"You okay?"

"That dog is going to be the death of me. Seriously, I don't know how many times he's nearly knocked me over."

Pale moonlight spilled in through the open door. Laura led the way into the dark, feeling at the walls for the light switch. Aidan set the suitcases on the wooden floor at the entrance as he tried to make out shapes in the dimly lit room. The lights flashed on with a *click*, blinding them both for a second.

Laura was on the other side of the room, standing by the light switch.

"Found it," she said, pleased with herself.

The inside was surprisingly modern for such an old house, a mix of modern decor and vintage furniture. The walls were painted a light shade of grey; an enormous stone fireplace stood proudly in the centre of a feature wall, a stag's head hung proudly above it like some sort of trophy. Beside the fireplace, five or six pieces of chopped wood were stacked inside a grungy metal crate. There was a large, black leather sofa in front of the fireplace, with a coffee table made of wood and cast iron at its feet. Aidan walked over to the coffee table and threw the folded missing persons poster on top of it.

Something Aidan hadn't expected was the huge, flatscreen TV to the left of the fireplace. A bookshelf, filled with books, DVDs and old board games, reached from floor to ceiling.

Laura counted three different lamps in the room: one freestanding; the other two on small tables throughout the room. Max was already curled up, watching them intently from a mustard-yellow chair in the corner of the room beside the bookshelf.

A chandelier hung in the middle of the living room, made from intertwined deer antlers that cast spiky, spiders-leg shadows onto the walls. Behind the sofa on the other side of the living room was a staircase that led up to the bedrooms.

"This is so much nicer than it looked online," Laura said, surprised.

"It's huge. Can we just move in and never leave?" Aidan laughed as he made his way back over to the front door. Kicking it closed, he picked up the suitcases, one in each hand. "I'll take these up to our room."

"Thanks, honey – make sure you pick the best one," she laughed. "I'll crack this open for us." Laura lifted out a bottle of red wine from her handbag and shimmied it from side to side.

"Sounds good to me," Aidan smiled, starting up the stairs.

He dropped the suitcases at the top of the stairs and started investigating the first floor of the house. A short hallway with five doors – one directly in front of him, two to his left and two more to his right – was painted in the same neutral shade of grey as the downstairs. He flicked on the hallway light and opened the door in front of him. It led through to another staircase. Aidan scrunched up his nose as the musty smell of damp and mothballs invaded his nostrils. Shadows drifted down the stairs like a river.

Must lead up to the attic, Aidan thought as he closed the door, reminding himself to investigate another day. Next were the doors to his left, one at either end of the hallway. He pushed open the first and turned on the light. It was a small bedroom with a single bed, a well-used wooden wardrobe and matching set of drawers, and a window looking out to the front yard. Aidan switched off the light and moved to the second door, opening it gently. A bedside lamp was already switched on, lighting the room with a low, orange glow. *The owner must have left it on by mistake.* There was a king-size bed that looked so plush and comfortable that it called out to him. He ran into the room and threw himself onto the bed face first. It was as comfy as it looked.

This must be what sleeping on a cloud must feel like.

This was the one. There were two bedside tables, one on either side of the bed, both with the same modern-looking lamp on top. Aidan reached over and turned on the unlit lamp. Rolling onto his back, he studied the rest of the room. Facing the bed, a large rectangular window stretched across the entire wall. There was a dark grey satin ottoman at the foot of the bed and a large, grey wardrobe against the wall.

In the corner beside the window was an antique bronze telescope.

Aidan rolled off the bed and made his way over to it. He knelt down and looked through the eyepiece. There was nothing to see except a blurred white light. He twisted the focus knob, and the blur grew clearer. The blurry white light was actually the battered landscape of the moon.

"Unreal." Aidan whispered to himself. He sat up and looked out the window to the backyard. There wasn't much to see in the dark except the glow of the moon glistening on the lake.

Aidan grabbed the two suitcases and threw them into the bedroom before heading back into the hallway to check the other two rooms. He walked to the other side of the hall and opened the first door to reveal a small office. A small writing desk looked out onto the backyard through a little window; an expensive, leather office chair was tucked under the desk. An extensive collection of books filled the bookshelf that made up the entire left side of the room. He left the office and opened the last door, which led to a modern bathroom; a luxurious, slate-tiled shower with a black metal shower head and matching basin and toilet, and a mirrored cabinet made from black pipes above the sink.

Downstairs, Laura was in the kitchen looking for two wine glasses. The kitchen-diner was modern and spacious with all the expected appliances. White wooden cupboards with black granite worktops. Rose gold cooking pots hung from hooks above the oven. A thick, wooden dining table – that looked like it had been cut straight from one of the massive pines outside – stood just to the right of the kitchen beside a long sliding door leading out onto the backyard. Laura pulled different cupboard doors open. She had found everything else – lots of plates, bowls, and coffee cups – but not a single wine glass. Finally, in the last cupboard she looked in, she found the glasses and tumblers. She took two out and unscrewed the cork from the wine bottle with a satisfying *pop*. She carried the bottle and two glasses into the living room as Aidan came down the stairs.

"You need to try that bed, it is… I can't even explain how good it is."

"Oh, you bet I'll be trying it out," she winked. She set the bottle and glasses on the coffee table and slumped down onto the sofa. "Should we start the fire?"

"Yeah, it's quite cold in here." Aidan made his way over to the fireplace and started stacking wood into the fire.

"Do you think they ever found him?" Laura asked, picking up the poster from the coffee table and unfolding it.

"Who?" Aidan asked, having almost forgotten about the poster of the missing man.

"The man in the poster."

"Oh, yeah. I'm sure he's fine, honey," Aidan said as he struck a match and lit the firelighters. "Or he doesn't want to be found. Lots of people just get up and leave one day and start over with a new life." Aidan wanted to believe the words coming out of his mouth, but he wouldn't allow himself to consider the alternative. The fire began to grow; yellow and orange flames danced over the wood like a ballet.

"Yeah… you're probably right. I have heard that, actually, on one of those true crime podcasts. There was a girl… I can't remember her name. The police and her family all thought she'd been abducted and searched for her for years. They did TV interviews, had search parties out looking for her – the whole nine yards. But it turned out that in the middle of the night, she'd snuck out of her house, hitchhiked to the other side of the country, and started a new life. New name and everything. And one night she just happened to catch one of those specials on the TV – you know, children that have vanished throughout the years – and there she was. A photo of her childhood self and her parents – old, now – still pleading for information about her. So, after… I think it said fifteen years – she finally reached out to her family and told them everything. It's crazy, right?"

"That is crazy. Pass me the poster."

"What?"

"Pass me the poster."

Laura shuffled herself up from the sofa and handed Aidan the poster. He took it from her and scrunched it up into a ball.

"What are you doing?" Laura asked.

He threw the scrunched-up piece of paper into the fire. Aidan's knees cracked as he stood up. Too many years of sitting behind his desk had wrung havoc on his knees and back. He walked over to Laura and picked up his glass of wine and took a mouthful. Laura wrapped her fingers around his belt and pulled him down beside her on the sofa.

"Let's not talk or think about that stuff anymore," he said. "Let's just enjoy the peace and each other's company."

"Sounds perfect." Laura took the wine glass from his hand and set it on the coffee table without taking her eyes off his. She grabbed his shirt and pulled him towards her, kissing him with her perfectly soft lips. Even now, after all these years together, she still made all his worries and anxieties melt away when she kissed him. She gently stroked her hand along the side of his face and over his rough stubble as he held her tightly in his arms.

"I love you," she said softly.

"I love you too."

She began unbuttoning his shirt as they kissed. Aidan grabbed the bottom of her t-shirt and pulled it off over her head, throwing it in Max's direction. The dog bounced up from the yellow chair, sighed, and walked into the kitchen, laying down beside the back door. Their breathing grew quicker. Aidan kissed her again. He cupped and gently squeezed one of her breasts while his free hand worked the button on her jeans. Slowly, she pulled herself away, got up from the sofa and held out her hand to Aidan. On his feet, he grabbed her hand and pulled her quickly to him. He kissed her again, then threw her over his shoulder. She screamed and laughed as he carried her up the stairs to their bedroom.

***

A loud crashing sound jolted Aidan from his sleep. His heart hammered in his chest. Quickly, he turned to Laura. She was still fast asleep, with the covers pulled up to her chin.

The room was dark, except for the moonlight filtering through the window. Max was still asleep on top of the ottoman. *Some guard dog you are,* Aidan thought. He lay perfectly still in bed for a moment, listening for any other sounds, but none came. Feeling a little silly, he grabbed his phone and unlocked it. Three in the morning. He pulled himself up and sat at the edge of the bed, rubbing the crust from his eyes. The cold from his heavy, sweat-covered t-shirt was giving him the chills, so he pulled it off and threw it into the corner. Still half-asleep, Aidan stumbled to his feet and shuffled towards the bathroom like a zombie from a cheesy horror film. He pushed open the bathroom door and switched on the light, startled by his own reflection in the fancy cabinet mirror. He threw four pills into his mouth and washed them down with a mouthful of tap water, then splashed some over his face. The shock of the cold made the hairs at the back of his neck stand up, but the water felt refreshing on his skin. He placed the almost-empty pill bottles back into the cabinet.

As he pulled the cabinet door, a black shadow darted across the mirror and disappeared behind his reflection. The air left his lungs in an instant. He slammed the door closed. The mirror shattered into large shards and he reeled back, turning around. Nothing was there. The bathroom was still. The only sound came from the running tap.

"Get a grip of yourself," Aidan whispered, rubbing his eyes. After a moment, his breathing returned to normal. He looked at the cracked mirror, then at the pieces shattered in the sink. "Shit." He turned off the tap and started back to the bedroom, embarrassed.

The creaking sound of a door opening somewhere downstairs echoed up through the house.

Aidan froze. *It's all in your head.* He stood at the bedroom doorway, his eyes squeezed shut, terrified. *Get a fucking grip of yourself!* the voice inside his head screamed. Aidan looked in on Laura and Max, both still sound asleep. Neither had heard a thing. He took a deep breath through clenched teeth and crept toward the top of the stairs and listened. All he could hear was the quick thudding of his heartbeat in his ears. He looked down the stairs into the darkness of the living room.

Footsteps charged across the wooden floor. A door banged shut.

Fear sparked down Aidan's spine like a bolt of lightning. *There's someone in the house.* He started down the stairs, taking them two at a time. The living room was dark and motionless, like nobody had been there. He pulled on the front doorhandle. Locked. Nothing was out of place; everything was as they'd left it. Beside the fireplace, he spotted an iron poker and hastily made his way towards it. He grasped it; the weight of the poker was good in his hand.

There was a door under the stairs that he hadn't noticed until now.

Slowly, he made his way towards it. He tried his best to settle his breathing, to listen for any movement, but it was no use. Fear had a hold of him, and it wasn't letting go. Aidan crept through the darkness of the living room, never taking his eyes off the door. The iron poker rattled in his clenched fist. He expected an intruder to jump out and attack him at any second.

A glass shattered on the floor. Aidan winced. *Shit.* He had bumped into the coffee table and knocked over a wine glass. *It's now or never, do it, do it!*

Aidan leapt over the sofa, the iron poker raised above his head, ready to strike down at whoever was on the other side of the door. He reached out and twisted the doorhandle.

It was locked.

Taken aback for a moment, he shook his head to clear his thoughts. *The kitchen.* Quietly, Aidan turned and pushed the kitchen door – already slightly ajar – all the way open with his foot. His entire body was shaking. The room was silent. Quickly, he flicked on the light switch and raised the poker over his head. Nothing was out of place in there, either.

Confused, Aidan lowered the poker to his side. He went to the kitchen window and pulled the handle. Locked. He hurried to the back door that led to the garden and the lake. It was also locked. There was no sign of a break-in, or that anyone other than them had been in the house.

His eyes suddenly felt heavy as his legs turned to jelly. Aidan steadied himself against the kitchen table and set the poker down. Rubbing his hands over his face, he took a couple of deep breaths. *Go get some sleep or you're going to go insane.* After a moment, he turned off the kitchen light and headed into the living room.

Aidan stopped dead in his tracks. The door under the stairs was ajar. *No! There's no way. It was locked… it was…*

He swung the door open and looked inside, wishing he still had the iron poker. It was pitch black. Aidan took a step inside and saw a thin staircase that went down another level. A basement. Hesitantly, he took another few steps down, looking for the light switch.

A freezing blast of air, colder than the rest of the house, rushed at him from the basement like an invisible tornado. His breath swelled out in front of him in a cloud. Finally, he felt the shape of the light switch on the wall and flicked it on. A blinding white flash filled the basement and stairs as the lightbulb blew. Bright white, red and yellow lights flashed in front of Aidan's eyes. He fumbled about in the dark, trying to feel for anything that could steady him. The weakness in his legs finally won and they gave out from under him. Aidan tumbled down the basement stairs.

The feeling of falling jolted Aidan awake.

Sunlight filled the bedroom, streaming in through the window. Birds sang loudly outside. Aidan sat up in the bed, his mind racing at a hundred miles per hour. Laura was sitting beside him, sipping on her morning coffee and reading a paperback.

"Good morning, sleepyhead," Laura said, looking up from her book. Aidan looked at her, baffled. Panic filled her face.

"What's wrong?"

"It... it was so... real." Aidan said.

"Was it the girl in the yellow raincoat?" Laura asked, setting her book and coffee on the bedside table.

"No... no, it wasn't her. You... did you hear anything last night? Banging sounds or anything?"

"No, I didn't hear anything, honey." Laura could see the fear in Aidan's watery eyes, "it was just a bad dream, sweetie. The first night in a new place is always uncomfortable."

Aidan didn't reply right away. His eyes flickered from side to side as he replayed the memory of last night over and over in his head. He rubbed a hand over his face and sighed. "Yeah... you're right. It must have been another nightmare."

Laura leaned over and kissed him on the cheek. The tightness in his stomach instantly softened, and he watched as she got out of bed and headed to the bathroom. Aidan picked his phone up from the bedside table. Still no service.

"Hey, Aidan..." Laura called.

"Yeah?"

"Why is the mirror in the bathroom broken?"

CHAPTER FIVE

The autumn sun blazed in the sky as Aidan and Laura drove through the neighbourhood towards town. A group of kids wearing backpacks and dressed for school stood at the edge of a white picket fence as their friend waved bye to their parents. Two teenagers, a boy and a girl who weren't so eager to get to school, walked hand in hand down the street. The boy pulled out a cigarette and checked the coast was clear before slipping it between his lips and sparking it up. The girl shook her head at him and slapped it out of his mouth. The boy stopped in his tracks, stunned. Aidan chuckled to himself as they drove past. *I'd kill for a smoke right now*, he thought, unknowingly tapping his feet in the footwell as he fidgeted with his fingers.

"What's so funny?" Laura asked, glad for the show of emotion.

"It's nothing."

"No, tell me," Laura smiled as she glanced over at Aidan, then back to the road.

"We drove past a couple who reminded me of us when we were younger, that's all."

Laura's smile grew. "Aww, that's nice. I wish I'd seen them." She looked into the rear view mirror to see the couple, but now they were just two small, dark figures in the distance.

A thunderstorm was roaring inside Aidan's head. He squeezed his eyes shut and rubbed at his temples.

"What's up, honey? You've been off since we got up." Laura's sea-blue eyes widened as the smile dissolved from her face.

Aidan shook his head and sighed. He had tried to put it past him, to shrug it off as a strange coincidence, but it was no use. The thoughts just kept going, over and over in his head, like a record skipping on the same beat. "I still can't get my head around that mirror being cracked this morning. I can't stop thinking about it. It's giving me a headache."

"It's only a mirror, it's no big deal. We can replace it before we leave."

"I'm not worried about that!" Aidan snapped. He rubbed a hand over his face and took a deep breath. "I'm sorry, I didn't mean to…"

"It's okay." Laura's lips tightened.

"It happened in my dream… in my nightmare, I mean. I can't remember everything that happened, but I can remember the mirror breaking. I remember that part clearly."

Laura thought for a second, then said, "It was probably broken already and we never noticed. It's no big deal. All kinds of random things pop up in our dreams."

Aidan shook his head. "No, it wasn't broken before we went to bed. I'm sure of it."

"I don't know. Could you have been sleepwalking and broken it by mistake? People have done crazier things in their sleep. I heard about a man, one time, who murdered his wife during a nightmare. He was dreaming someone was trying to kill him. Hell, some people have even had sex while being completely asleep." Laura smiled and slapped Aidan's thigh, giving it a tight squeeze. It sent tingles shooting up Aidan's leg.

He lifted Laura's hand to his mouth and kissed it.

"Hopefully you don't murder me in your sleep," she smiled, "but if you ever wanna try the other thing, I'm fine with that."

"You're probably right, sweetie. I'm just being silly." Aidan said. He had never sleepwalked before, not even when he was a kid. *It could be a symptom of the medication,* he thought. *Another thing to add to the list of issues you have to deal with. Next you'll be waking up, naked, halfway down the street in the freezing cold with your junk all out for the world to see. You'll be getting arrested for indecent exposure.*

***

Laura pulled into the car park of Robinsons General Store. It surprised Aidan to see that parking was free; he was used to paying an extortionate amount per hour back in Fallbridge. *That's a nice perk of small town living I could get used to,* Aidan thought. Fresh sea air swept through the town, mixing with the earthy scent of the pine trees and the oaks surrounding the rest of Elmwood.

Aidan inhaled the fresh air, filling his lungs with the deepest breath he had ever taken in his life. *Another first.* The grocery store stood at the corner of the town square; at the entrance was a row of interconnected shopping trollies. Flower baskets hung from either side of the automatic doors and a fold-out wooden sign stood on the footpath, inviting potential shoppers inside. Bright white, bold letters jumped from the sign's black background:

We're open! Come on in.

The sound of ringing bells from the boats bobbing up and down in the nearby harbour echoed through the town. The fresh air had calmed the storm brewing in Aidan's head; at least for now, anyway.

Aidan stopped. "I'm gonna love you and leave you, honey."

"What? Are you seriously going to make me do the shopping by myself?" Laura replied, sounding peeved.

"I'm sorry, you know I hate grocery shopping. I'll just slow you down."

"Okay," Laura sighed. "Well, what are you going to do instead?"

"I'm going to find the pharmacy and get these filled up," he took the pill bottles from his coat pocket and shook them in the air. "I'll meet you back here. It shouldn't take me too long."

"Fine, but –"

Aidan leaned in and kissed her, then started towards the town square before she could say anything else. He turned the corner onto Main Street and looked back to make sure Laura wasn't following him. She wasn't. The last pills rattled in their bottles like Tic Tacs. He looked down at them in his hand.

"No more," he said out loud. Then he dropped the pill bottles into a bin as he passed by.

He hated taking them, always had. They made him feel numb, like he wasn't even a person anymore. A shadow of the man he once was. *They weren't helping anyway, and now I might be sleepwalking on top of everything else. I'm better off without them.* His stomach tingled with a flurry of butterflies. He felt bad lying to Laura, but she'd be stone cold against him coming off his medication. To take his mind off it, he reached into his coat pocket, pulled out the packet of cigarettes, stuck one between his lips and lit it. The butterflies melted away with each long draw. *There goes the fresh air.*

Main Street was fairly busy, giving the small town a familiar, pleasant buzz. People came in and out of the stores lining the square. Chatter and laughter floated down the street from a coffee shop a couple of doors up. Across the street, Aidan saw a small bookstore. Outside, two trollies were filled with battered paperbacks; a sign stuck to each trolly said, *used books, individually priced*. Intrigued, he crossed the street, took one last drag and flicked the cigarette butt to the ground and stomped it out.

"Asshole," a man said as he pushed past, shaking his head.

"Hey, fuck you!" Aidan yelled back.

"How about you pick up after yourself, city boy?" The man flipped Aidan the bird and carried on walking up Main Street.

"What the hell?" Aidan whispered to himself as he walked into the bookstore.

The store was a lot smaller inside than it looked; the unforgettable scent of mottled paper filled the air. The smell reminded Aidan of when he was younger, back when his mother had used to take him to the Fallbridge City Library every month. His favourites were science fiction and horror novels, and he would check out his limit every time. Without fail, his mother always used to say he would never read them all on time, but every month he would prove her wrong.

The aisles were tight, filled with dusty bookshelves in every direction. Dust motes floated in the air, twinkling in the haze coming in through the front windows. Aidan had to shuffle sideways to fit down some of the aisles as he searched for the horror section. It had been a while since he'd gotten stuck into a good book, and he could think of nothing better than losing himself in one while relaxing at the Lake House. *Maybe I could make this a weekly thing*, he thought.

Finally he found the horror section. As usual it wasn't huge; he scanned a couple of shelves, but couldn't see anything that caught his eye.

Disappointed, he turned and started making his way back

through the store. A round table near the entrance caught his eye. Three stacks of books were piled next to each other in a pyramid shape beside a sign that read: *Local Authors*. Aidan picked one up. It was called *The Hauntings of Elmwood*. It was the front cover that had grabbed his attention.

Under the title was a grainy, black-and-white photograph of the Lake House. He turned it over to read the back:

Creep into the dark history of Elmwood and explore the depths of horror that surround this picturesque coastal town, from the lady of the lighthouse to the most notorious haunted house in –

"I wouldn't bother with that one," a female voice said. Aidan looked up from the book. A woman walked out from behind the cash register and stood in front of him. She was pretty. She looked like she was in her mid-twenties. Pink hair hung effortlessly over her shoulders as the overhead lights shone off her nose ring like a piece of glitter. A name tag that read *Bex* hung limply from her Fleetwood Mac t-shirt. She leaned in and whispered, "I know the author and he isn't very good." She pointed with her thumb to a man with a short, greying beard, stacking books onto shelves at the back of the store.

Aidan laughed and set the book down. "I'm Aidan."

"Hey, I'm Bex." They shook hands. "So, when did you arrive in Elmwood?"

"Um … how?"

"I'm psychic." Bex grimaced, squeezing her eyes shut. "Sorry, that was weird," she shook her head. Aidan could see the heat rising from her neck. "I'm kidding. Elmwood is a small place, so we notice when there's someone new in town."

"I guess that's why some guy called me an asshole city boy outside."

Bex burst out laughing. The man stacking the books looked down at her disapprovingly. She squeezed her mouth into tight slits, trying to suppress her laughter.

"Don't take it to heart," Bex said, still chuckling to herself.

"It probably didn't help that I threw my cigarette butt on the ground."

"Well, in that case you are an asshole." Bex smiled as Aidan nodded in admittance. "So, you're staying in the Lake House?"

"You reading my mind again?"

"Nope," she said, glancing down at the book. Aidan followed her gaze and instantly felt stupid. "Besides, it's the only nice place left to stay in Elmwood since they renovated it, but you wouldn't catch me staying there. No way."

"Why's that?"

"Isn't that why you're here?" Bex asked, confused.

"What do you mean?"

"People come from all over to stay in the Lake House. It's the most haunted house in Elmwood. The book might be shitty, but the stories…"

An icy chill shot through Aidan's spine, all the way to his toes, as the words left her lips. His stomach tingled like millions of insects were trying to crawl their way out of him.

"Shit," Bex exhaled as she watched the smile drop from Aidan's face. "I'm so sorry." She fumbled with her hands, not knowing what to do. "I thought you knew."

"People actually come here to…"

"Well yeah, that or they come here to go *hunting*, and …" she looked Aidan up and down, "you don't look like the hunting type to me."

"Why would anyone want to stay in a haunted house?"

"I don't know – bragging rights, I guess? To say they stayed in the most haunted –"

"You don't really believe all that, do you?" Aidan asked, cutting her off before she could say it again.

Bex hesitated for a moment, not sure what to say. "Um…

yeah, I guess. Everyone grows up here hearing the stories of the town, and especially the Lake House. We used to tease and dare each other as kids to go up to the house and knock on the door, but we would all chicken out. I don't know if they're all true, or just urban legends passed down through generation to generation... but you'd be hard-pressed to find someone in Elmwood who doesn't have at least a bit of childhood fear over that house. If you went by that book though, you'd think every inch of this town had something lurking in the shadows." Bex forced a giggle, trying to lighten the mood.

"Are you sure? I've been inside, and it doesn't look like a haunted house to me."

"Oh, believe me when I tell you, some messed up shit happened in that house."

The storm slowly started growing again in Aidan's mind.

"If I haven't sent you running to the hills, I could tell you about it sometime, if you'd like? Maybe over a drink?"

Aidan shook the thoughts from his mind. "Wha... um, yeah, that would be great." He smiled at her, not knowing what she had just said.

"Great!" Bex buzzed. Excitement gleamed in her eyes as her smile stretched from ear to ear. She hurried over to the cash register and ripped off a piece of paper from the receipt roll. Aidan pulled out his phone and checked the time.

"Shit, I have to go. It was nice meeting you." Aidan waved at Bex and started for the door.

"Hey, wait." Bex scribbled something down on the piece of paper and hurried to the door past Aidan, stopping him from leaving. She handed him the piece of paper. The smile beamed across her face. "See you later, city boy," Bex teased, moving out of the way. Her sweet perfume danced around him as she disappeared into the sea of books. Aidan looked down at the crumpled-up piece of paper as he left the store.

Curious, he opened it up. Her phone number, signed with her name and a little heart.

Aidan smirked as he stared at the number, crumpled it up, and threw it in a bin, walking back down Main Street towards the grocery store.

A crow perched on top of a streetlight cawed as it kept a watchful eye over Elmwood.

CHAPTER SIX

"Did you know?" Aidan asked, placing a can of chopped tomatoes in the cupboard. His mind buzzed with hundreds of questions. It was like someone was battering a wasp's nest inside his head and the wasps had finally had enough. Stinging the soft tissue in his skull over and over until he couldn't contain them anymore.

"Know what?" Laura said, puzzled, as she carried on stocking the fridge. They hadn't spoken since the car ride home, and most of that conversation had been one-way on her part. Aidan had answered her questions with various grunts and stared blankly out the window at the passing trees. She knew he was in his head, knew the signs all too well now. The eyes that always looked darker when he was deep in thought. The twitching under his right eye. Navigating the next couple of minutes would be like trying to traverse a minefield without blowing herself to pieces, and she had been growing tired of it. Tired of tiptoeing constantly around Aidan. All she wanted to do was relax, spend time with her husband and mend their marriage, putting the past behind them.

"Come on, you can tell me if you did," Aidan said as he turned and leaned on the countertop. Max got up from the kitchen floor and padded into the living room to get away before the impending yelling started to hurt his ears.

"I don't have a clue what you're talking about, Aidan." She closed the fridge and started filling the freezer.

"I won't be angry, I promise."

Laura slammed the freezer closed and spun around to face him. "What the hell are you talking about?"

Silence surrounded them for a moment.

Aidan fidgeted with his fingers. A twitch began knocking at the side of his eye.

"Did you know, before booking this place," he rolled his head as he looked around the room, "that it's the most haunted house in Elmwood?"

Laura frowned. "What?" She shook her head, laughing at the words that had just left his mouth. "Is that seriously what you've been worrying about this entire time?"

Aidan picked at his knuckles. "Well, did you?"

"What kind of question is that? Do you really think I went online, looked this place up, saw it was – *supposedly* – haunted, and said to myself, 'That would be a great place to go to relax with my husband'?"

Aidan looked down at his feet, wishing now that he'd never said anything, but there was no going back now.

"You don't honestly believe that nonsense, do you?"

"Well… I don't know. It would explain the mirror."

"Jesus Christ, Aidan! Will you give it a rest about that damn mirror? You broke it while sleepwalking, or it was already broken. But I can tell you one thing: it definitely wasn't a ghost."

"But I –"

"How did you even hear about this, anyway?" Laura interrupted him again. He hadn't seen her this angry in a long time.

"I was talking to a… local, earlier, and they told me –"

"Aidan …" Laura closed her eyes and rubbed at the bridge of her nose.

"They told me that this place is famous, or whatever. That people come from all over to stay here."

"I don't want to talk about this anymore."

"We could –"

"I'm done."

Before Aidan could say anything else, Laura stormed out, disappeared up the stairs and slammed the bedroom door so hard that the photo frames on the kitchen walls shuddered.

Max cautiously peeked around the corner.

"Come here, boy," Aidan said, defeated, kneeling down to the floor. Max sauntered into the kitchen and over to Aidan. His tail wagged carelessly as Aidan scratched the sacred spot behind his ears, then moved to his stomach. Max loved every second.

***

A blood-red haze blazed across the sky as the sun began to fall, casting long shadows from the trees that looked like outstretched fingers. The axe came down, splitting a small piece of wood in two.

Aidan had been out in the garden splitting firewood for the last hour. They had burned through their first stack the night before.

Laura hadn't spoken a word to him all afternoon. The only times she had reappeared since their fight were to make frequent trips to the kitchen and fill her wine glass, so he thought he'd put himself to good use. The day had been warm for late Autumn; a lone summer's day that had gotten lost along the way somehow. Sweat ran down Aidan's bare back as he split another piece of wood. The thud of the axe hitting the tree stump echoed through the surrounding forest.

He stuck the axe into the stump and took a quick swig of beer. The back door squeaked open.

Laura walked out into the dying light wearing a thin, yellow dress that billowed in the gentle breeze, wine glass in hand. She was stunning. Dead leaves crunched under her bare feet as she walked to the edge of the lake. Laura never seemed to get any more than a buzz on, no matter what she drank. She could always drink Aidan and their friends under the table and get up the next morning without even a hint of a hangover. Aidan hated it. Sometimes his hangovers lasted days, the epic ones weeks.

He watched as Max followed her to the lake, his curly ears flopping from side to side as he trotted after her. She walked past Aidan without saying a word. A fly buzzed around his sweaty face. He swatted at it absent-mindedly.

Go apologise, dip shit! He grabbed his t-shirt and wiped the sweat away from his face, then downed the rest of his beer. *For courage.*

He threw the t-shirt onto the grass and went to Laura.

Laura stood at the edge of the lake, watching the light show play out as the sun hit the water just right. She took another sip of wine as she heard Aidan coming up behind her. She didn't turn to face him.

His dirty hands wrapped around her waist. She could feel his warm breath as he gently kissed the back of her neck. Goosebumps erupted all over her body. She loved it when he kissed her there, and she knew that he knew it too. His mouth moved to her ear. He nibbled on it for a second and whispered, "I'm sorry."

Laura closed her eyes, took a deep breath, then turned around. She could tell by the look on his face – the kind of look that Max pulled when he had done something he shouldn't have – that he truly was sorry. The burning inside her cooled a little. She still wasn't happy with him, but he'd apologised, and accepting that was better than fighting for the rest of the day. She wrapped her arms around him, pulled his sticky body against hers, and kissed him.

"It's okay," she whispered back, giving him a tight-lipped smile.

Aidan bent down and picked up a stick from the ground, throwing it into the lake.

Max leapt from the sunspot on the grass where he had been lazing and jumped in after it. He grabbed hold of the stick with his mouth and doggy-paddled his way to the edge of the lake. Lumbering out, he shook his body, throwing cold water over Aidan and Laura.

"Max!" Laura laughed, holding her hand out in an attempt to stop the water from hitting her.

Without a care in the world, Max took the stick and went back to his spot in the sun and began gnawing on it. Aidan held his hand out to Laura. She took it.

"Where are we going?" she asked. Aidan nodded towards a little wooden pier around the edge of the lake.

The wood creaked under their feet as they walked to the end of the pier. Aidan slipped off his converse, rolled up his jeans to just above the ankles and sat at the edge of the pier, dangling his feet in the cold water. Laura lifted her dress and sat next to him, resting her head on his shoulder. The water made their feet tingle, but neither of them cared. They sat at the edge of the pier in silence, staring out at the beautiful, setting sun. The bright pinks and reds that lit up the sky reflected on the water like a painting as a light mist danced over the surface of the lake.

***

Aidan sat hunkered on his knees, throwing chunks of wood into the fire. It was pitch black outside, and they had spent the last half hour making the living room as cosy as possible. Soft yellow light spilled across the room from the many lamps. The smell of burning wood gave the room the aroma of a log cabin, and they'd laid blankets over the sofa to curl up in. Laura walked in carrying the pizza and set it down on top of the coffee table.

"Can you grab the wine and some glasses please?" Laura asked.

"Sure thing."

Aidan walked into the kitchen and uncorked the bottle of red on the counter, took two glasses from the cupboard, and went back into the living room. Laura was already sitting on the sofa with her legs pulled up tightly against her chest, a slice of pizza in one hand and the TV remote in the other. Aidan set the glasses on the table and filled them both generously.

"Thank you, honey," Laura said.

Aidan sat next to her and lifted a slice for himself, shovelling it into his mouth.

"Anything good?" he asked, but it came out as *ann fing ood*.

"What?" Laura laughed.

Aidan gulped the mouthful of molten cheese and crust, then flapped his hand in front of his mouth to cool it down. "Anything good on?" he said finally.

"Nothing at all." Laura left the TV on the local news channel while they ate. It must have been a slow news day in Elmwood, because the only major stories were a lost dog who'd been reunited with its owner, and a local man arrested for being drunk and disorderly. "Would it kill them to give us Netflix?" she protested, throwing her last pizza crust onto the plate, then turned off the TV.

Aidan laughed, his mouth full. Laura topped up their glasses and wrapped a blanket around herself.

"Some difference to the news in Fallbridge," Aidan said.

"That's true," Laura nodded.

"Right, we aren't sitting here all night talking about the news. Or lack of it." Aidan got up and walked over to the bookshelf. He scanned the old books and worked his way down, taking another bite from the pizza slice in his hand. There were board games on the middle shelf: *Monopoly*; *The Game of Life*; *Guess Who*. Then one caught his eye.

Ouija.

Aidan threw the last chunk of his pizza to Max, who rushed into the kitchen to make sure no one could take it off him. Aidan pulled the board game out of the shelf and blew the dust off it.

"How about this?" he said, turning to Laura and shaking the box in his hands.

Laura looked up. "No," she shook her head. "Are you serious? Especially after today."

"Aww, come on. I've always wanted to play this. I wanted one so bad when I was a kid, but my mum wouldn't buy me it."

"Yeah, with good reason."

"We could see if the locals were telling the truth or not," Aidan teased.

"I don't think playing with that is a good idea."

"I didn't think you believed in all that… what did you call it? Nonsense?"

"I don't."

"Then what are you worried about?" Aidan scoffed. "It's for ages eight and up." He pointed at the age recommendation on the corner of the box.

He stood there like a child in a toy store with a stupid grin stretched across his face, gripping the box against his chest. Laura rolled her eyes and sighed. "Fine."

"Yes!" Aidan exclaimed.

He cleared the pizza remnants off the coffee table by

throwing them into Max's bowl. Moved the wine glasses aside and carefully opened the box as if he was afraid of breaking the contents. He placed the wooden board on top of the table, set the plastic planchette down, and hurried back around to the sofa. He caught Laura throwing a brooding look in his direction.

"If it weirds you out, we don't have to play it. I just thought it would be a bit of fun."

"Just one game, then I'm going to bed," she said sharply. She had a feeling deep in her gut that this would end badly, that it could send Aidan off again.

"Okay, that's fair." Aidan shuffled himself to the edge of the sofa and gently placed two fingers onto the planchette. He turned his head and looked at Laura, who sighed and unwrapped herself from her blanket, then placed her fingers next to his.

"Do you know how to play it?" Laura asked.

"No idea," Aidan chuckled nervously. "Only what I've seen in the movies."

"Well, that's great." Laura rolled her eyes, then smirked at Aidan.

"Close your eyes and just focus, okay?"

"Okay."

They closed their eyes and Aidan began sliding the planchette around in clockwise circles, then brought it to a stop in the centre of the board. The room was silent. The only sound was the crackling of the fire. Aidan could feel his heart beating a little harder in his chest.

"If anyone is here with us, please let us know by communicating through the board."

Everything was quiet.

"Did you live here?" Laura asked. The planchette stayed perfectly still.

"Is this house haunted?"

They sat in the deafening quiet, waiting for any kind of answer or slight movement of the planchette.

"Did you die in this house?" Aidan said. Frustration cracked in his voice.

Nothing.

"Well, that was a load of shit," Aidan sighed.

Laura snorted. She hadn't realised until then that her entire body had been tensed. Aidan moved the planchette onto *Goodbye* and they took their fingers off the piece of plastic.

"What a waste of time," Aidan said as he reached over and picked up his glass of wine. He poured the rest down his throat without tasting it.

"What did you expect to happen?"

"I don't know." His face reddened slightly, then set the empty glass back on the table. "Something, anything." He couldn't believe he'd thought a stupid kids' game would actually have worked.

"Well, I'm going to bed." Laura stood up and began turning off the lamps around the living room, leaving the board and glasses on the table to be cleared away in the morning. The fire had already burned itself down to deep, red embers. She held her hand out to Aidan. "Come on, I know something we could do to pass the time."

She had that cheeky glint in her eye that Aidan loved. He took her hand, and they went upstairs to the bedroom.

Slowly, the basement door creaked open.

CHAPTER SEVEN

"Aidan," a deep voice whispered.

"Ai-daaaan..." it said again, drawing out the name like a mother gently waking her sleeping child. Aidan stirred in the bed as his eyes cracked open. For a moment, the world was dark and blurry. He rubbed the sleep crust from his eyes, pulled himself up, and leaned against the headboard.

"Aidan."

He turned and looked at Laura, fast asleep next to him. Max slept in his usual place on top of the ottoman. Aidan reached down and picked up his phone. The light blinded him, then his eyes adjusted. 2.55 a.m. Shadows filled the room, cast by the dull moonlight shining through the window. The house was quiet; the only sound came from the gentle breathing and snores of Laura and Max.

Aidan smacked his dry lips together. His tongue felt like a rough piece of jerky. Still half-asleep, he swung his legs out of bed and pulled himself to his feet. His knees cracked and creaked like hinges that needed oiling as he headed downstairs to get a glass of water. *Am I sleepwalking?* he thought as he shuffled to the kitchen.

He didn't notice the basement door ajar.

Taking a glass from the cupboard, he filled it under the tap and began gulping it down.

"AIDAN!"

His entire body jolted. For a second, he thought something had electrocuted him. The tumbler fell from his hand and smashed on the floor, scattering water and fragments of broken glass around his feet. All the hairs on his body stood on end. Aidan looked around the kitchen, but couldn't see anyone. He took a step back from the sink, forgetting about the broken glass. A shard ripped into the sole of his foot.

"Shit!"

White hot pain shot up his leg. Aidan stumbled towards the table, walking on the side of his foot, manoeuvring awkwardly around the sharp mess on the tiles, then dropped himself into a chair. He lifted his foot, resting his shin on the opposite thigh. The glass shard was sticking out about a half inch. Just looking at it made him wince. He reached for it, hesitated, then pulled his hand back.

Just do it. Pull it out, you pussy.

He took three quick breaths and went for it. The piece of glass came out easily, but the chunk was larger than it had looked. It made Aidan think of icebergs; the way there was so much more under the surface than you could see above. Warm blood leaked from the wound and dripped to the floor. He flicked the piece of bloodstained glass to the floor with the others, not caring that he was bleeding, just relieved the glass was out of his foot.

Remembering the voice, Aidan looked around the room without getting up. A part of him knew there would be no one there; the voice he'd heard had come from inside his head, it must have.

I really am going crazy. A cold sweat covered his body and made his skin feel clammy, like a dead fish.

"Out here," the voice said.

You're dreaming. It's all a dream, Aidan told himself, despite the throbbing in his foot telling him otherwise. He limped towards the door, unable to stop himself. *Don't go out there*, he thought, but he couldn't stop.

He unlocked the door and swung it open. A bone-rattling, icy breeze blew in from outside, bringing with it dead leaves and the scent of the autumn night. Aidan stepped out onto the back porch, leaving a trail of bloody footprints behind him in the kitchen. Moonlight sparkled on the surface of the lake. The wind howled all around him. He hugged himself for warmth, but it wasn't much use.

"*Come to me*," the dark voice groaned in the wind, louder now.

One by one, he took the porch steps down to the garden.

What are you doing? Stop walking, you idiot!

"*Over here*," the voice beckoned. It was coming from the treeline at the edge of the forest, hidden within the shadows of the tall pines and oaks. Dead leaves and pine needles crunched under his feet as he moved. His teeth chattered in his head. It sounded like they were trying to send him a message in morse code. He grunted as he tried to regain control of his legs. No response. His arms were also useless. It was like his body had a mind of its own, like it had reduced him to a passenger.

Still able to shake his head, he went to speak, to call out to the voice, but nothing came out. His lips wouldn't move. All he could do was grunt, like he had tape covering his mouth. His heart hammered in his chest as a muffled scream hid behind his lips.

His legs marched him towards the forest. In the moonlight, he could only make out the first row of trees, and beyond them an endless darkness. *Don't go in there*, Aidan pleaded with himself. *Please don't go in there.*

Tears fell from his wide, marble eyes.

A twig snapped. Something moved. Something in the

forest, just beyond the tree line. Aidan grunted, willing himself to stop. It was useless. *What the fuck is that?* His heart was in his throat. He imagined himself throwing it up, stomping it into the dirt and continuing to walk, his legs taking his lifeless head along for the ride.

Something moved again. Aidan got a quick glimpse of it. Whatever it was, it was darker than the emptiness beyond the trees. He shook his head from side to side, like a child trying to move its mouth away from a spoonful of medicine. Too afraid to even blink, Aidan could do nothing as his legs dragged him towards the thing in the forest.

"Enough," the dark voice whispered.

At last his legs finally came to a stop between two pine trees at the cusp of the emptiness. The only sound was his heavy breathing and the rustling of the leaves in the wind. He peered into the blackness.

Unwillingly, he dropped to his knees. He tried to move, but he had no control over his body. A deep roar erupted from within the emptiness. The trees whistled and swayed as wind blasted through the forest. The wind spiralled around Aidan, engulfing him like a tornado; contorting as it circled, thickening into something that looked like smoke. It grew darker and darker until it was impossibly dark, darker than any shadow or night Aidan had ever seen. The smoke snuffed out the moonlight, the trees, the Lake House, until that darkness was all that remained. Aidan's mouth dropped open. He tried to force it closed, but nothing happened.

An arm of swirling black smoke slithered out towards Aidan like the growing root of a tree. His eyes almost popped out from their sockets as he grunted, unable to move any part of his body now and unable to look away from the darkness that crept towards him. His mouth ripped open. Smoke billowed down Aidan's throat. He gaged and choked. Shadows spread across his eyes like ink until they were black holes. More arms splintered out from the swirling smoke, covering Aidan's face and body until he and the darkness were one.

"CAAAWWWW!"

Aidan jolted awake, screaming. He scuffled, grabbing at his face and eyes before calming down and letting out an enormous sigh.

It was just a dream. Of course it was…

Before Aidan took his hands away from his eyes, he knew something wasn't right. He could hear the rustling of tress in the gentle breeze and feel the cool air against his damp skin. Slowly, he moved his hands from his face. The early morning light stung his eyes. He was lying on his back in the dead leaves and moss at the edge of the forest, looking up at the blue sky. He sat up, confused, and pulled his foot across his leg. There was no cut, not even a mark or scratch. Just dirt, leaves, and pine needles stuck to his feet.

Jesus, I really am sleepwalking.

"CAAAWWWW!"

The sound startled Aidan. He looked over his shoulder back towards the house.

A crow stood on the handle of the axe, still wedged into the tree stump, watching Aidan with its tiny beady eyes. It cawed again, then took off into the forest.

CHAPTER EIGHT

The frying pan hissed as Aidan scraped in cubed chunks of tofu. Thankfully, he had woken before Laura. The last thing he wanted was for her to see him sleeping out in the garden in his boxers. If she'd seen that, she'd have him handcuffed to the bed next time. *And not in a good way,* he thought.

After Aidan had woken up, he'd come back inside to look for the smashed glass or the bloody footprints on the floor. Neither were there. The glass was beside the sink, sparkling in the morning light, looking as good as new. No sharp pieces on the floor and no blood, either.

Well, why would there be? Aidan looked down again at his dirty, uncut feet. He could distinctly remember cutting himself after dropping the glass; the sharp white pain that followed; the coppery scent of blood and then pulling the hefty chuck from the sole of his foot. It had all been so real that Aidan would have bet his life on it. But here it was, staring him in the face: the undeniable truth that he had dreamed it all. He headed towards the stairs and stopped at the basement door. Noticing it was open slightly, he pulled it the rest of the way and looked down into the dark.

Cold air emanated up from the basement and brushed his bare legs. The dark shadows of the basement flooded his mind with images of the swirling, black smoke from his nightmare. He shivered, then shut the door and tiptoed upstairs. The door to the bedroom was still open. Laura had the covers pulled up over her head and Max snored happily on the ottoman. Aidan grabbed some fresh clothes and headed for the shower, ready to wash away all the dirt and memories of the night.

He stirred tofu in the pan and added some paprika for good measure. Incredible smells filled the house, and it wasn't long before he could hear Laura thumping about upstairs, finally getting out of bed. Max had already come down and was outside in the garden, barking at the ducks in the pond.

"Something smells amazing," Laura said, making her way down the stairs.

"It's your favourite."

"Tofu breakfast burrito?" Laura came into the kitchen, her eyes wide with excitement.

Aidan smiled when he saw her. She was wearing his old Metallica t-shirt, the one that barely covered her bum.

She saw the way he was looking at her and scoffed. "You're up early," she said, almost questioning, as she went to the coffee machine, pulling down the hem of the t-shirt in an attempt to cover herself a little more.

"Yeah, I couldn't get back to sleep, so I thought I'd make a start on the day."

The coffee machine buzzed in the background as Laura wrapped her arms around Aidan. He added some chopped mushrooms to the pan, then turned to face her.

"I'm so lucky to have such a great husband," she said as she stroked the side of Aidan's face. Without thinking, Aidan flinched from her. The memory of the dark arm reaching out towards him from the forest flashed in his mind.

Laura snapped her hand back as if she'd touched

something hot.

"What happened? Did I hurt you?" Laura said, confused.

Aidan squeezed his eyes shut. "No… no, it's nothing," he said, shaking his head.

"Are you sure? It didn't seem like nothing."

Max scraped against the back door to be let back inside. Aidan took Laura's hand and kissed it.

"It's nothing," he lied. "Your hands were cold, that's all."

Laura frowned. They were quiet for a long minute. Aidan finally let Max in, who had given up scraping and crying at the door and begun barking obnoxiously. Laura poured herself a coffee.

"You want a cup?" she asked, shaking an empty mug in the air.

"Sure, thanks."

Laura poured Aidan a coffee while he wrapped their breakfast burritos and took them to the dining table. Bright autumn sunlight shone through the kitchen windows, making the dust motes sparkle.

"I'm going to head into town soon to take some photos and explore a little. Do you want to come with me?" Aidan asked, biting into his burrito.

"No, I'm okay. I want to stay here and relax for a while. I still haven't gotten over that drive."

Aidan nodded as he took another mouthful. Max sat next to Laura, looking up at her with his big puppy eyes. Drool dripped from his mouth at the smell of their breakfast. He kept lifting his paw, setting it on Laura's lap and whimpering. Unable to resist the powers of his cuteness, Laura pulled a part of her burrito off and threw it onto the floor. Max bolted after it, scooped it up, and made his way into the living room with the prize in his mouth.

***

Aidan stared at himself in the bedroom mirror. The purple under his eyes had darkened so that it almost looked like the beginnings of a pair of black eyes. His stubble had turned more into a short, shaggy beard. Laura hated when his facial hair got too long. She said it tickled her lips when they kissed, so Aidan always kept it trimmed. *I'll shave it when I come back.* He grabbed his coat from the wardrobe, checked the settings on the camera hanging around his neck, and started downstairs.

Laura was leaning over the countertop in the kitchen, still wearing his old t-shirt. There was a soft *crack!* as Aidan came up behind her and spanked her on the bum. Laura jumped and grabbed her bum cheek.

"Jesus, that stung," Laura laughed, rubbing at her cheek. Aidan wrapped his arms around her and pulled her in close, kissing her on her forehead.

"You sure you don't want to come?"

"Yeah, I'm sure. I'm going to grab a shower and have a pamper day."

"Okay, honey." Max came over and started scraping Aidan's leg with his paw. "Sorry, boy, I can't take you with me," he said, as if Max would understand. "I'll take you for a walk around the lake when I get back later, okay?" Aidan gave Laura one last kiss on the cheek. "I'll see you later," he said, starting for the front door.

"Love you!" Laura called out.

"Love you too," Aidan smiled at her as he shut the door behind him.

***

It was a beautiful Saturday afternoon. The sun was bright in the sky and the air was crisp. A river of dried, red leaves crunched below Aidan's feet as he walked down the footpath towards town. He pulled out his box of cigarettes, sliding one between his lips and sparking it up.

Birds sang in the coloured elms lining the footpath as he walked through a neighbourhood of identical redbrick houses. Two young girls whizzed past him on their bikes, ringing their bells. One girl was lagging behind, calling out to her friend to wait for her. Aidan felt good being out in the fresh air, taking photos again just for the fun of it. The nightmare had almost faded to the back of his mind, stored away with all the bad dreams he'd ever had since he was a kid.

"Good afternoon," a man said, out watering his lawn. The grass was perfectly cut, a shade of green so bright it was unnatural.

"Afternoon," Aidan smiled as he walked past, still not used to the friendliness of small-town living. Back in Fallbridge, you could be stabbed in the middle of the street and people would still walk over you to get to their next meeting.

"I hope you enjoy your stay in Elmwood."

Aidan lifted his hand in the air in a feeble attempt at a wave without looking back at the man. Up ahead, there was an entrance between two green, well-trimmed hedges, and a wooden sign that read *Gray's Park*. Aidan took one last draw off his cigarette and went to throw it to the ground, but stopped himself at the last second.

Instead, he walked to a bin at the entrance of the park and stubbed it out on the ashtray.

The park was beautiful. A narrow tarmac path weaved its way through tall oak and hawthorn trees. Wooden benches along the pathway sat empty. Instead, people sat on the grass and leaves in the sun. One couple sat on the grass eating a picnic; another man sat at the base of a massive oak, reading a paperback in the shade. Aidan turned on the camera and lifted the viewfinder to his eye. He snapped a handful of photos of the couple enjoying their picnic as they smiled and fed each other strawberries, then some macro shots showing the texture of the bark of an old tree. He shut the camera off and carried on through the park. Leaves fell from the trees all around him like snow. *Laura would love this place,* he thought. In the middle of the park was a small pond. Thousands of coins glistened through the water like twinkling fairy lights. In the centre of the pond stood the bronze statue of a man, looking proudly out over the park. He wore a hat that reminded Aidan of the kind a pirate would wear. A plaque at its feet read: *Johnathan Gray, Founder of Elmwood.* Aidan reached into his pocket, fished out a coin, and flicked it into the pond.

***

After showering and finally getting dressed, Laura lay sprawled out along the sofa, her long legs dangled over the edge, swinging back and forth. The house was almost silent; the only sounds came from the *tick, tick, tick* of a clock mounted on the wall and from Max, chewing on a bone in a sunspot that shone in through the living room window. She pulled her phone from her pocket; no service. Hardly surprised, she threw it on top of the coffee table, where it landed on the Ouija board.

The board and planchette were still sitting as they'd left them the night before. Just looking at them gave her the creeps. Growing up, she'd heard stories about people becoming possessed after playing with them, or opening portals to other dimensions. She didn't believe any of that now, of course, but the nervous feeling she'd gotten as a kid stuck with her and right now, staring at it, she could feel her stomach dancing as it had when she was little. So that was that. She sprung up from the sofa and boxed it back up as quickly as she could, trying her best to not hold on to it for too long, then placed it back in the bookshelf.

Now what? she thought, looking around the living room.

A *thump* came from upstairs, muffled through the floorboards. Laura looked up at the ceiling as if she might be able to see through it. It sounded like something had fallen over.

Max paid no attention to the thud and carried on gnawing on his bone.

The thought that she was all alone in a strange house crossed Laura's mind for the first time. She remembered what Aidan had said about the locals. She shook the thoughts from her head. The fact Max hadn't reacted to the sound soothed her, if only a little.

It's nothing, you're just being stupid. It was probably just your suitcase falling over… actually, yeah, that's definitely what it was. Look, even Max thinks you're mental.

Max was sitting up, taking a break from his bone. He stared at Laura with his head cocked sideways. She stared back at him, turning her head to mimic his. Board, Max licked his nose and went back to his bone.

Another thumping sound came from upstairs.

Laura picked up the fire poker – better safe than sorry – and ran up the stairs and into their bedroom. Nothing was out of place. Nothing was on the floor. Both their suitcases were where they had left them.

"Must have been the pipes," Laura murmured as she turned and walked back into the hallway. The door that led to the attic crept open; its hinges shrieked like fingernails being scraped down a chalkboard until it came to a stop. Laura walked over and pushed it the rest of the way with the fire poker. A shiver ran down Laura's spine as she looked up the stairs into the dark.

With the poker held tightly in her hand, she clicked on the light switch and started up the staircase. The wooden stairs groaned under her feet as she walked up into the attic. The smell of damp and mould reminded her of her grandma's house. The attic was mostly empty, bar a few pieces of furniture, an old set of drawers and an empty bookshelf. Piled up in one corner were a few boxes of rotten, soggy newspapers. Laura wrinkled her nose as the smell grew stronger. She scanned the room before turning to leave. Something caught her eye.

In the far corner of the attic beside the bookshelf was a strange-looking wall. There was something off about it; part of the wall, she realised, was sitting out about an inch further than the rest.

Something clicked as Laura ran her fingers down the protruding edge.

She could feel cool air on her fingertips. *It's a door. A hidden door.* Her heart quickened as she gripped the edge with both hands. She wrapped her fingers around the protruding part of the door as best she could and pulled as hard as she could.

The door was stiff, but finally it scraped open. Dust and God-knows-what-else fell to the hardwood floor. Laura coughed as she waved her hand in the air to clear some of the dust choking her.

Behind the hidden door was a small room no bigger than a closet. Old, dusty boxes filled the room, all piled on top of the other. Two had fallen to the ground, and the top had ripped open. Its contents – mainly books – were all scattered out across the floor.

Max barked from downstairs, but Laura ignored him.

She knelt and picked up one of the books and blew the dust off. It looked like she'd blown a grey storm cloud into the room. Laura opened the book. The pages had aged and turned a dirty yellow colour. There was something written in neat cursive on the first page. Laura brushed her hand across the gritty paper.

It read: *Journal of Nicolas Wright.*

CHAPTER NINE

Aidan sat slumped in a worn-out oxblood Chesterfield in *The Roast House*, the coffee shop on Main Street. The inviting aroma of coffee had called to him as he walked down the street, drawing him in like a snake charmer. The inside surprised him. It was a cosy space that he would never have guessed would be in Elmwood. A dozen paintings glowed brightly under spotlights, like art in a museum. Large, walnut bookshelves covered an entire wall, filled from top to bottom with a mixture of fiction and non-fiction books. Along the window that looked back out onto Main Street was a tall, slender wooden table with six metal stools underneath. Soothing folk music played quietly in the background.

The barista, a man in his early twenties, was busy making coffee. He sang along to the song that played over the speakers without a care in the world. From what Aidan could tell, he was the only staff member working. Besides Aidan, there was only one other person in the shop: a man who sat alone by the window, sipping on his coffee and staring out. A couple of other people had come in, but they had bought their coffees to go. Aidan enjoyed the quiet as he flicked through the photos he had taken earlier in the day.

He had been to the lighthouse and gotten some great

pictures. In one, the lighthouse stood tall and mighty as white waves crashed upon the rocks at the edge of the cliff below. Aidan had then made his way to the harbour and taken some candid photographs of the fishermen as they worked. He flicked to the next photo. An elderly fisherman, preparing bait for the day ahead.

He wore a bright yellow coat. The bait had stained the sleeves red. Aidan hurried past the next couple of images without looking at them. The sight of the yellow raincoat reminded him of Emily Pembrook. Aidan squeezed his eyes shut. The sound of heavy rain hitting the ground slowly drowned out the music of the coffee shop. The hum of the coffee machine now sounded like the rumble of an idling car's engine. All the sounds were all too familiar to Aidan.

No, no, no, how is this happening?

He shivered; his wet clothes clung to him as puffs of white mist swirled out from his mouth like a steam train with each breath. He grimaced as he cracked open his eyes. The dark road stretched out in front of him as he stood beside his car in the pouring rain. Puddles splashed under his feet as he dragged himself to the front of the car. The road ahead of him was lit by the headlights. He glanced down to where Emily's body lay at the side of the road.

She wasn't there.

Aidan frowned. Something was different. It was all different. He looked around the dark road but couldn't see anything.

Everything went silent. The rain fell, but it made no sound. Curious, he placed his hand on the car; it was still running. He could feel the vibrations rattling up his arm, but could no longer hear the engine. He looked back towards the only illuminated part of the road.

The strength in his legs gave out, and he stumbled backwards, his breath stuck in his throat.

Emily stood at the side of the road, the light reflecting brightly off her raincoat. A red scar wrapped around her throat like a necklace, that strange, unknown symbol still carved into her forehead. She stared at him with her unnaturally blue skin, her eyes as wide as full moons. She reached out towards Aidan and took a step forward. Aidan stumbled backwards and hit his back on the open car door.

"I need to speak to you," Emily said. Her voice sounded raspy.

Aidan's hands shook uncontrollably.

"It's important." She took another step forward.

"I... how..."

"The Darkness is everywhere. He sees everything, knows everything... and he has seen *you*, Aidan."

"What?" Aidan shook his head. "What are you talking about? How do you know my name?"

"The Darkness is as old as life itself. He is everywhere. There is no escaping him. I thought I could leave, that I could get away, but he found me... and he will find you. There is no escaping the Darkness."

"What's the Darkness?" Aidan asked in a trembling voice. The words had left his lips before he even realised.

"Evil." Emily stared deep into Aidan's eyes. "You have been touched by the Darkness. He has chosen you."

"Chosen me?" Aidan whispered. Images of the dark smoke swirling around him engulfed his mind. He saw the arm reaching out towards him, coughed as he remembered it forcing its way down into his throat.

"They must feed him... he is always hungry."

"Who?" Aidan frowned as he shook his head. "How do you know all this?"

Emily reached up and touched the symbol carved into her forehead. She smiled and said, "Here you go sir, one black coffee in a takeaway cup." Aidan blinked. The world came back into focus. The music grew louder; he could smell coffee. He rubbed at his eyes and looked up at the source of the voice. The barista was standing beside him, coffee in hand. Aidan squinted in the bright light. "Is everything okay, sir?" the barista asked as he set the coffee down on the table.

Aidan cleared his throat. "Yeah... yeah, sorry," he forced a chuckle.

"Well, if you need anything else, I'll be right over there." The barista pointed back to the counter.

"That's great, thank you," Aidan said, catching his breath.

Aidan set his camera down and took a hot sip of coffee.

What the fuck was that?

He sighed. From the corner of his eye, he could see the man at the other side of the shop staring over at him. Aidan turned and looked at him. The man quickly looked away.

"Fuck's his problem?" Aidan said under his breath. He began fidgeting with his fingers, then pulled his phone from his pocket to give them something to do. *Still no service.* He tapped the WiFi icon, and a list of available networks filled the screen. They all had padlock icons beside them. He scrolled down and saw one that read: *ROASTHOUSEWIFI.*

There was no padlock, so he tapped it impatiently. This was the closest he had been to the outside world since arriving in Elmwood. Part of him enjoyed the lack of social media, but it had become so ingrained into his routine that he couldn't stop himself when given the opportunity.

The WiFi finally connected, and his phone buzzed immediately with incoming emails and notifications. He swiped the Facebook notifications off the screen. There was a list of new emails, five of which were from his brother, Will. He opened the first.

Hey little bro, just thought I'd shoot you a message to see if you arrived safely. By the way, where did you guys go off to?

Anyway, hope you have a lovely time, you both deserve it. Have

fun and if you need anything, just give me a call.
Will.

Aidan closed the email and deleted the rest without reading them.

The sound of a cup being set down on the table made him look up from his phone. *Now what?*

The man who had been staring over at him had shuffled his way behind the coffee table and now he sat down, facing Aidan.

"Um, can I help you?" Aidan asked, slipping his phone back into his pocket.

The man looked like he was in his late thirties; he had scruffy, longish black hair that had started to go grey at the sides. He was in a long black peacoat, with a red checked shirt underneath and black skinny jeans. The man rustled his book bag as he set it down beside him.

"Hey, I'm Jack," he said finally. His voice had a huskiness to it.

Aidan didn't know what to do. People didn't just come and sit with you in Fallbridge. So he did the only thing that came to mind; he reached out and shook Jack's hand.

"Hey, I'm Aidan," he replied.

"Is everything alright? You were muttering to yourself for a while there. Looked like you went somewhere else." Jack stared right at him with his intense, brown, bloodshot eyes.

Heat rose up Aidan's neck as he looked away. "Oh... ah... yeah, I'm fine."

Jack nodded and took a sip of coffee. "So what brought you to Elmwood?"

"Jesus, does everybody know about us arriving? If it wasn't so weird, I'd feel like some kind of celebrity."

Jack laughed. "I guess it is kind of strange. We're a small town, so when someone new arrives... news spreads fast."

"Yeah, you aren't joking," Aidan said as he took another

drink.

"So what brings you to town?"

"Um… my wife and I got here a couple days ago. We just wanted to get away from Fallbridge for a while, get some fresh air for a change."

"Ah, the big smoke. It's been a while since I've been to Fallbridge."

"You aren't missing much." They laughed, then the conversation died off into awkward silence.

"Let me guess," Jack said, "you're staying in the Lake House?"

Aidan hesitated for a second, looking down at his coffee and shaking his head. All these questions made him feel uncomfortable, like he was being interrogated.

"You're a braver man than me," Jack said, before Aidan had a chance to answer.

"Why's that?"

"The Lake House has… a reputation, around town. Most of the locals stay well away from that place."

"So I've heard."

"Oh, is that right?"

"Bex – in the bookstore – told me about it."

"Did she now? Did she tell you about Nicolas Wright?" Jack looked hard at Aidan, the playfulness gone from his voice.

"Who?"

"Never mind." Jack looked over his shoulders around the empty coffee shop, then leaned in closer towards Aidan and opening his mouth to say something else.

The bell above the coffee shop door rang as it swung open, interrupting him. Dead leaves blew in from outside. Jack's eyes hardened as he watched the door. Aidan turned to see who the other man was staring at. It was a tall man in his late forties, with slicked-back grey hair, dressed in a black suit and tie. He walked towards the counter.

An Elmwood Police Department badge, polished to perfection, shone from his belt. Aidan could see the gun hanging from its holster under his blazer. As he walked past them, the grey-haired man stared at Jack for a long moment before turning his eyes on Aidan.

"Gentlemen," the man in the suit said, nodding at Aidan as he walked to the counter.

Jack had stiffened in his seat. He didn't take his eyes off the man until he could hear him making his order, then he leaned in closer towards Aidan. His voice was a whisper. "I live in the cottage at the end of Little Rock Road. If you need to talk, that's where you'll find me." Jack reached into his bag and pulled out a piece of paper and a red marker. He quickly scribbled something down and folded the piece of paper. Aidan couldn't see what he had written.

Jack looked over his shoulder towards the police officer, saw that he wasn't watching them, and slid the piece of paper across the coffee table to Aidan. "Take it," Jack said, staring at Aidan with a wide, intense eyes. Aidan snatched the piece of paper and scrunched it up in his fist.

Jack drank the rest of his coffee in one gulp, before wiping his mouth with his sleeve. He picked up his bag, slung it over his shoulder, and stood up. The police officer was looking over at them. Jack stepped out from behind the coffee table and stopped beside Aidan.

"Open it when you're alone," he whispered, then he turned and glared at the police officer. He patted Aidan's shoulder and walked out of the coffee shop. The police officer picked up his coffee from the counter and walked towards the exit, shaking his head.

"Welcome to Elmwood," said the grey-haired man as he walked past Aidan.

The bell above the door rang as it closed behind him.

The piece of paper burned in his hand like a piece of hot coal, begging him to open it. He slid it into his pocket and grabbed hold of his camera. He threw it over his neck, then hurried out the door, throwing a cigarette into his mouth and finishing it in three long draws. Aidan darted to Gray's Park and found a bench that was off the pathway. He looked around him to make sure no one was nearby, then pulled the piece of paper from his pocket. The coffee was turning on him. He swallowed back the saliva that filled his mouth.

He looked at the paper in the palm of his hand for a moment, then opened it up. It was another missing persons poster.

Missing: Sophie Henderson, aged nine. Last seen walking home from school on Wednesday, April 5th. If you have seen this girl or have any relevant information, please contact the Elmwood Police Department.

There was a message, scribbled in bright red marker scribbled across the poster:

DON'T GO INTO THE WOODS!

CHAPTER TEN

Frantic barking surged from the house. Aidan's stomach sank as he approached the iron gates. Max almost never barked, not like this. The most Aidan had ever heard from the dog was a pitiful, gruff sound when he wanted something, or a whimper to get out and do his business. Aidan hurried through the gates and rushed up the driveway towards the house. Smoke billowed out from the tall chimney, fading into the early evening sky; the frenzied barking grew louder as he approached the house. The door thumped off the wall as Aidan burst into the living room, knocking a picture to the floor. Laura jumped to her feet from the sofa.

"Jesus Christ, Aidan! You scared the hell out of me," she yelled, her heart in her throat. Aidan could barely hear her. Max scraped at the back door in the kitchen, scoring visible claw marks into the wood.

"What the hell's going on?" Aidan shouted over the barking. Laura's eyes were puffy and bloodshot. She wiped her runny nose with her sleeve. Aidan rushed to her and wrapped his arms around her. "What's wrong?"

Laura looked down at a stack of old dusty books on the coffee table. "We need to talk."

"Let's go outside. I can barely hear you over that fucking

dog."

Aidan stormed into the kitchen. Max's barking made his eardrums rattle like there was an earthquake inside his head.

"Max!" he yelled, but the dog didn't take any notice of him. "What the hell has gotten into you?"

He unlocked the door and pushed it open. Max burst out the door and ran through the garden towards the lake, then turned back to Aidan and started barking again.

"He's been like this all day," Laura said as she came into the kitchen, holding one of the dusty books. "I don't know what's wrong with him. I've tried letting him out, thinking he needed to pee or whatever, but all he does is stand there and bark back at me. So I brought him back inside. He just won't stop."

Max stared at them, then back towards the trees at the edge of the lake. Aidan's ears rang like fire alarms. "I think he wants us to follow him."

***

They walked hand in hand along the pathway that ran around the edge of the lake. Bright red and yellow leaves crunched under their feet as the sinking sun set the sky ablaze. Max walked just ahead of them, sniffing the ground. Thankfully, the barking had stopped, but he still seemed on edge. He would stop every couple of feet and look around as if he could sense something in the gloom of the early evening.

"So what did you want to talk about?" Aidan asked as he watched Max.

Laura sniffed, then handed the book to Aidan.

He held it in his hand and stared at it, perplexed. "A book?"

"I heard a thump earlier and went looking around the house to find out what it was. I went up to the third floor."

Laura wiped at her nose and sniffed again. "Anyway, when I went up, I saw a part of the wall that looked weird. So I went over to it and…" she lowered her voice to a whisper, "it was a secret door."

"A secret door?"

Laura grabbed his arm and scolded him with wide, blaring eyes that screamed for him to whisper. "Yes," she said quietly. "It only went to a tiny room filled with old boxes. I didn't think much of it – I thought maybe the owner forgot to close it properly before we arrived or something. Well, some of the boxes had fallen to the ground and thrown loads of these books across the floor." She tapped on the book in Aidan's hand. "I picked one up and opened it and, well…" Her voice broke as she shook her head. "Just open it."

Aidan opened up the book to the first page.

Journal of Nicolas Wright.

Aidan stopped dead in his tracks and glowered at the writing on the page. He couldn't speak. The saliva in his mouth dried up.

"I only read a couple of the entries before I had to stop. It's so horrible, Aidan. He wrote everything that he did – to *all* of them – in *explicit* detail."

"Them?" Aidan croaked.

"He was a serial killer, Aidan. A monster. And he lived in this house." Laura pointed back to the lake house. Tears gathered in her eyes; finally, the dam holding them back burst. Aidan pulled her tightly to his chest and wrapped his arms around her. His face scrunched up in frustration as he shook his head, fighting with his thoughts.

"I have something to show you too," Aidan said finally. He reached into his coat pocket, hesitated for a moment, then pulled out the folded piece of paper and handed it to Laura. He said nothing, just bowed his head towards the paper.

Laura frowned as she opened it. "What… what the hell is

this?" The piece of paper shook in her trembling hand.

"I don't think we should stay here anymore," Aidan said, his voice coming out stronger than he'd thought it would. "There's something not right about this place. I know it sounds crazy, but I just have this bad feeling that I can't shake."

"It doesn't sound crazy at all, not after –"

Max erupted with frantic barks, cutting her off as he sprinted down the path, back towards the house.

"Max!" Aidan yelled.

Max stopped at the tree line at the edge of the forest. He barked furiously at something in the trees. Aidan and Laura ran towards him.

"Max, stop that!" Laura yelled. Max ignored her.

"He's probably just seen an animal or something," Aidan said, trying to convince himself, remembering his nightmare from the night before. "Max, come on boy!" he yelled, slapping his thigh.

"What's he doing?" Laura asked.

"I've no idea. Max, come on!"

"I've never seen him act like this before."

"Here, take this." Aidan handed her Nicolas' journal. "Hey! Max!"

A crow cawed from a tree, but Aidan didn't notice. He looked through the trees to see if he could spot what had rattled the dog so much, but he couldn't see anything in the dark shadows of the forest.

"Max!" Aidan reached out to grab a hold of Max. His fingertips brushed the edge of his collar as the dog leapt forward and took off into the woods. Aidan stumbled and almost fell, but he steadied himself. "Max, get back here!" he yelled. A large vein bulged in his neck. He turned to Laura and said, "You stay here, I'll go get him."

"Wait!" Laura cried. "What about this?" She held up the

missing person poster at Aidan. It flapped in her hand like a white flag.

DON'T GO INTO THE WOODS.

"Forget that. I have to go after him."

Max's barking grew distant as the animal thrust deeper into the woods.

"But –"

"I have to go."

"Let me come too."

"No, stay here."

"But I –"

"Laura, please," he held her tightly by the shoulders. He could feel her blood racing through her body. "The longer I wait, the further he'll go. I need you to stay here, in case he comes back, okay?"

She turned her head away from him. Aidan leaned in and kissed her on the head, then turned and faced the forest.

The tall pine trees towered over him like ancient giants. He felt tiny in comparison. The forest was too dark to see anything past the first couple of rows of trees. Max's barks echoed through the woods, getting quieter each time. Aidan took one last look at Laura. Her gaze pleaded with him to stay, but she said nothing. Aidan took a deep breath and stepped into the darkness of the woods.

***

Aidan trudged forward, pushing deeper into the woods. Spiderwebs stuck to his face as he swiped at the low-hanging branches. Aidan would have seen the plumes of his breath if it hadn't been so dark. Even in the early evening, it felt more like twilight under the cover of the huge evergreens, and what little light there had been was fading fast. He reached into his pocket and pulled out his phone. The feeble torchlight didn't help much, only illuminating a few feet in front of him. The trees hissed and creaked in the wind above him as they swayed back and forth.

There were no birds singing inside the woods. The only noise was the groaning of the trees, the sound of his heavy breathing, and Max's faint barks echoing through the forest. Aidan didn't have a clue which direction to go. The barking sounded like it was straight in front of him one second; then it would be to his right, then his left, then in front of him again.

"Max! Come on, boy!" Aidan called. His voice shouted back at him. The forest floor was soft under his feet, covered with spongy, light green moss, pine needles and leaves that muffled the sound of his footsteps. The insects were back in his stomach, scurrying around inside him. He turned around to see his route back to the lake house, but everything looked the same. His breathing quickened.

One thing at a time, Aidan. He stopped and leaned against one of the enormous trunks and took a deep breath. *Find Max first, then figure out how to get back.*

A branch snapped.

What the fuck was that?

Blood pounded in Aidan's ears as he pressed himself against the tree trunk. His phone fell slack in his sweaty hand as he stared wide-eyed into the blackness of the woods to see what had made the sound. He hadn't noticed that he'd been holding his breath until his lungs screamed at him for air.

Aidan dropped to his knees and gasped as air filled his lungs. White spots danced in front of his eyes. His mouth filled with saliva, but he swallowed it back down. The image of the dark shape from his dream flashed in his mind's eye. Aidan slapped himself across the side of the face.

Get a grip. It was just a dream; it wasn't real.

Something ran past him. Closer this time. He could hear

the twigs on the ground breaking as it darted past. Aidan snapped up onto his feet and shone his light out into the wall of darkness.

Nothing.

"Hello!" Aidan called. His voice sounded small.

Everything was quiet.

His eyes were like two craters as he tried to see through the dark. Max's faint barking barely reached him now.

This place goes on for miles and miles, and he could be anywhere.

The magnitude of the task ahead finally hit him. Aidan gathered himself, determined to find Max, and marched on through the woods, watching for any movement in the trees.

***

The forest grew denser the deeper Aidan walked. The overgrowth had scratched his hands to hell. It was completely dark now, and it had been some time since Aidan last heard Max bark. He tried not to think about it and pushed on, knowing that now wasn't the time to overthink – or he would never find Max or, for that matter, get out of the woods himself.

A strange, rotten smell drifted through the trees. Aidan gagged, then spat out a mouthful of phlegm. The phone's battery was dying and the pale light from the torch threatened to go out any minute, plunging him into blinding darkness.

"Max! Where are you?" Aidan yelled. "Come on, boy. Let's go home!"

The smell grew more wretched with each step. Aidan lifted the collar of his coat and pulled it across his face to cover his nose. It gave little protection against the horrible stench, but it was something.

Aidan tripped over something protruding from the forest

floor, and fell forward, headfirst, smacking his head on the base of a tree. The phone flew out of his hand as he hit the forest floor with a *thud*. Sharp pain rattled through his skull and it throbbed like it had its own heartbeat.

Aidan groaned as he rolled over onto his back. He reached up and touched the right side of his forehead. The gash on his head burned when he touched it, it felt like a caged animal was trying to escape from his skull. He jerked his hand away from the wound as if it had actually burned him. Warm blood ran down his face and dripped into his ear. Groggily, he pulled himself to his feet. The world – or, at least, what he could see of it – spun around him. It felt like he had just come off the waltzer ride at a fairground.

Shit, where's the phone?

He held his arms out like a tightrope walker to steady himself, searching the small area around him. *Please don't let it be broken*, he said to himself. *If it's broken, you have no chance of getting out of here tonight.*

He took an uneasy step forward on his wobbly legs, taking his time with each step like a person trying to walk on a boat in rough seas. But he was fighting a losing battle. Two steps later, and he was back down on his knees. The rancid smell was almost unbearable now. Even breathing through his mouth was useless; he could almost taste the rot. Aidan coughed and gagged. The food in his stomach fought to come up. On his hands and knees, he crawled forward, dragging himself over the forest floor.

There was a faint glow up ahead. Aidan stopped and rubbed at his eyes to make sure he was really seeing it.

His heart fluttered at the sight. His entire body tingled, and the spinning of the world slowed. The muscles in his arms and legs didn't feel as weak. He rushed towards the glow of the phone, still on his hands and knees, never taking his eyes off the light.

The phone sat at the edge of a ditch, screen down so that light only spilled out from the sides. The torch beam shone up into the never-ending sky and faded to nothing. Aidan reached out to pick it up, but his light-headedness made him lose balance again. In a panic, he threw his arms out in front of him to stop himself from falling.

His hands landed in something cold and gooey that went up to his elbows. In the dark, he had no idea what it was. The strange substance made a slurping sound as he pulled his arms free. He wiped the goo from his arms, flicking it to the ground, and picked up his phone. The light hit his arm and turned a crimson red.

Aidan knew what the smell was.

He shone the light into the ditch. It took his eyes a second to adjust. Something that looked like a broken branch stuck out from the ground. It looked like the tree's bark had peeled off to show the pale wood underneath. Then he saw another, and another. Aidan shined the light further over the ditch.

It wasn't wood at all. They were bones. Part of a ribcage. The cold, gooey substance was a cocktail of decomposing, liquefied organs.

Aidan's entire body shook. He couldn't hold it in any longer. Finally, he lost the fight with his stomach and threw up at the edge of the ditch.

Aidan looked back, his eyes wide with terror. He scanned the rest of the ditch with the torch. The ragged pit was full of human remains. Skulls, bones, decomposing bodies. The stench of dried blood and decomposition forced itself inside his nose. There was no escaping it. Aidan froze on all fours at the edge of the ditch. He wanted to get up, to run away, but he couldn't take his eyes off the gore.

Then, at the other side of the ditch, a small backpack caught his eye. His lungs emptied as if someone had kicked him in the stomach.

Piled in with all the bones and flesh, just beyond the backpack, was a small body with a mess of blond hair. Little Sophie Henderson, the girl in the missing poster, sat at the edge of the ditch. Her empty, lifeless eye sockets stared back at him. Her skin had turned a sickly, dark green colour and mould had grown up the side of her face.

Aidan threw up again. Tears streamed down his face, but he couldn't remember when he had started to cry. He scrambled to his uneasy feet, unable to stop the tears. He ran as far and as quickly as his legs would take him through the forest, no idea where he was going.

All he knew was he needed to get away from the horror.

CHAPTER ELEVEN

Aidan had disappeared a couple of hours ago, and Max's barking had stopped at least an hour after. Before going back inside, Laura had sat and waited for them both to come back at the picnic table in the garden. She'd wanted to stay out of the house for as long as she could, preferably until she was no longer alone. The house had loomed over her like some forgotten god waiting to eat her whole. She'd imagined herself going back inside and the door closing on her like a giant mouth eating her alive. A long shiver ran down her spine. The late evening had brought a cool breeze along with it. Laura stood on the picnic table, her arms crossed over her body, looking at the tree line.

"Aidan!" she called, but there was no reply. She stood waiting a while longer, hoping they would show up.

But they never did. So reluctantly, she went inside.

Laura left the back door open so she could listen for any sound from Aidan or Max. There was a sinking feeling in her stomach that only grew stronger the longer she was alone. She went to the kitchen, filled a glass of water, and downed it with a faint hope that it would settle her stomach a little. It didn't. So she pulled the cork from the wine bottle and poured herself a generous glass.

She fidgeted at the dining table, looking out the open door, unable to settle, listening for a sound from outside. *Where are they?* she thought. *Max couldn't have gotten that far.*

Then it hit her like a freight train. *What if Aidan's hurt? What if he's unconscious, lying in the woods somewhere?* Her mind whirled with different questions, different scenarios. Making her feel dizzy.

Something squeaked in the living room.

Laura turned towards the noise and watched as the basement door under the stairs creaked open. For a second, she couldn't breathe. A gust of wind blew in from outside and swirled around the house. The door moved again. Laura relaxed, finally able to breathe. *It's just the wind.*

She sighed and got up from the table, wine glass still in hand, and started for the door. She peeked around the door, looking down the staircase into the dark basement. The smell of damp and stale air drifted up the stairs. She slammed the door shut, making sure it wouldn't blow open again. Then she rested her forehead on the cold wood, closed her eyes and took a deep breath.

BANG!

The sound cut through the silent house like a knife. Laura's skeleton almost jumped out of her skin. The wine glass fell from her hand and smashed on the wooden floor. Pieces of glass scattered everywhere.

Shit!

She turned to face the source of the noise. A box lay on the floor beside the bookcase. It was the Ouija game. Pieces of broken glass crunched under her feet as Laura walked to the box. She picked it up and slid it back into its place on the shelf, then turned away.

Something hit her on the back of the legs, then landed on the floor.

Laura hesitated for a moment. She squeezed her eyes shut

as her entire body shook. A single tear fell over her cheek. *This isn't happening. It can't be happening!* Every part of her was screaming for her to get out, to leave the house and wait outside until Aidan came back. Even if it meant sitting out in the cold.

If he comes back, that is.

Laura shook her head, annoyed at herself for even thinking about it, then opened her eyes. She wiped away the damp trail left by the tear and took a deep breath. The Ouija box was on the floor again. She turned and picked it up. As soon as Laura's fingers touched the box, a wave of calm swept over her.

Her shakes slowed, then stopped. The panic that had filled her chest no longer existed. All her muscles relaxed. Then something happened that she could have never expected:

She smiled.

Laura carried the box to the coffee table, swiped the journals to the floor, and set the box down like a museum worker handling a fragile piece of history. She opened the box and set the board and planchette on the table.

There was a look in her eye, a glint that hadn't been there since the day she'd found out she was pregnant.

***

Aidan rushed through the trees in no particular direction. The torch beam of the phone in his hand flashed on the passing trees like a strobe light. His tears stung the cuts and scratches on his face he had earned by forcing himself through the low-hanging branches. There was no way of knowing where he was, or how deep into the woods he had gone. The sickening smell of rotting flesh had finally faded away, so he slowed to a stop, leaning over with his hands on his knees as he tried to catch his breath. Blood ran down his face from the gash on his forehead, painting half his face red. His mouth tasted of pennies.

Wind howled through the woods like a banshee. The trees swung and hissed all around him. Aidan sat up and looked around the dark forest of giants, feeling more alone than he had ever felt in his entire life.

I'm lost, fuck! What am I going to do? I'm going to fucking die in here.

Aidan clenched his sweaty hair between his fingers, the dire reality of his situation finally setting in. He cried.

A bark echoed through the woods. The first in God-knows-how-long. It sounded close. Aidan sniffed, then stood as quietly as he could, holding his breath to help him hear better, to make sure it wasn't just in his head.

Another bark. It was just up ahead.

Max?

Aidan's heart leapt into his throat at the sound. His red-stained teeth gleamed in the dark.

"Max!" Aidan screamed, taking off towards the sound, ducking and weaving his way around the trees.

Max barked again.

"I'm coming, boy!" Aidan still had no idea where he was or how he was going to get back home, but that didn't matter now. Soon he would have Max and he wouldn't be alone. He could figure out the rest after.

Up ahead, the claustrophobic dark eased a little as the trees thinned. Aidan didn't have to fight as hard to make his way through them. A faint, blue glow from the half-moon lit up the forest in front of him. He stopped and basked in the pale light, relieved for the break from the suffocating darkness. Even the wind seemed to have calmed down. He reached his arms up towards the tall trees as if he was trying to snatch the moon from the sky.

Something moved beyond the light.

"Max?" Aidan called out.

A branch snapped behind him. Aidan spun around. He squinted to see better, but he couldn't see anything.

"Come on, Max!"

Something brushed against a tree trunk. The entire tree leaned forward, blocking out some of the moonlight. Aidan stumbled back, expecting the tree to come down on top of him.

Another tree moved, then another. The moonlight grew dimmer and dimmer. Aidan didn't know what to do except stand in the small beam of light as if it would protect him somehow.

Then he saw it.

A hand – at least, what Aidan could only guess was a hand – wrapped around the trunk of a tree, somehow darker than the blackness of the woods beyond.

"What the fuck…"

Three unnaturally long fingers gripped the bark. The tree groaned and protested. Wood snapped and cracked as the trunk moved forward, extinguishing the last of the moonlight and throwing Aidan into the blinding dark once again. He tried to run, but his legs had stopped working. *Just like in the nightmare.* He pulled at his frozen legs, but it was no use.

In the limited light, the thing that was darker than night slithered around the trees. Aidan followed it with his head, never taking his eyes off it. Piss ran down his leg as the dark thing stepped out from behind a tree towards him. One by one, trees dissolved into the dark as the shape crept towards Aidan.

Leaves crunched on the forest floor behind Aidan. Something was running, and fast. The sound grew louder and louder. Aidan whirled around to look – Max leapt out from the woods behind him.

He landed at Aidan's feet with a skid, hunched over, lips

curled and baring his teeth. A low, guttural growl rumbled in his throat as he stared down the dark thing. Max hammered out a defensive bark, but the thing kept coming. In a flash, Max leapt at it.

"Max, no!"

The dog grabbed hold of the dark shape's arm, digging his teeth into its pitch-black flesh. Thunder rumbled, and the ground shook under Aidan's feet. The thing swung Max around in the air like a rag doll, but he held on tight. The shape stumbled back – then swiped Max away with a second, unnaturally long arm, sending him tumbling through the air.

Max slammed against a tree with a yelp and landed on the forest floor. The tight grip that held Aidan in place loosened, and he ran. Kneeling down beside the dog, Aidan looked back towards the shape, his teeth clenched and fury in his eyes, but the dark thing had gone.

Max whimpered.

"I'm here, boy." Aidan cupped his hands around Max's head.

Max looked up at him, his enormous eyes filled with terror.

"No, no, no, no," Aidan gasped as he laid his hand on Max's chest. Three huge claw marks had opened up the side of his chest, turning his golden fur a dark crimson. Aidan could see his ribs and muscle through the gouges. His chest rose and fell in fast, shallow movements as he tried to catch a breath. Aidan's heart sank while he stroked the dog's head. Tears filled his eyes. Max gently licked Aidan's hand then lowered his head, exhausted. "You're going to be okay. Everything's going to be okay."

Aidan looked at his phone to check how much battery it had left. It went dark.

"Fuck!"

He wrapped his arms under Max and lifted him up into his arms. *I'll get you home, boy. Somehow and some way, I'll get you back, don't you worry.*

Max whimpered with the movement. To slow the bleeding, Aidan held him tightly against his chest, groaning as he pulled himself to his feet. He looked around in the darkness with no idea how to get back to the house.

"This way," a faint voice called from the shadows.

Aidan squinted into the dark. Something shone through the shadows like the glow of a lantern. Light, then dark, light, then dark as it moved through the trees. He squeezed his eyes closed to clear the tears. The glow grew a little stronger. Aidan gripped Max in his arms and took a couple of steps towards the strange light. As he got closer, the light grew clearer.

It wasn't a lantern at all. It was a yellow raincoat.

"Come on, we have to hurry!" Emily said. Aidan looked down at Max. His breathing had begun to slow. Emily took off into the woods, her raincoat shining like a flare in the night. Aidan ran after her, holding Max as steady as he could. "This way!"

Her voice echoed through the woods. Aidan's lungs were on fire when he caught up to her. She weaved around the trees, dodging the overgrowth and ditches as if she knew every inch of the forest. In the shadows at his back, Aidan could hear the trees swaying and groaning as they closed in on him, the branches reaching out for him like long claws.

"Laura!" Aidan screamed.

***

Laura placed both her hands on the planchette and called out. "Who wants to speak with me?"

Silence.

"You were trying to get my attention. You have it. What do you want to tell me?"

Laura thought she could feel the plastic planchette move slightly under her fingers, but she wasn't sure if it was all in her head. "I think I can feel you... you need to try harder to move it." The planchette vibrated violently under her fingers, rattling against the wood of the board. Her heart pounded hard in her chest.

The planchette jerked to the left side of the board. Laura gasped, snatching her fingers away. She squeezed her eyes shut, cursing herself.

"I'm sorry, I wasn't expecting that," she said to the empty room. She lowered them back down, feeling the electricity between her fingers. "What do you –"

Before Laura could finish, the planchette took off, moving around the board in a circular motion. She grinned as she watched with the wonder of a child.

The planchette stopped jerkily on some of the letters. *U-M-U-S-T-H-E-L-P.*

"Help? Are you in trouble?" Laura asked. Her body tingled with goosebumps. It felt like there was a current running from her head to her toes.

The planchette kept moving. *E-V-I-L-I-S-C-O-M-I-N-G.*

"Evil?" Laura whispered. Her hands slid effortlessly over the board.

T-H-E-M-A-S-K-S.

"Masks? I don't understand." Laura shook her head.

The planchette spelt out *B-E-W-A-R-E*, then slid across to the drawing of the moon in the top corner of the board.

A noise echoed faintly from outside. The planchette suddenly stopped.

Laura's eyes felt heavy, like she had just woken from a deep sleep. She took her fingers off the planchette and sat up, wiping at her eyes. She heard the noise again, but couldn't make out what it was.

Then again, clearer this time.

"Aidan?" Laura whispered.

"Laura!" Aidan yelled. His voice echoed from the woods. Laura's heart swelled as she jumped up from the sofa, then bolted through the kitchen and rushed outside to the garden.

"Aidan!"

***

Aidan heard Laura calling his name. He was close now. Emily weaved in and out of the trees and he followed closely behind.

"Almost there!" she called, without looking back. Aidan's arms trembled with the weight of the dog hugged to his chest. His legs grew weaker, quickly turning to jelly. He only hoped he would make it back to the house before they gave out.

Laura called his name again. Up ahead, he saw something in-between the trees. A glimmer of moonlight shone at the edge of the woods.

That has to be it.

Emily ran towards the light. Aidan squeezed Max tighter to his body and followed. As Emily reached the edge of the woods, she erupted into hundreds of fireflies.

"Laura!" Aidan screamed as he finally broke through the trees into the garden. Laura rushed towards him, her eyes wide with panic.

"Oh my God! What happened?" Laura gasped. Her eyes shifted back and forth from Aidan to Max, both covered in blood.

"Go inside and call the police. Use the landline in the kitchen," Aidan said breathlessly.

"What happened, Aidan?" Laura demanded. Tears streamed down her face.

"Laura, go phone the police now!" Aidan snapped. Max

felt like a tonne weight in his arms, and he didn't know how much longer he could hold on to him. "Tell them there are bodies in the woods." Laura stopped and looked at Aidan in disbelief as he trudged past her, focused only on getting to the house.

"Wha…"

"Go!" Aidan yelled, growing impatient, his legs ready to give out at any second.

Laura sprinted past them to the house and into the kitchen. *Come on, just a little further.*

Aidan groaned as he stomped up the steps and into the kitchen. He leaned Max's weight onto his weary legs and swiped his arm out across the dining table, throwing everything onto the floor and gently laying Max on top. Every breath burned like saltwater filling his lungs. Sweat stung his eyes, and the dried blood on his face made his skin feel tight. Laura was on the phone to the emergency dispatcher. The phone shook visibly in her hand.

"Yes, we need police… and an ambulance. My… my husband and my dog have been attacked. My husband says… he said there are bodies in the woods… yes… Jesus…"

Laura trailed off, seeing the three claw marks up Max's side for the first time. All the blood in her body cooled all at once.

Aidan ran up the stairs to the bathroom, taking two at a time, grabbed all the towels he could find and hurried back down to the kitchen. Max had lost a lot of blood and his breathing was almost non-existent. Aidan took one towel and held it tightly against the wounds on Max's side to slow down the bleeding. Within seconds, dark red blood had saturated the towel. Laura stumbled with the phone still in her hand, forgetting to hang up.

A small voice from the receiver said, *"Ma'am are you still there? Ma'am? Stay where you are, a unit is on the way."* The voice turned to a hum as the call ended. She threw the receiver on the table and picked up a towel and handed it to Aidan. The blood-soaked towel dropped to the floor with a wet *slop.* The clean, white towel turned red before their eyes. Laura stroked Max's head, her face wet with tears. Max watched her with his puppy-like eyes and let out quiet whimpers.

"What happened?" Laura whispered, scared to speak any louder. Aidan stared at Laura. He looked like he had been through the wars with his bloodshot eyes and blood-stained, cut up face.

"I looked for him everywhere. It was getting dark so quickly," Aidan said as he tried to catch his breath. "My phone's torch was useless. He kept getting further and further away until I couldn't even hear him anymore… I tripped over something and fell and hit my head. That's when I saw them… there were so many… her eyes." Tears fell down Aidan's face, turning red in the dried blood.

"Saw who? Whose eyes?" Laura asked. Aidan was silent for a moment. His mouth was open, but nothing would come out. He took a deep breath.

"Sophie," Aidan sobbed. "The girl from the poster. I found her." He shook his head. "I can't unsee her eyes."

Laura wrapped her arm around Aidan and pulled herself in close, wiping away his tears, not knowing what to say.

"There was something… something in the woods. I've no clue what it was. The thing was huge, and it came for me, but…" Aidan looked down at Max and stoked his matted fur. "He saved me. If it wasn't for him, I'd be dead right now."

Max started hyperventilating, his tail tucked tightly between his legs while his legs kicked frantically on the table like he was trying to run away. Aidan held him down to make sure he wouldn't fall off.

"It's okay boy, it's okay," Aidan said. Panic filled Max's

eyes as he looked for Aidan and Laura. Aidan could feel his tiny heart thumping quicker and quicker in his chest.

"Aidan, what do we do?" Laura's voice trembled.

"I don't know, I don't know!"

Aidan threw the blood-soaked towel to the ground beside the first one. Picked up the fresh towel from the table and pressed down as hard as he could on the wounds. Laura sat on the kitchen floor, her head resting against his, looking into his eyes and stroking his head. "Everything's going to be okay. You're a good boy, aren't you? Yes, you're the best boy," Laura sobbed.

Max cracked opened his mouth and licked the tears rolling down Laura's cheek. His tongue felt cold and dry on her skin. A long breath left his body and his tongue went limp, falling to the side of his mouth.

Laura stared into his glazed eyes. "Max... Max?" Laura whispered. Aidan grasped the blood-soaked towel in his hands and slammed it to the ground. The strength left his legs, and he fell to the floor. Laura sobbed, unable to catch her breath.

Aidan wrapped his arms tightly around her as her heart broke. They sat there for what felt like an eternity, just holding each other.

CHAPTER TWELVE

Laura and Aidan sat in silence in the living room. Laura sobbed into her jumper and Aidan stared off into the distance with glazed eyes, not really looking at anything at all. His head throbbed. Dried blood still covered half his face. Max's body lay on the kitchen table, covered with a blood-stained sheet. Wailing sirens grew louder.

The sound snapped Aidan out of his daze. Blue and red flashing lights bounced off the walls outside as an ambulance and a police car pulled up outside the house. Aidan groaned as he pulled himself to his feet. The muscles in his legs had gone stiff, and they burned when he moved.

Laura looked up at him through tear-filled eyes as he scraped his feet along the wooden floor towards the front door. *My husband has aged ten years since this morning*, she thought grimly as she watched him pull open the door. Aidan held his arm in the air, shielding his eyes from the blinding, flashing lights.

The driver and passenger-side doors of the police cruiser opened in unison. Two silhouetted officers got out, leaving the flashing lights on, and walked towards Aidan. One officer took off their hat as they approached.

"Good evening, sir. We received a call about an attack. And

something about bodies in the woods?" an officer said, a questioning tone to the words. He had a raspy voice that sounded like he smoked too much and drank whiskey like water. When they reached the front door, the dim porch light gave their silhouettes features. Aidan recognised the raspy-voiced man immediately. The officer from the coffee shop ran a hand through his silver, swept-back hair, then held it out towards Aidan. "I'm Detective Walker."

Aidan went to shake the detective's hand and stopped.

Detective Walker stared at the dried blood on Aidan's hand and withdrew his own. "That's probably for the best, son." He rubbed his hand on his suit trousers. "This is Officer Foster."

He gestured to the officer beside him. Officer Foster was a young man; he must have been in his early twenties, but he looked much younger. The *Elmwood P.D.* badge glittered proudly on his chest. Beads of sweat glistened in the light on his forehead as he stared wide-eyed at Aidan. *Is this kid even old enough to shave?* Aidan thought to himself. The paramedics took out a large bag from the back of the ambulance and started towards Aidan and the officers.

"Detective Walker, Officer Foster," Aidan nodded, sidestepping from the door. "Please come in."

Laura jumped up from the sofa, wiping her tears away with her sleeve as the two officers and the paramedics came into the room.

"Good evening, ma'am," Walker said, his face as hard as coal. "I'm Detective Walker and this is Officer Foster."

"I'm…" she sniffed, "Laura Crain."

The officers didn't offer a handshake this time. Officer Foster spied the blood-stained sheet in the kitchen and nudged Walker. Foster rested his hand on top of the gun strapped to his waist. Walker frowned at him and shook his head. Foster hesitated, then lifted his hand, settling it down by his side.

"Sorry, I'm…" Aidan said as he rubbed at his face, sending dried flakes of blood drifting to the ground. "I'm Aidan. Aidan Crain. Sorry, my head is scattered at the minute."

"It's okay, sir. It's been one hell of a night from the looks of it." Walker looked Aidan up and down. His clothes were stained dark red from Max's blood. "You should let the paramedics take a look at you, then we can have a chat about what happened." Walker gestured with his hand towards the kitchen. "You too, ma'am. Let's get you checked out as well."

The two paramedics hurried into the kitchen. They glanced at the blood-stained sheet covering Max's body, then back to each other. The female paramedic shrugged, then began to pull out chairs from the table. Laura went to Aidan and threw his arm around her shoulder.

"Come on, honey," she said as she helped Aidan into the kitchen.

"If you don't mind, were going to have a quick look around," Walker said.

"That's fine," Aidan said without looking back.

***

Detective Walker waited until Aidan and Laura were out of the room, then grabbed Foster by the scruff and pushed him up against the wall.

"Are you some kind of fucking idiot?" he hissed. "I should take that God-damned pistol off you right now and send you back to the station. You fucking useless piece of shit!"

"I'm sorry –" Foster mumbled.

Walker loosened his grip on the young man and smoothed out his uniform. "I'm sorry *what*?"

"I'm sorry, sir."

Walker stared at him for a long moment. Finally, he

nodded. "Now make yourself useful and do as I say, got it?"

Officer Foster nodded, then hurried to the other side of the room.

A piece of glass crunched under Walker's foot. He looked down at the shattered wine glass, then pulled out a small, black flipbook and pen from his pocket and started taking notes.

Male, visibly shaken, clothes bloody. Take for evidence and have tested.

Female, in shock, but doing better than the male.

Broken glass on the floor. Possible struggle.

"Sir. Look at this," Foster called. Walker sighed, then looked over at the officer. He stood at the coffee table, holding the Ouija board up to his chest.

Walker scribbled down *Ouija board* in his notebook, then went to Foster.

"What the hell do you think this is all about?" Foster said.

"I don't know," Walker said, studying the board.

"Do you think…" Foster whispered as he leaned in closer, "that this is some kind of ritual, or some shit? Like, they killed their dog as some kind of offering –"

Walker looked at Foster and the younger man stopped talking immediately. "You know what I think," Walker said, shaking his head. "I think you're some extra kind of stupid who watches too many damn horror movies. Now get your sorry ass back in the cruiser and I'll deal with you when we get back to the station."

"But you've heard the stories about this place, don't you think –"

"Now!"

Foster looked up at him like a scolded puppy with its tail between its legs.

"Well, what are you waiting for?"

Foster threw the Ouija board onto the sofa and headed for

the door.

***

Laura sat in one chair having her blood pressure taken while Aidan sat in another, one of the paramedics shone a torch the size of a pen into his eyes. They both had their backs to Max.

"All right, ma'am, your vitals seem fine. Take some paracetamol and have an early night," a female paramedic said. The other had switched the torch off and was rustling around in their bag. Bright balls of light danced in front of Aidan's eyes.

"Thank you," Laura said, then she turned in her chair and faced the living room. It sounded like the officers might have been arguing in there, but she couldn't make out what was being said.

The paramedic who had been working on Aidan pulled out a packet of alcohol wipes from the bag. "This will sting a little," the paramedic said. Aidan knew he was lying. It was going to *hurt*. The man began wiping the dried blood from the gash on Aidan's forehead. He grimaced as the alcohol worked its way into the wound.

"So what happened?" the female paramedic asked, snapping off her latex gloves. The front door slammed shut.

"I was about to ask the same question," Walker said as he moved into the kitchen, eyeing the blood-stained sheet that covered Max and the soaked towels laying on the floor. "Dispatch told us you and your dog were attacked – where, exactly, did that happen?"

Aidan squeezed his eyes shut, inhaling through his teeth as pain wracked him.

"I was in the forest... something attacked me. I don't know what it was, some kind of animal maybe," Aidan shook his head. "Max, he jumped in and saved me, but..." Aidan opened one eye and swallowed as he looked at the sheet. Walker, who was standing next to the table, lifted a corner of the sheet and looked under it to see Max's body.

"It must have been one hell of an animal to do that," Walker looked at Aidan with slitted eyes and dropped the sheet. "Tell me, Aidan, how did you and your dog end up in the woods at night?"

"We were walking around the lake and he saw something in the woods..." Aidan winced as the paramedic cleaned his head with a fresh wipe. "He took off after... whatever it was. It wasn't like him, he's... he *had*... never done anything like that before. So I ran in after him. It got dark real quick, and I only had my phone light to see. I tripped over something and banged my head." Aidan pointed at the gaping wound. "That's when I found..." Aidan trailed off.

Walked flicked open his notebook. "We'll have to get the vet out to have a look at him and determine what animal could have caused this. I'll call Mr. Stine in the morning." He wrote a note and underlined it. "And where were you during all of this, miss?"

Laura stared into the living room with glazed eyes.

"Miss?" Walker said, a little louder.

"Huh?" Laura said, shaking her head and blinking heavily. She looked like she had just woken up. "Sorry, I was... somewhere else. What did you say?"

Walker eyed the empty wine bottles on the counter, scribbled something in his notebook, and looked back to Laura. "Where were you during all this?" He gestured to the chaos in the kitchen.

"Um, I was here. Aidan was in the forest."

Walker nodded and jotted *wife was home* in his notebook.

"What about the bodies?" Aidan snapped.

"Ah yes, the human remains." Walker licked his forefinger and flipped to a new page in his notebook. "So, where in the forest did you see these *human remains*?"

Aidan could hear the scepticism in Walker's voice, but ignored it.

"I don't know. It was dark, and I was lost, but there was this smell, a horrible smell," Aidan's nose wrinkled as the memory played back in his head. "It was after I hit my head. They were all in... they were all piled in a ditch."

Walker wrote in his notepad.

"One of them was that little girl. Sophie Henderson."

Walker stopped and glared at him. "How do you know about Sophie Henderson?" His eyes were focused on Aidan with intense interest.

"I saw her missing poster."

"And you're sure it was her?"

"I think so, yes." The image of her empty eye sockets flashed in his mind, sending a shiver down his spine.

"So you admit it was hard to see?"

"Yes, it was hard to see, but –"

"So it might not have been Sophie?"

"I saw her... Do you seriously think I'm fucking making this up?"

"Aidan!" Laura snapped. Both men backed down.

Aidan pulled his face away from the paramedic. His hands clenched so tightly that his nails dug into his palms.

"It's okay," Walker said, looking at Laura, then back at Aidan. "I understand that you're upset and frustrated, but I need to know for sure. Was it Sophie Henderson?"

Aidan leaned forward and looked him directly in the eyes and said, "It was."

Walker closed his little notebook and put it and the pen back into his pocket, running a hand through his hair.

"Excuse me," Walker said, then left for the cruiser.

"You're going to need stitches," the paramedic said finally. "But I think you'll be fine with the adhesive ones." She shuffled through the bag and pulled out a small packet. "You'll have one heck of a headache tonight, and maybe tomorrow, too. You'll probably be left with a small scar, but nothing serious," she said, applying the stitches to the gash on Aidan's head.

"Okay, thanks."

"Both of you get some rest."

They nodded. The paramedics packed up their things and left. Laura helped Aidan to his feet. His knees cracked and his muscles felt like hot pokers as they shuffled to the front door.

The red and blue lights still flashed in the dark. Detective Walker was standing by the cruiser, talking to Foster, who didn't look pleased. The older man turned and saw Aidan and Laura standing at the front door and headed to them.

"It's too dark to do any kind of search tonight, but do you think you could show us tomorrow where you found the bodies?" Walker asked.

"You want me to come with you?" Aidan asked, surprised.

"Of course. Do you think you could guide us to where you found them?"

"I… I don't…" Aidan stuttered. Laura pulled him in and held him tightly in her arms. "I can try. If we get a whiff of that smell, we won't miss it."

"All right. I'll be back first thing in the morning with a search party. The Elmwood police department isn't huge, but we'll do what we can." Walker pointed over to Foster, pouting in the cruiser. "Officer Foster will keep the first watch tonight."

"First watch?" Laura asked.

"It's just a precaution, ma'am." Another police cruiser pulled up at the house. "I'll see you bright and early."

Walker strolled to the second car and got inside. The police cruiser turned off its flashing lights and headed down the driveway, followed by the ambulance.

***

Walker flicked through his notes, mumbling under his breath.

"Everything all right, boss?" Officer Cross asked from the driver's seat.

Walker closed his notebook and turned to him. "Just a feeling," he said. "I don't know what it is, but that man's hiding something."

CHAPTER THIRTEEN

It had been a long night – the longest Aidan could remember, and one they both wanted to forget – and now all Aidan wanted to do was take his dirty clothes off, have a shower and try as hard as he could to fall asleep.

The building was quiet now. Motionless. The quiet made Aidan feel as if the house was closing in around him, so he went to the old record player in the corner of the room and flicked through the collection. He didn't recognise a single one. Giving up and just needing the quiet to end, he pulled out a random record. The cover was of a middle-aged man sitting on a stool holding an acoustic guitar, grinning back at him. He slid the record out of its sleeve, placed it on the player, and dropped the needle. A faint crackle filled the room before the first song started. Aidan peeled back the curtain and looked out the window. Officer Foster was sitting in the cruiser, fast asleep; mouth wide open, catching flies. *That's a great help.*

Laura walked in from the kitchen with a bottle of whiskey in hand. She glanced at the sheet covering Max as she passed, and felt the pressure building behind her eyes.

"Who's this?" Laura asked, anything to distract herself before the tears started up again.

"No idea," Aidan shook his head, still looking out the window. Aidan gestured out with his thumb and turned to her. "He's really working hard out there."

"I don't understand why we need someone to keep watch," she said. "I mean, what are they watching for?" Laura set the bottle down on the coffee table.

Aidan thought about the dark thing that had come at him in the woods. "I don't know, sweetie. It's not like he's doing much watching, anyway."

"Maybe he's here to keep an eye on us," Laura said as she picked up the Ouija board and threw it like a frisbee into the corner of the room.

"Maybe he is," Aidan said with raised eyebrows. He unscrewed the whiskey bottle and took a swig. Laura snatched the bottle from Aidan and took a mouthful. Her eyes were red and puffy. Mascara had run down her face, leaving long black streaks that looked like spider legs coming from her eyes.

"I need to talk to you." Laura sighed. "Something happened earlier. I don't know how to…" she took another swig and grimaced as the whiskey burned going down her throat.

"Laura, what happened?" Aidan took the bottle from her and set it on the table.

"I… I don't even know how to…"

"Just try." Aidan took her hands in his. They were cold and trembling, so he squeezed them a little tighter. His head throbbed, but he ignored it.

"It was like something came over me – a *calmness* is the only way I can explain it. You know I don't believe in any of that stuff… you know I wouldn't make any of it up."

"What stuff?" Aidan said, confused.

Laura sighed, her eyes squeezed into tight slits. "Ghosts."

The word struggled to leave her lips. Aidan leaned back on

the sofa, his forehead wrinkled into a frown.

"When you were in the woods, something strange happened." Aidan took another swig and nodded for her to continue. "I was sitting at the dining table waiting for you and the... the Ouija board fell from the shelf. It scared me half to death. I thought I might not have put it back on the shelf properly, and it was just a coincidence that it fell when it did. So I stuffed it back in, but... it fell out again."

Saying nothing, Aidan handed her the bottle.

She took it from him and gulped it down. There was a fire ablaze in her stomach, but the warmth comforted her. She gazed blankly into the flickering flames of the fire; yellows and oranges danced off her pupils. "I picked it up and then this... this feeling came over me. I don't really know how to explain it... it was like I was in a dream and the feeling was telling me not to be scared, and I wasn't. I felt like I had to protect it, like... a mother's instinct or something. It wanted me to open the Ouija and use it, so I did." She took another mouthful. "I put my fingers on the planchette and started asking questions... and..." She looked at Aidan wide eyed. "I... I got a response."

Aidan was still. "What did it say?"

"That it needed help." Laura paused for a moment, then took a deep breath. "And that... evil was coming. Then something about masks. I don't know what any of it means, but... I need to help them. I can't explain why, I just have this feeling..." Tears filled her eyes again. "You believe me, don't you?"

Aidan sat motionless, staring back at Laura, deep in thought. "Of course I believe you," he said finally, wrapping his arms around her. Her face was smothered in his chest, her cries muffled. He wanted to tell her about the dark thing in the woods and about Emily guiding him through the forest back to her. But even he didn't understand what it was, or how any of it was possible.

They had been through enough for one day.

I'll tell her about it all, about everything, but just not today.

The record had stopped playing, but neither of them noticed. A low, static hiss crackled from the record player as Aidan stroked Laura's head. "You know I'll always be here for you. And if you think we should stay to help them... well, then we'll stay."

"Are you sure?" Laura said, climbing up from Aidan's chest.

"I'm sure." Aidan grabbed the bottle of whiskey and guzzled down a mouthful. Grimacing, he said, "Let's go to bed."

Laura leaned in and kissed him. Alcohol rushed to Aidan's head as he stood up. The room span around him, slowing as he steadied himself. He shut off the hissing record player and went to the kitchen. Laura watched from the bottom of the stairs, her eyes filling up again. She felt like she had cried enough for an entire year in one day and didn't know how there were any tears left in her, but somehow, they kept on coming.

Aidan stopped by Max's body and gently pulled the sheet back from his face, stroking his head. "Sleep tight, boy. We love you."

Laura wiped away the tears with the corner of her sleeve. Aidan leaned over and gave Max a kiss on the head before covering him again.

Laura went straight to bed, and Aidan climbed into the shower. The scalding water stung his sore, scratched body but soothed the aches in his muscles. The water at his feet turned a brownish-red colour as dirt and blood ran off him, the horror washing itself away.

Aidan leaned against the wall and pressed his eyes closed, letting the water run over his face.

***

The bedroom was dark, save for the dim glow from the bedside lamp. Laura was fast asleep next to Aidan, snoring into her pillow. He was glad she'd allowed her exhaustion to take over, but he found that he couldn't do the same. He stared at the ceiling, unable to feel even the slightest grip of the Sandman.

It wasn't the memories of the hellish day that kept him awake; it was the eerie quiet of the house without Max in it.

The room spun around him; his eyes somersaulted as they tried to keep up. Aidan rolled onto his side to slow the spinning down. It worked a little. Laura wriggled beside him, pulling the cover over her head. Aidan tapped the screen of his phone on the bedside table. It lit the room in a bright blue glow that forced him to squint.

It was 3 a.m. Again.

He locked the phone, sending the room back into blackness. Flashes of colour beamed in front of his eyes like a kaleidoscope. His brain throbbed like a caged animal trying to break free of his skull, and the spinning had started to make his stomach turn. As he lay in bed, his thoughts turned to the people he had found in the forest, which didn't help his stomach much.

Then he thought of little Sophie. Her hollow eyes haunted him even while he was awake. He wondered what her life was like. Did she enjoy school? What did she want to be when she grew up? What happened to her? He thought about her parents and what they must be going through. The endless torture of wondering what they could have done differently.

Then it hit him.

Tomorrow, her parents' torment would end with her body

finally being found.

Only, it wouldn't end. Not really. It would evolve into a new, more erosive kind of torture instead. The kind that would dig a trench in their minds and make them wish everything could go back to the way things were before. They'd tell themselves that everything was their fault and that they'd do anything to be with their little girl again. She'd occupy their minds from morning to night. Thoughts of who'd done this to their little girl and the unspeakable things that she must have gone through would slowly drive them insane, eating away at them both until they were nothing but empty shells.

Aidan's heart fell to the pit of his stomach. A cold tear crept out of his eye and ran down into the pillow as he stared blankly at the wall. He wiped at the trail left from the tear with the quilt cover and begged for sleep to come and take him away, even if only for an hour or two.

A floorboard squeaked in the hallway and for a second Aidan thought it was Max, then reality smacked him like a steam train. The bedroom door creaked open a couple of inches, splitting the room in half with the light from the hallway. Aidan bolted upright in bed and scanned the room. His ears boomed with the pounding of his heart. Laura stirred in her sleep but didn't wake. For a second Aidan thought about waking her, then decided against it. *Just the wind*, he told himself. *There must be a window open somewhere, that's all*. He shuffled back into bed and pulled the covers up to his chin, leaving the door slightly ajar, and closed his eyes.

A strange scratching sound came from under the bed. It sounded like a mouse gnawing on the floorboards. He listened but refused to open his eyes.

The scratching grew louder.

Then another sound. Aidan couldn't quite tell what it was. He thought it sounded like something sliding. Unable to stop himself, he opened his eyes and leaned forward. The springs of the mattress squeaked as he peeked over the edge of the bed and looked at the bedroom floor.

There was nothing there.

An arm sprung out from under the bed and grasped the floor, digging its fingernails into the wood. Aidan sprung back, his wide eyes locked on it, unable to tear them away. The arm was a greenish colour with spots of black mould; the fingernails splintered and broke as they scraped over the floorboards, pulling a head forward from under the bed.

It was a woman. Patchy, thin hair clung to her scalp and draped over her face.

The corpse pulled itself with one arm further out from the bed and stared up at Aidan with long-dead, grey eyes. She looked at him and a horrible groan escaped her lipless mouth. For a second, Aidan forgot how to breathe. The naked corpse pulled itself further from under the bed, revealing the torn flesh that had ripped apart at her waist. Black, liquified intestines sprawled out from her like tentacles, leaving a blackish-red trail of gore on the floor behind it. She stopped and rolled onto her side, her pleading, grey eyes locked onto Aidan's. She let out another wheezy groan that sounded like a gasping cry for help, lifting her arm out towards him. Before her decaying hand could grasp Aidan, he leapt from the bed, scrambled to the bedroom door, and flicked on the light.

The light blinded him for a moment, then his eyes adjusted.

The room was empty.

Laura shot up in bed, screaming. She looked around the room, disoriented by the blinding light. Finally, she saw Aidan standing by the door.

"What happened?" she gasped. Her hand rested on her chest to slow her thundering heart.

Aidan looked back to where the corpse had been and shook his head. He wiped his hand over his face and sighed. "It's nothing… forget it, sorry I woke you."

"Sorry you woke me? You almost scared me half to death."

"I'm sorry. Go back to sleep."

"Aidan, tell me what happened."

"I… I thought I saw something."

"What was it? What did you see?" Laura was fully awake now and looking intently at Aidan.

"It was nothing, forget –"

"Tell me!"

Aidan took a step back. "I thought I saw a woman."

"Where?" Laura demanded, looking around the room. She didn't seem scared – more curious than anything else.

"She… she crawled out from under the bed. Look, I know what it sounds like, but…"

Laura swung herself over the edge of the bed and looked underneath, then sighed with disappointment as she came back up. "What did she look like?"

Aidan squeezed his eyes shut. "I'd rather not, Laura."

"But I believe you."

"It's got nothing to do with that," Aidan said, shaking his head. "I just… don't want to talk about it."

Laura glared at him and said something through her teeth, but Aidan couldn't make it out. She threw herself back down onto and bed and turned away from him, pulling the covers up over her head. "Turn the light off," she snapped.

Aidan sighed, switched off the light and headed downstairs.

In the dimly lit living room, Aidan filled himself a glass of whiskey and downed it in one fiery gulp, then poured another. He slumped down onto the sofa, spilling some of his whiskey on the way down. He didn't care. His torn, blood-stained jacket lay over the arm of the sofa. Aidan stared at it for a moment, wishing he had just thrown the damn thing into the bin. He took a sip of whiskey, then fumbled around in the pockets of the coat for his pack of cigarettes. The box had been crushed and a handful of cigarettes had broken and turned to loose tobacco. Sinking back into the sofa, Aidan pulled out one that was still intact, lit it, and inhaled a stress-crushing draw.

I'm not crazy, he told himself, over and over in his head

The long shadows in the living room danced in the low light. They made Aidan feel uneasily. A part of him expected one of them to dart across the room at any second. He took another long, satisfying draw and a fiery gulp of whiskey, setting the empty glass on the coffee table, then picked up one of the dusty journals.

He opened it up, flicked the ash into the empty glass, and began to read.

February 4th 1980

I woke up in the forest this morning. The voice called out to me again last night. This time, I followed it deeper into the woods than I ever had before.

I think it's guiding me to something, but I don't know what yet. Perhaps to a place — or to him? It reminds me of the story of Johnathan Gray, guided here by the voice of God. Told to create a settlement in the land that the voice had brought him to. Told that if he and the other settlers did as God asked, then he and the town would prosper.

I've always wondered what God asked them to do. Well, this voice, this calling... it has me thinking. Could it be that same voice?

I wonder if Fiona hears it, too. Maybe I'll ask her.

Maybe I'm just going crazy.

Reading the journal entry made Aidan's spine tingle. He

wasn't sure if it was reading the inner thoughts of a serial killer that was unnerving, or the fact that – if he'd ever kept one – this could have been a page from his very own journal. Aidan flicked through the next couple of pages without bothering to read what Nicolas Wright had written. Then he stopped.

On one page, there was no journal entry, only a crudely drawn symbol that filled the entire page.

The symbol looked strangely familiar to Aidan, but he couldn't remember where or when he had seen it before. It was a *V* shape with a plus symbol – or a cross, he supposed – through the middle. Aidan stared at it in awe, the way someone would stare at a beautiful sunset or a magnificent landscape, unable to pry his gaze from it. The world dissolved all around him until all he could see was the symbol. He lifted the cigarette to his lips to take another draw, but the cigarette had burned to ash all the way to the butt.

Didn't I just light this?

Something pounded on the front door, startling him. The journal fell onto his chest with a *thump*. Greyish-blue light spilled through the windows. *Morning already?* Aidan thought as he looked around the room. His back cracked like old floorboards as he sat up from the sofa and threw the cigarette butt into the empty glass.

"Mr. Crain?" a muffled voice called from behind the rattling door.

CHAPTER FOURTEEN

The hammering on the door continued. The ceiling creaked and groaned as Laura scrambled upstairs to get dressed. Aidan set the journal on the table, then looked up at the clock on the wall. It was 7 a.m. Early morning light crept through the large living room windows; the greyish-blue hue made the room look like it was underwater.

"I'm coming!" Aidan yelled, rubbing the back of his neck as he walked over to answer the door. Laura came beating down the stairs, pulling her arms through a t-shirt as Aidan opened up.

Officer Foster – along with a bald, slender man who looked to be in his fifties, dressed in a tweed suit and holding a leather briefcase – stood on the porch.

"Good morning, sir. This is Mr. Stine, the local vet. He's come to take Max." Officer Foster gestured to the man standing beside him. Foster's scruffy hair stuck up on end and the dark purple rings under his eyes hung down like hammocks. He looked how Aidan felt, although Aidan thought he'd probably look a lot worse if he saw himself in a mirror. He reached out and shook the vet's hand.

"I was told your dog was attacked last night and sadly passed away. I'm sorry for your loss, Mr. and Mrs. Crain,"

Mr. Stine said. "May I come in?"

"Yes, of course, thank you. Please come in," Aidan replied, shuffling with his robe as he held the door open for Foster and Mr Stine. "Sorry about this," Aidan gestured to his messy robe as he closed the door behind them, "I didn't expect you this early."

"Is this a bad time?" Stine asked.

"No, not at all," Aidan lied. "Just through here." He nodded towards the kitchen.

"Would anyone like a coffee?" Laura asked.

"No thank you, sweetheart," Stine replied.

"I'd love one, thank you Mrs. Crain."

"No problem, officer. How do you take it?"

"Just black, please. Thank you."

"Coming right up." Laura moved to the counter, flicked on the kettle, and pulled out three mugs. Aidan, Foster and Mr. Stine stood in a semi-circle around the stained sheet covering Max on the kitchen table. The kitchen had taken on a coppery aroma overnight. Laura covered her mouth and swung the back door open to air out the smell.

"Have you thought about how you would like to deal with Max's remains?" Stine asked.

Laura and Aidan shared a look. The thought hadn't crossed their minds in all the chaos of the night before.

"Um… no, not really, sorry," Aidan said finally.

"What would you suggest? We've never dealt with anything like this before, so we don't know what our options are," Laura said, crossing her arms.

"Well, seeing as you're not from here, I imagine you would like to take Max home with you when you leave. So I would suggest cremation." Stine threw his briefcase onto the countertop and flicked it open. He pulled out some leaflets and handed them to Laura. "These will explain the process and costs in more detail."

Aidan walked away from the kitchen table and sat back down on the sofa. Laura quickly shuffled through the leaflets, then set them on the counter. The kettle clicked off, and the rumbling faded into the silence of the room. Mr. Stine took a quick glance under the bloodstained sheet, then quickly dropped it and stood beside Foster at the doorway between the kitchen and the living room.

"How long would it take?" Laura asked, handing Foster his coffee before joining Aidan on the sofa.

"At least two or three days, I'm afraid."

"Why so long?" Aidan asked. Foster slurped at his coffee.

Mr. Stine hesitated for a moment. "We don't have our own cremation facilities at the clinic. So we have to use the equipment at the funeral home and that means we have to wait our turn, unfortunately," he sighed. "The joys of a small town."

Foster added nothing to the conversation. He was happy enough getting some caffeine into his system.

"Don't worry, I will get him home to you as soon as possible, I promise." Stine rocked slightly from side to side, awkwardly looking down at his feet. "If you would like to say your last goodbyes, now is the time."

Aidan sighed and pulled himself up from the sofa. He held his hand out to Laura, who sat with her mug cupped tightly in her hands, staring at him sullenly. She squeezed her lips together, set the mug on the table, and took his hand. Aidan led them into the kitchen. The blood on the sheet had turned a dark brown and stuck to Max's matted fur. Aidan reached out and peeled back the cover, revealing his golden-haired head.

Dark, lifeless eyes stared blankly into space.

Laura leaned down and gave their boy one last kiss goodbye, running her hand over his cold fur. She could feel the tears coming; there was no stopping them. She shot up, pushed past Aidan, and hurried out into the back garden. Aidan watched as she took off towards the lake, her soft sobs echoing in the early morning air. He knelt down and gently stroked Max's long, curly-haired ears.

"Goodbye, boy. I love you." Aidan's voice cracked. He leaned in and kissed Max on his cold, dry nose. "Thank you, Mr. Stine," he said as he got back to his feet. Stine pulled a large blanket out from his briefcase and threw it over max.

"I'll call you when he's ready to be picked up. We can discuss payment then."

Aidan nodded. He couldn't bear to watch Max be taken away, so instead he went outside to find Laura. She was sitting on the picnic table, her head in her hands, crying. Aidan went and sat next to her and wrapped his arms tightly around her.

"I can't believe this is happening. It feels like a nightmare that I can't wake up from," Laura moaned, her voice muffled. Aidan stroked his hand over her back.

There was a cautious knock at the back door. Aidan turned; it was Foster.

"Detective Walker won't be long. You should get ready," he said, and then he left.

***

Aidan pulled a t-shirt over his head and stared out the bedroom window at the grey, overcast day. It had started to rain and the thought of trudging through the wet and the cold, searching for bodies, was an unpleasant one – and one Aidan never thought he would never have to experience. Laura was in the kitchen making herself some breakfast. She had asked Aidan if he wanted some, but he'd said no. He had little appetite, and although Laura insisted he should eat something – even a piece of toast – before heading out, Aidan refused. The memory alone of the vile smell waiting for him in the woods made his stomach turn, and the thought of throwing up in front of the officers only made him more certain he wanted nothing to eat.

A police cruiser and a black pickup turned into the driveway and pulled up at the front of the house. Aidan slipped on his shoes and headed down the stairs.

"They're here," he said as he grabbed his coat and the box of cigarettes from the coffee table.

"Be careful," Laura said, standing at the kitchen doorway with a greasy spatula in her hand. Her face was hard as stone. Aidan slid into his coat and stuffed the box of cigarettes into the pocket. She had spotted the cigarettes when Mr. Stine was looking over Max, but had decided not to say anything to Aidan. *If it helps him get through this mess, then let him smoke as many as he wants. I'll help him quit when we get back home.*

"I will, sweetie," Aidan said as he went to her and kissed her. He shook his head. "I wish I didn't have to do this."

"I know," she said, gently stroking his scratched cheek. "I wish you didn't have to either."

"I love you." Aidan kissed her again, then turned and walked out the front door.

"I love you too," Laura whispered.

Aidan lit a cigarette as Detective Walker got out from the pickup, wearing a fresh-pressed suit. His badge gleamed from his waist as he tugged up his trousers. Two officers stepped out of the cruiser, both dressed in identical black uniforms with *Elmwood P.D.* badges sewn onto the arms, a pair of handcuffs, and a gun holstered on each of their belts. One officer looked like he should be in a retirement home, not part of a search party, and the other must have been in his early thirties. *This is it?* Aidan thought. The last thing he wanted to do was step foot into the woods again, but again he didn't have a choice; at least this time he wouldn't be alone if that thing came for him.

"Detective. How are you this morning?" Aidan asked as he headed towards Walker with his hand outstretched. Walker took a firm grip of his hand and shook it.

"Oh, not too bad. Had my morning coffee and I'm raring to go. I can't say the same about these two, though." Walker pointed at the two officers with his thumb and chuckled as he pulled a heavy coat from the back of the pickup. "How are you, Mr Crain; did you manage to get any sleep?"

"Please, Aidan is fine. And I've definitely had better nights, let's just say that." He took a long drag of his cigarette and dropped it to the gravel, stomping it out under his foot.

"Didn't think you'd get any," Walker smiled and nodded. "How's the head?"

"A little sore, but I'll survive." Aidan gently touched the stitches on his forehead. It stung a little, but he didn't let the pain register on his face.

"Glad to hear it. How's your wife doing?"

"She's struggling, but she's strong. Stronger than me, anyway," Aidan nodded to himself. "She'll be okay in time."

"That's good," Walker said, brushing his silver hair back with his hand. "This is Officer Young and Officer Cross. They'll be joining us today." He gestured to the two officers who had made their way over to them. The older officer's shirt buttons strained around his bulging gut as he leaned on the front of Walker's pickup. "Young, if your fat ass scratches my paint, I swear to God."

Young got off the pickup in a hurry and wiped at the truck with his sleeve.

Officer Cross shook his head. "Isn't it time you retired, old man?"

Aidan laughed quietly to himself.

"I could still beat your ass up and down this driveway, you little shit," Young spat.

"Nice to meet you both," Aidan interjected, wincing at the realisation he was standing among Elmwood's finest. "Is this everyone? Just us four?"

"I'm afraid so," Walker said.

"Why, are we not good enough for you, city boy?" Officer Young jabbed.

"No, of course. I was just expecting more people, that's all."

"Well, this is what we have, and don't be taking any notice of this one," Walker pointed to Young. "Grumpy fuck."

Young growled under his breath as Walker went to the back of his truck and lifted out a black backpack. From inside, he pulled out four large torches, handing one to each of them. "Oh, and before I forget. Do you still have your clothes from last night?"

"Yeah, why?"

"I'll need to take them to the station. For... well, for evidence."

"Um, yeah, that's... no problem. Want me to get them for you?"

"I'll get them later, if that's okay with you."

Aidan nodded.

"All right, let's go."

Walker turned and headed through the gate that led to the back garden, followed closely by the two officers. Aidan watched as they disappeared through the gate, rubbed his hand over his face, then followed.

***

Laura tossed the scraps of her breakfast into the bin and put the plate in the sink just in time to see Aidan and the others head into the woods. *Please be safe*, she thought to herself as she watched them disappear through the trees. The rumbling kettle clicked, then went still. Laura poured the boiling water into the French press and made herself another well-needed coffee. The absence of Max pottering about the house brought a lump to her throat. She'd even missed him begging for food while she was trying to eat.

Everything's different now.

She hurried from the kitchen into the living room and set the mug on the coffee table, lit the fire, and slumped down onto the sofa. She noticed the half-empty bottle of whiskey and the crushed cigarette butt in the empty glass beside the stack of journals. *Did he sleep down here last night?* she thought as she set them to the side.

Then the memory came to her, like a forgotten dream to the forefront of her mind. She took a quick swig of coffee, burning the roof of her mouth, then shuffled around on the sofa to get a better look at the entire living room.

"Hello?" Laura called out. The house was quiet except for the crackling of the fire and the rain hitting the window. "Do you want to talk to me again?"

Silence.

"Was it you that my husband saw last night?"

Nothing.

An idea popped into Laura's head. One time, when Aidan had made her watch one of those ghost-hunting shows, the investigators – or hunters, or whatever they were called – tried to make contact by recording themselves asking the ghosts questions. Laura had always thought it was all bullshit, manufactured to make the show seem more interesting. What good was a ghost-hunting show without ghosts, after all? But now, since her experience the day before, she wasn't so sure. *No harm in trying,* she thought as she pulled out her phone. Her heart thundered in her chest. It wasn't fear. No; it was excitement. Laura gripped the phone tightly in her hand, the voice recorder app open and ready to go. She clicked the red *record* button, and the timer started.

***

The need for the bulky, high-powered torches was clear from the second they stepped foot into the woods. Under the cover of the trees, it looked more like twilight inside the forest than the beginning of early afternoon. Aidan was grateful for the proper torch this time as he swept the bright, powerful beam through the trees. He looked constantly over his shoulder and into the darker parts of the forest for movement between the trees. The rain hitting the leaves sounded like typewriter keys being punched, over and over. Detective Walker and the two officers moved methodically in a straight line, side by side, following Aidan. He only hoped that he wouldn't get them all lost. Everything inside the forest looked the same to him.

Their breath billowed out in puffs of white, then faded into nothing as they trudged over the soft forest floor. Aidan's fingers burned with the cold. *Find the bodies and get out of here as quickly as possible,* Aidan told himself over and over.

"I wish I had one of these last night," Aidan said, shaking the torch.

"I can't believe this is what I'm doing on my day off," Officer Young whinged, ignoring him.

"Come on now, all you'd be doing if you weren't out here is playing with yourself. Or are you so old your junk doesn't work anymore?" Cross teased.

"Fuck you!" Young pushed him.

Cross hopped on one foot, almost losing his balance as he laughed.

"Young!" Detective Walker snapped. The officer turned to protest, but thought better of it.

The forest was silent, completely devoid of any sound besides the crunch of the leaves and pine needles under their feet and the punching of the rain.

"So, Aidan, why did the two of you come to Elmwood?" Walker asked.

"Oh… we just wanted a change of scenery. To get away from the city and into the fresh air for a while. This wasn't exactly what I had in mind."

"Yeah, I bet," Walker shook his head. "I've heard things are pretty wild in Fallbridge at the minute."

"Yeah. It's a mess alright."

"What's the matter, can't ya handle the big smoke?" Young teased.

"Shut up, Young!" Walker barked, pointing his finger in the old man's face.

"It's okay, honestly, I –"

"So, you're a photographer, right?" Walker said, interrupting Aidan, continuing the conversation as if he hadn't just exploded.

Aidan stared at the detective, bewildered. *Of course he's looked me up. What else does he know?*

"Yeah… that's right."

"I saw the camera on your table in the Roast House."

"Oh right, yeah," Aidan laughed weakly. "I thought I recognised you."

"It's a small town, as I'm sure you've figured out by now."

"Yeah, some people knew my business even before I did."

Cautious laughter tapered off into silence. Thin, broken branches hung from the side of a tree up ahead of them. Aidan pointed them out, and Walker hurried in front of him to the tree. He looked at the broken branches, then hunched down to inspect the forest floor. Aidan watched curiously as Walker run his hand over the moss, brushing a slight impression in the ground.

"What is it?" Cross asked.

"A footprint," Walker said as he stood up. "What size

shoes do you wear, Aidan?"

"An eleven."

Walker nodded to himself as he looked down at the print. "Looks like an eleven to me. And by the looks of this tree, I'd say the owner came through here in a hurry."

"Yeah, that sounds about right." Aidan said, thinking back to bolting through the woods.

"Let's keep going this way. Hopefully, you trampled us a path to exactly where you ended up last night."

"Here's hoping," jabbed Young.

Walker took the lead, and Aidan and the two officers followed closely behind. Through the gaps in the trees, random streaks of dull sunlight streaked into the forest, sparkling like glitter off the wet leaves and spider webs hanging from tree to tree. Aidan thought it was strange seeing this place beautiful – almost peaceful – unlike the nightmare he'd lived through the night before. A wave of relief washed over Aidan when Walker took the lead. For the last hour he had been walking blindly through the woods, and the fact they'd come across this pathway was nothing short of a miracle. The tightness in his stomach loosened, but only a little. They still had bodies to find.

"I've been wanting to ask you something all day," Young said. Aidan rolled his eyes, expecting another sarcastic remark.

"Sure, go ahead," Aidan sighed.

"How can you stay in that house?"

Walker looked over his shoulder at them, shaking his head.

"It isn't so bad," Aidan lied, thinking of the sleepless nights he'd had since arriving.

"I've been in that house once, and I never want to step foot in it again."

"You know, you're the third or fourth person to say that to me since I arrived."

"I heard the stories growing up, like everyone else in town," Cross said.

"Believe me, if you saw what I did, you wouldn't want to go anywhere near it. Just standing in the driveway earlier was close enough for me." Young shivered as if someone had walked on his grave.

"Why? What happened that was so bad?" Aidan asked.

"You all don't really believe that shit, do you?" Walker asked with a grim smile.

"You're damn right I do," Young said with a deep, wrinkled frown.

"I snuck in one time when I was a kid," Cross said, "back when the place was a wreck. And I swear to God, something charged at me. I near pissed my pants."

"What did you do?" Aidan asked.

"I got the hell out of there, that's what I did," Cross said.

Detective Walker burst out laughing. The sound of his bellowing laughter echoed back at them, as if the forest was joining in on the gag. Cross scowled at him.

Aidan didn't laugh.

"Screw you!" Cross yelled, which only made Walker laugh more.

"I might have to put that little confession on your record, breaking and entering. Trespassing," Walker said, wiping a tear from his eye. Officer Cross flipped him the bird.

"When I got called out there for the case..." Young trailed off. Aidan caught it; a look, from Walker, that said *don't say another word*. And that was the end of the conversation. The laughter from only moments ago was now an awkward silence that lingered in the air like a foul smell.

Aidan shone his flashlight around the surrounding trees. There was something familiar about this part of the forest. But if he was right, then the horrible smell should have hit them by now. All he could smell was the pine trees and the damp earth.

"This looks familiar," Aidan said. "Yeah, this is it!" He pointed the beam of his flashlight at a group of trees a few yards up ahead.

Walker looked to where Aidan was pointing. "You sure?"

"Yes, definitely. I tripped over something here – that's how I did this," he pointed to the stitches on his head. Aidan shone his light along the forest floor and found a tree root breaking out of the ground. "There, that must be what I tripped over. The ditch should be just a few feet ahead."

The officers hurried towards the ditch. Instantly, everything felt real. Aidan's hands tightened into white-knuckled fists as butterflies fluttered in his stomach.

"We should be able to smell it by now," Aidan said, shaking his head, confused.

"I can't smell anything," Young said.

"Me neither," Cross said, sniffing the air.

Aidan slowed to a stop a couple of feet away from the edge of the ditch. "I can't go any further, I can't see that again." He leaned his back against a tree as sweat trickled down his head.

"That's okay," Walker said.

Detective Walker and the two officers stepped cautiously towards the ditch. There wasn't a sound. Everyone was tense, focused on the moment. The men stood at the edge of the pit, lighting it up with their torches.

"You sure this is the place?" Walker asked, turning back to Aidan.

"Yeah, this is it. It has to be," Aidan said.

Young and Cross looked back towards Aidan, then at each other. Young shook his head as he muttered something under his breath.

Walker stepped down into the ditch.

"No! Don't go down there," Aidan yelled, but it was too

late.

"Is this some kind of joke?" Walker yelled out from the ditch.

"What do you mean?" Aidan asked. *How could it be a joke? He should be knee-deep in rot and gore.*

"There's nothing here. Come see for yourself."

"What?" Aidan shook his head and hurried to the ditch, pushing past Young and Cross.

Walker was right. The ditch was empty. There was no sign of any bones or decomposing bodies; no blood. Nothing. Even his vomit was gone.

"How..." Aidan stuttered, "they were here last night, I swear."

Aidan was sure of it and sure that this was the right place, but there was nothing here. The ditch looked just like the rest of the forest floor, covered in moss, dead leaves and pine needles.

Untouched.

He thought of the gunge up to his elbows and how every inch of the ditch had been filled with bones and body parts in a soup of liquified rot. But by the looks of the ditch now there hadn't had so much as a drop of rain, never mind blood.

"How is this possible?"

He stood at the edge of the ditch, his head shaking from side to side, unable to believe his own eyes.

"Is this a joke to you?" Officer Young snapped.

"No, of course not!"

"Then why bring us out here?"

"They were *here*."

"You're full of shit," Young shouted. "Dead bodies don't just get up and leave. We aren't living in a Romero movie."

Aidan stalled, trying to find the right words to say. He couldn't find them.

"Look, everyone, just calm the fuck down!" Walker

interrupted, holding his arms up in the air, still standing in the middle of the ditch. "I believe you."

"Detective, you can't be fucking serious!" Young yelled.

"Do not speak to me like that again, officer, or I'll force you into retirement!"

Young looked down at his feet like a scolded child.

"I believe you saw something," Walker continued.

"Thank you!"

"But," he held up a finger, "clearly it wasn't what you thought. You hit your head pretty hard, and head injuries can cause hallucinations."

"Detective, it was real."

"Yes, to you maybe. But in reality..." Walker gestured out to the surrounding emptiness.

"But –"

"But nothing," Walker snapped.

"Well, what about Max? I didn't hallucinate what happened to him."

Walker didn't answer. Cross helped pull him out from the ditch as Young glared at Aidan, pushing past him with his shoulder and knocking him to the side. The three of them headed through the forest back towards the house.

"Are you seriously leaving? I didn't make this up!" Aidan yelled, but none of them answered. The officers were out of eyeshot now, and Aidan knew he should hurry and catch up with them or they would leave him in the forest.

A twig snapped to his right. It sounded close. He swung the torch beam towards the sound.

Emily Pembrook stood at the base of a large pine. The yellow hood of her soaking wet coat was pulled up over her head, covering her face in shadow. She shook her head slowly from side to side.

A crow cawed like a siren from high in a tree. Aidan almost jumped out of his skin, swung around towards the sound, and spied the crow as it flew into the forest. He looked back at Emily, but she had gone. He stood at the edge of the ditch, listening to the rain and the distant sound of the officers making their way back through the forest.

Emily had been trying to warn him of something, but of what he didn't know. Was it the forest? The house?

The officers?

There was something about Detective Walker that had made Aidan weary of him. He couldn't quite put his finger on it, but the turning in Aidan's gut told him not to trust him.

CHAPTER FIFTEEN

Aidan caught up with the officers and walked the rest of the way to the Lake House a few steps behind them. No one spoke. Their banter from earlier was now a distant memory. Aidan studied them all carefully, trying to read their body language and watching for strange looks, but it was useless. None of the men gave anything away, besides their burning frustration towards him. When they got back to the house, Walker took all the torches from them and tossed them into the back of his pickup. Young and Cross got into their cruiser and left without saying a word.

"Look, I just wanna –" Aidan started.

Walker grabbed him by the arm and pulled Aidan in close, holding him there with a vice-like grip. Walker's warm body odour stung Aidan's nose as he leaned in and whispered into his ear. "If I were you, I'd make my stay here in Elmwood a quick one. You better hope I don't see you again."

Walker pushed Aidan away, climbed inside his pickup, and sped off down the driveway.

***

Aidan sat at the edge of the lake in the crisp autumn air, his sore feet hanging in the cool water. The rain had finally stopped, and Aidan didn't want to go inside to Laura. He didn't want to tell her how badly the search had gone and just wanted some time alone. Before migrating to the lakeside, he had crept inside and grabbed a journal from the coffee table. Thankfully Laura hadn't been there; he guessed she must have been upstairs somewhere or in the shower. So he took the book and hurried out to the lake before she could come down and look for him. He felt like a terrible husband for avoiding her, but he just needed some time to process what had happened and to figure out what the hell was going on.

Since he'd opened the journal, he couldn't pry his eyes away. He focused on every word scribbled on the page, trying to absorb as much information as he could.

February 10th 1980

It called me again today, the voice from the trees. It pulls on me like a magnet. I asked Fiona if she had heard anything strange, but she just gave me a disquieted look and said no, she hadn't.

She hasn't been acting herself lately. She's been distant, quiet, as if she's somewhere else in her mind.

February 12th 1980

I went into the woods tonight while Fiona was asleep. The voice told me to do things for him. Horrible, unspeakable things that I can't even write. I don't know what's going on; I think I'm losing my mind.

Fiona is still acting strangely. She stared into the fire for over two hours today without saying a word. Every time I ask her if she's okay, she tells me she's all right, but clearly she isn't.

We used to be so close, so loving, but she's changed. Ever since we moved into this house.

February 20th 1980

Why am I even writing this? What good is it going to do? She's gone, my wife's gone, she left me. Fiona's dead. I found her in the bathtub. The water was so red.

She sliced her wrists right up to the elbow.

Why would she do this to me? I loved her so much, I would have given anything for her. Why didn't she talk to me? Why didn't I press her more when I was certain something was wrong?

She's still in the bathtub.

I don't know what to do.

I cried for help, and he spoke to me. The voice. He told me he can bring my wife back. He told me to bring her to him, that there is a special place, a sacred place in the woods. He told me he would guide me there.

I'm going to take her.

I need her back.

"What the fuck...?"

Aidan snapped the journal closed and set it beside him on the pier. He squeezed his eyes shut, trying to take control of the thoughts running rampant in his mind. *Could it be the same voice I'm hearing? I woke up in the woods, too. I don't know if I'm going crazy or if it's crazy to accept the voice is real? I guess I'd prefer to be going crazy. Did this have anything to do with the bodies in the woods? Is it all connected?*

If so, how?

He lit a cigarette. The tobacco helped a little. The light autumn breeze was cool, but refreshing against his skin. His feet had gone numb some time ago, but he didn't mind. The surrounding trees reflected on the perfectly-still water like an oil painting, covering the lake with a mix of bright reds and oranges. Aidan sat and stared at the natural beauty, getting lost in it, wishing his life could be this peaceful.

The back door squeaked as Laura pushed it open with her foot. She made her way down towards the lake with a cup of coffee in each hand, walking carefully down the steps and trying her best not to spill any. Aidan crushed his cigarette into the decking of the pier and flicked the butt into the lake.

"Here you go," Laura said as she handed Aidan a cup. He picked up the journal and set it on his lap, shimmying over so she could sit down next to him. "Getting some reading in?" Laura said, shuffling closer to Aidan and eyeing up the journal in his lap.

"Yeah, you weren't joking when you said it was messed up." Aidan set his coffee mug on top of the book.

"I love this view," Laura said, changing the subject.

"It's beautiful," Aidan said, then took a cautious sip of coffee that still burned his tongue. He dreaded Laura asking him about the search. It was the last thing he wanted to talk about, especially today, but it was unavoidable and most likely the reason she'd come out to sit with him.

"You've been avoiding me," Laura said, getting straight to the point.

The words hit him like daggers. "I'm sorry," Aidan sighed as he ran a heavy hand across his face.

"What's the matter?"

"It's nothing… don't worry about it." He took another burning sip of coffee.

"It's not nothing. What happened?"

He stared across to the other side of the lake, unable to even look at her. "We didn't find anything in the woods," Aidan mumbled through clenched teeth.

"What do you mean? You couldn't find the place?"

"No, I mean, we found nothing!" Aidan snapped. His lips pressed into tight slits as he shook his head, regretting the outburst instantly. Laura recoiled. "I'm sorry," he said, steadying his breathing. "We found the place, I'm sure of it… but it was empty."

Laura looked puzzled. "How is that possible?"

"It isn't. Detective Walker said I must've been hallucinating after I hit my head, but I smelt them, I *saw* them, I did. It was real."

"I believe you," Laura said matter-of-factly as she placed her warm hand on top of his.

"Laura, there was nothing there, nothing at all," Aidan said, shaking his head. "It was as undisturbed as the rest of the forest. I don't know what to believe anymore. Either way, my eyes have lied to me at least once. But something strange is going on, that's a fact, and Detective Walker has something to do with it."

"How's that?" Laura asked.

"Something isn't right about him. He was too quick to dismiss everything, even last night. Then before he left, he threatened me."

"He what?" Laura snapped. Red, fiery blood pumped into her head.

"Yeah," Aidan let out a lifeless laugh.

"He can't do that."

Aidan nodded. "But like I said, he's hiding something, I'm sure of it. And I guess it has something to do with everything that's been going on."

"Even the things in the house?"

"Maybe."

"Well, screw him! Who the hell does he think he is? You're not the kind of person who makes things up. So if you say you saw them, then I believe you. And if you think this detective has something to do with all this, then I believe that too."

Aidan leaned in and kissed her. Laura rested her head on

his shoulder. It was good to have it out in the open; like it had lifted a weight off his shoulders. He wanted to tell her about the voice, about seeing Emily and about the dark thing in the forest, but he thought what he had said was enough for today. No need to pile it on all at once.

Laura sat up, frowning. Aidan could tell she was in her head because she looked exactly like he did when he did the same thing.

"What's the matter?" Aidan asked.

"I don't know if now is a good time… but –"

"What is it?" Aidan asked, twisting to face her. His arms tingled with panic.

"I did something earlier and…" she nodded to herself, "I think you should see it, or… listen to it, even."

Aidan looked at her, bemused, as she reached into her jeans pocket and pulled out her phone. She unlocked it and swiped at the screen with her thumb. "Here," she said finally, handing the phone over to Aidan. The screen said *REC. 001*.

Aidan pressed *play*.

The recording hissed to life. White noise crackled through the speaker. Laura watched Aidan eagerly.

Laura's voice burst through the static hiss.

"Do you remember me?" Ambient, white noise fizzled for a few moments. *"My name's Laura, what's your name?"*

Laura didn't take her eyes off him, studying his face while he listened to the recording. Then, in the silence, Aidan thought he picked up on something, something that was different from the rest of the static, but he couldn't make it out.

"What did you mean when you said evil was coming?" Laura's voice continued.

"The darkness," a small voice whispered distantly through the static. The voice sounded female, childlike. Aidan looked up at Laura, but she was fixed on the phone. Every hair on

his body stood on end.

"*Why are you here?*"

"*Trapped,*" the voice whispered again.

"Holy shit, this is incredible!" Aidan exclaimed.

"Shush, listen." Laura pressed a finger against his lips.

"*Can you see me?*" Laura's voice went on. The static continued for a few seconds, then a loud, dark gurgling noise that sounded like a strange scream flooded the speakers.

The recording stopped.

Aidan's heart pounded. "What the fuck was that?" he said, holding the phone away from him as if the thing that the scream had belonged to was about to jump out from it. Laura shook her head.

"I've no idea. I didn't hear anything when I was asking the questions. No voice, no scream, nothing. It was like I was talking to myself."

"That's mental," Aidan said, handing the phone back to Laura. "I can't believe it actually worked. You actually caught a voice and… whatever the hell that was, at the end."

"It's the same person who reached out to me through the Ouija. She needs our help, Aidan."

"How are we meant to help her?"

Laura shrugged. "We need to do *something*."

"Play it again." Aidan said.

Laura clicked *play*, and they listened again. It was just as exhilarating the second time around.

"Do you have any idea what you have done?"

Laura stared at Aidan blankly.

"You have proof that life after death exists. That ghosts exist. It makes you wonder what else might exist out there." The vastness of Aidan's own question made his head hurt. He rubbed at his temples. "This day just keeps getting weirder and weirder."

Laura noticed the dark rings under Aidan's eyes. The stress

from the last couple days, plastered over his face like a billboard.

"I have an idea," she said, "and it's got nothing to do with ghosts."

"What's that?" Aidan asked.

"The other day, I saw a cute little bar in town. We should go, have a couple of drinks and forget about all this madness for a while."

Aidan smiled. That sounded perfect. They could put the strains of the last couple of days behind them, even if only for a few hours.

"Yeah, that sounds great."

"Yes!" Laura exclaimed and gave herself a little clap. "We can get dressed up and make a night of it. Come on, let's get ready."

Laura jumped up from the pier and held her hand out towards Aidan. She wore the bright, beautiful smile that made Aidan's heart swell. He loved seeing her like this. He took her hand, and she helped him to his feet.

They started for the house, excited to spend some quality time together and pretend – if only for one night – that the nightmare they were living in didn't exist.

CHAPTER SIXTEEN

The sky burned an autumn orange as the sun set over Elmwood. Aidan stood in front of the mirrored door of the wardrobe in the bedroom, dressing himself. He wore his favourite light blue shirt with skinny black jeans. It wasn't fashion-week worthy, but this was as close to a tuxedo as Aidan would get. Even on their wedding day, he hadn't worn a suit; he always said they were uncomfortable and unnatural. The last time he'd worn one was at his mother's funeral, and he'd sworn then that he never would again.

Laura pushed open the bedroom door. "How do I look?" she asked.

Aidan turned to her. His jaw almost hit the floor.

Laura stood in the doorway, brushing and pulling at a tight, fitted black dress that showed off her curves perfectly. Her flowing brown hair hung over one shoulder and her smoky eyes made her look like a film noir heroine. Aidan couldn't take his eyes off her.

"You look incredible."

"Is it too much?" Laura asked nervously.

"No! Not at all."

Heat pricked at her cheeks as she made her way over to Aidan. "You look very handsome yourself," she said as she fixed the collar of his shirt. Aidan smiled. She stretched up and kissed him on the chin with her silky red lips, leaving a print from her lipstick. In an instant, Aidan dropped to his hunkers and wrapped his arms firmly around Laura's legs, lifting her up over his shoulder as if she weighed as much as one of the pillows on the bed, and spun her around. She laughed and screamed, gripping onto a fistful of his shirt. He carried her over to the bed and gently laid her down.

Her dress had climbed up her to her waist, showing off her toned legs and her lacy, royal-blue underwear. Aidan climbed on top of her, the bedsprings creaking under them, and kissed her neck. Goosebumps tingled over her entire body like waves starting in her head and flowing down to her toes, then back up again.

Gently, he ran his fingertips up her inner thigh. "Maybe we should just stay here and I can have you all to myself," Aidan whispered in her ear, his breath sending another wave of goosebumps down her body.

"Then we would've gotten all dressed up for nothing," Laura said breathlessly.

"It wouldn't be for *nothing*. I'd get to take them off you," Aidan laughed.

Laura grasped his shirt and in one swift move, rolled him onto his back so she was on top of him. Reaching down, she unbuckled his belt and undid the buttons of his jeans. Aidan pulled her down to him and kissed her while he slid a hand under her lacy underwear.

A feeling suddenly came over Laura, and not a pleasant one.

Every muscle in her body tightened.

The indescribable feeling of peeping eyes watching them took over her. A gnawing at the back of her mind made her feel like they were on show for some unseen voyeur. She wondered if Aidan could feel it too.

"We need to get out of this house," Laura whispered.

"Why? Aren't you having fun?" Aidan asked as he continued to kiss her neck.

"I am," she lied as she sat up. "But I wanna get out of here for a while."

"What's the matter? Did I do something wrong?"

"No, not at all. I…" she looked around at the empty room. "I just wanna go out. But I promise, when we get back, you can do whatever you want to me," Laura said, giving him a cheesy wink.

Aidan laughed and started buttoning up his jeans. "Okay, fine, but I'm holding you to that."

Laura forced out a chuckle.

"I'm going to fix my makeup," she said, and she hurried out of the room.

***

Aidan locked the front door behind him and headed for the car. Laura, already in the passenger seat, sat clutching her purse tightly in her hands, eagerly waiting to leave. He knew something was up with her. She'd been acting strange for the last half hour, but he promised himself he wouldn't bring it up, not tonight anyway. With everything that had happened, he couldn't blame her.

Tonight, they were leaving this mess behind them and living the stress-free vacation they had so desperately come here for. The evening air had turned chilly, the coldest it had been since they had arrived. A half-moon shone like a broken silver coin in the black, empty sky. Aidan reached for the car's door handle.

A flapping sound from behind him stopped him in his tracks. He looked over his shoulder, back towards the house where the sound had come from. A crow as dark as the night sky stood on the porch. Its large, beaked head twitched to one side, watching him defiantly with its small beady eyes.

What the hell? He shook his head and got into the car. *No, not tonight.*

They drove through the sleepy town towards the marina. All the shops had closed for the night and there were only a handful of people walking the downtown streets. Boats gently bobbed on the water as they pulled into the car park facing the harbour. The clatter of bells on the rocking boats resonated through the night air. The muffled hum of music mixed with the disembodied voices of multiple conversations bellowed from the bar behind them.

Aidan turned off the car and looked at his beautiful wife. *How did I get so lucky?* he thought to himself. He knew he hadn't been the greatest lately, and that Laura deserved so much better than him... but tonight was going to be different. Tonight was a new beginning, a chance for him to become the husband she deserved.

"You ready?" he asked with a smile.

"Yeah," Laura said, reaching for the doorhandle. Aidan grabbed her arm. She spun around and looked at him, wondering what he was doing. He leaned in and kissed her.

Laura squeezed her eyes shut. She could feel the kiss breaking through the bricks of her internal walls like a sledgehammer. Her body relaxed.

"I love you," Aidan said with his eyes still closed, lingering in the moment for a little longer. A serene smile crept in from the corners of Laura's mouth. The kiss made her entire body tingle. It reminded her of how she felt when she had her first kiss back when she was a girl. When even a kiss felt like it held all the magic in the world.

"I love you too."

They got out of the car and started hand in hand towards the pub across the road. Laura's dress flapped in the windy sea air. The chill cut through them like a razor. Aidan wrapped his arm around Laura and pulled her tightly against his body to keep her warm as they hurried towards the bright red glow of *The Anchor Bar's* neon sign.

The buzz from inside swelled in the night air as they approached. Two old, wrinkled men sat on a picnic bench out front having a smoke, deep in drunken conversation and oblivious to the chilly breeze that swirled around them. The *Anchor* was a small, humble bar, nothing flashy, but it served its purpose.

One of the old men – the one with a shaggy white beard scattered with chunks of food – caught in it, turned from his drunken partner and watched Aidan and Laura with glazed, almost-closed eyes as they passed.

"Hey... hey... you, you, should... you shouldn't..." the man slurred, then he roared, almost falling off his seat with a low, grunting laugh. He had three teeth sticking up like gravestones in his black hole of a mouth, and even those three didn't look like they planned on sticking around for much longer. Ignoring him, Aidan and Laura pushed open the door and went inside.

Half the town must have been in there. The smell of stale beer had soaked into the wooden beams overhead, lingering like an old ghost. Classic rock flooded the room along with the loud crackle of everyone talking over one another. There were couples, young and old. Groups of friends out for a night on the town and, of course, the old regular drunks that spent every day there, known by name by the waitressing staff. No pub was complete without them.

The place had an amazing vintage charm to it, filled with framed photos of all the previous owners and news clippings about the town. There were two old guns that looked like something that a pirate would use mounted to the wall and old fishing nets draped from the ceiling. A huge shark skull hung proudly above a small wood burner in the corner, and on the other side of the bar were two pool tables and an old jukebox, the kind with the fantastic multicoloured lights and bubbles that danced in a curve at the top. Aidan hadn't seen one of those in years. There were a handful of booths running along the entire length of the pub, filled with people chatting and socialising. A group of twenty-somethings played a drinking game called kings in one booth; a skinny guy with messy hair was losing badly and had turned a pale green colour.

A couple of locals, mainly the old regulars hunched over the bar, turned and stared at Aidan and Laura for a moment before returning to their drinks.

They walked up to the bar and sat on two of the stools. Laura looked at a drinks menu.

The bartender was a woman in her thirties. She had a natural beauty, and Aidan could tell just from looking at her that she took no shit from anyone. The men at the edge of the bar all hung onto her every word. One drunken man had been trying his luck with her.

"Come on…" he burped. "Come on, Emma, go to dinner with me. You know you want to."

Emma scrunched her nose up at the man and fake-gagged. "Stop being creepy, Steve, you're old enough to be my gramps. If you keep this shit up, I'll have to kick your ass out again," she cautioned while cleaning out a pint glass. "You should know better."

Steve scoffed, waving his hand at her in a shooing motion while downing the rest of his beer. He stumbled to his feet and turned to leave, then stopped. He looked at Aidan and Laura, who sat a couple of stools over from him.

"You," Steve said, pointing an unsteady finger at Aidan as he stumbled towards him. "You ruined my day off."

Aidan rolled his eyes, realising who was talking to him

before he'd even seen Steve's face.

"Officer Young," Aidan said with a sigh. "Working on the gut I see."

"You little shit. I oughtta –"

"If he's harassing you folks, let me know and I'll get him taken home," the barmaid said as she made her way over to them.

"Aw, you wouldn't do that to me, Emma," Steve teased.

"If you piss me off enough, you know fine rightly what I'd do, so leave these nice people in peace." Steve looked down at his feet. "Now what can I get for you two?"

"Can I get a whiskey on the rocks, please?"

"Sure thing. What can I get for you, darling?"

Laura looked up from the drinks menu.

"Um, can I just get a gin and tonic, please?"

"Not a problem."

"And get him a refill too," Aidan said, pointing with his thumb at Steve.

Emma nodded, filling the pint glass she was holding with a draught of beer and sliding it to Steve. He took the beer and went to the other side of the bar without even a thank you.

Asshole, Aidan thought.

"Don't mind him," Emma said as she pulled a wooden bowl full of peanuts from under the bar and set them between Aidan and Laura. "If you need anything, just holler."

"Thank you," Laura said.

Aidan stuffed his hand into the bowl of peanuts and threw a handful into his mouth. Emma came back and set their drinks down on top of two coasters.

"One whisky on the rocks and one gin and tonic."

"Cheers," Aidan said, sliding a twenty across the bar. "Keep the change."

Emma smiled, then went to the other side of the bar to serve another one of the old local drunks.

"Who was that?" Laura asked quietly.

"Oh, he was one of the officers from today. He's not my biggest fan."

"Yeah, I can tell," Laura laughed.

Aidan picked up his glass, held it in the air and turned to Laura. "To a new start."

Laura smiled and picked up her glass and they clinked them together. "To a new start," she echoed.

They both took a sip of their drinks. Laura grimaced.

"What's wrong?" Aidan laughed.

"That is one hell of a strong gin and tonic."

"You're welcome!" Emma yelled over from across the bar. Laura laughed and held her drink in the air, nodding in approval.

"Wanna play a game?" Aidan asked, pointing to a free pool table.

"Sure thing, I can kick your ass again like last time."

"Oh, you're on! Loser buys drinks for the rest of the night."

They picked up their glasses and hurried to the pool table before anyone else could get to it. Aidan jabbed the button, and the balls fell into the trap at the end of the table with a thunderous rumble. Laura swiped Aidan's drink, resting on the edge of the pool table and asking to be knocked over, and set both glasses down on a table and took a cue. Aidan pulled out the triangle and set up the balls while Laura stood at the other end of the table, eagerly chalking up her cue.

"I guess you're breaking then?"

"You betcha!"

Aidan rolled the white ball across the felt to Laura, spun the eight-ball in the centre and lifted the triangle. Laura set the ball up and leaned over the table, taking her aim. With a loud crack, she scattered the balls across the table, immediately potting two stripes.

"Are you serious?" Aidan protested with a chuckle,

throwing his arms up in the air.

A couple of people sat at the next table turned to stare over their shoulders at the commotion. Laura grinned.

Aidan went to the table and took a swig of whiskey. Laura potted another ball then lined up her next shot, missing narrowly.

"Shit!" Laura laughed.

"Oh, now you're screwed." Aidan picked up his cue and walked over to the table, chalking the tip. He lined up his shot and hit the ball as hard as he could, smashing the green ball into the pocket. "Whoa!" Aidan cheered.

Laura laughed, downing the last of her gin and tonic. "Lucky shot. Do you want another drink?"

"Sure thing. I'll take a beer, please."

Laura walked over to the bar and ordered two more drinks while Aidan lined up his next shot. He gently knocked the white ball towards the red; it grazed it, barely moving the ball at all. Aidan sighed and slumped his head in shame.

"That's what you get," Laura said, walking back from the bar with their drinks. She set them down on the table and picked up her cue. "Get yourself comfortable while I finish up here."

Aidan shook his head, grinning. He walked to the table, polished off the last of his whiskey, and started on the beer. Laura potted the rest of her balls with ease and moved onto the black eight-ball.

"Drowning your sorrows?" Laura asked, looking up from the cue at Aidan.

"Just finish the game," Aidan smirked. AC/DC blasted from the jukebox as Laura calmly tapped the white ball towards the black, knocking it straight into the corner pocket. Aidan hung his head and laughed.

"Seriously, what the hell! Were you some pool champion in a past life or something?" Aidan snickered. "Two out of three?"

"Nah, I wouldn't want to embarrass you in front of all these people by kicking your ass, *again*."

Aidan smirked with raised eyebrows as Laura sauntered to him, her face beaming with triumph. Aidan handed Laura her drink.

A group of women got up from their booth across from the pool table and left. "Shall we sit over there?" Laura asked, pointing to the empty booth.

"Sure, give me a sec. I'll meet you there."

Laura picked up her drink and started for the booth. Aidan, with his beer in hand, went over to the vintage jukebox. The neon lights lit his face in yellows and pinks. He flicked through the songbook, laughing to himself when he came across one of his and Laura's favourite songs, surprised to see it in a place like this. An acoustic love song called *Meant To Be* by a singer-songwriter called Sidney Thomas. Aidan pushed *B7* on the jukebox and the gentle strumming of the guitar charged the room. No one in the bar seemed to notice or mind the change in music. Aidan walked towards Laura who, sat in the booth, looked beautiful as always. She was in the middle of sipping her gin and tonic when suddenly she stopped, recognising the song playing from the jukebox. Her face lit up. Aidan set his beer on the table and reached out his hand.

"Can I have this dance?" Aidan asked. His stomach fluttered with butterflies.

She gently took a hold of it, laying her hand in his, and slowly stood up. Aidan pulled her in close as they danced in the middle of the bar. All eyes were on them, but they didn't care. Aidan wrapped his arms tightly around Laura's waist as they swayed back and forth. She twirled his hair around her fingers at the back of his neck as they stared deeply into each other's eyes.

"I haven't heard this since our wedding night," Laura said, resting her cheek on Aidan's chest. "I've missed this." Her eyes closed.

"Me too, honey," Aidan said, and kissed the top of her head. A couple of onlookers had gotten up and joined them; quickly, the bar filled with people slow dancing. "I'm sorry… for all of this," Aidan whispered.

"It isn't your fault." Laura looked up at him intently. "You've been through a lot lately, a hell of a lot. And I'm just glad to see *you* again tonight. The loving, fun, carefree man that I fell in love with." Laura held his head in her hands as they kissed, swaying back and forth to the beautiful music of Sidney Thomas.

Ding! Ding! Ding! Emma the bartender, rang a large brass bell at the end of the bar, snapping them out from their trance-like state.

"Last orders!" Emma yelled. Some of the old regulars groaned at the thought of leaving.

"Would you like another drink?" Aidan asked.

Laura grasped handfuls of his shirt and pulled him down towards her. "No, let's go home and pick up where we left off earlier," she smiled cheekily.

They downed the last of their drinks in a hurry. Laura guided Aidan by the hand through the crowd, then out the door. The ice-cold breeze cut through them like a knife. "What do you think of our chances of getting a taxi?" Laura asked, wrapping her arms tightly around herself. Aidan looked around at the empty town, not hopeful.

"I'll just drive us home."

"No, you can't."

"It'll be fine, I only had two drinks."

"Are you sure you'll be okay?"

Aidan nodded. They walked past the picnic table where the two drunkards had been earlier.

Aidan had to do a double-take to make sure his weren't tricking him. *You've got to be kidding me.*

Stood on the picnic table was a crow, watching them as they walked by.

It couldn't be the same one, could it?

Aidan looked back over his shoulder just as the crow flew away.

***

There were no other cars on the road. Elmwood had turned into a ghost town. All the houses were now in complete darkness, the people inside dreaming the night away. Laura gripped Aidan's thigh and squeezed it tight, then ran her fingertips up towards his crotch. Aidan's entire leg tingled with ecstasy. He leaned over to give her a kiss.

"Look out!" Laura gasped.

Aidan shot back into his seat, his heart in his throat, and slammed on the brakes. The tyres screeched down the tarmac. Illuminated by the dull orange glow of the streetlights, someone or something dressed in black had stepped out in front of the car.

They had a stag's skull for a head.

Aidan swerved away from the thing, losing control of the car. The wheels groaned. Laura screamed.

The sour smell of burning rubber lilted around them.

Aidan spun the steering wheel left, then right in an attempt to get control of the car, but it was no use. The car spun out, skidding across the road, smashing headfirst into one of the massive oak trees at the side of the road.

Everything went dark.

CHAPTER SEVENTEEN

Aidan blinked heavily, like he was waking up from a full night's sleep. His head hammered. In front of him, the tips of pine trees swayed back and forth; the night sky was so dark that even the light of the stars didn't shine through. He could have sworn he had seen a half-moon earlier, but now it was gone.

He swept his arms out, feeling the forest floor under his fingertips, and sat up. "Laura?" he called. Only his own voice called back. Dead leaves and pine needles stuck to his back. A thick fog crept through the trees. Something felt off about this place. He felt it in his gut. He rubbed at his temples, trying to settle the pounding in his skull, but it didn't help any. After a while, he got to his feet and looked around.

The fog glowed with an eerie blue light, like clouds flashing in a lightning storm. It was so thick that Aidan could only see a couple of feet ahead of him. He looked up at the night sky again. Then it hit him all at once. The trees. They were moving, but there was no sound, no swaying hiss – not even the sound of the whistling wind.

What the hell is going on?

Dead silence.

"Laura!" Aidan yelled again. His voice was the only sound,

and it echoed through the forest, sounding more and more like an unfamiliar voice shouting her name back at him. Everything was quiet. The leaves under Aidan's feet didn't even crunch as he walked cautiously through the woods, not knowing where he was or where he was going.

Aidan knew something had happened to Laura, something bad, but he couldn't remember what. He fought with himself, trying to remember, but it was like trying to remember a dream after waking up. The harder he tried, the further it faded.

Aidan stopped dead in his tracks at a sudden noise. Sitting in silence, he listened intently.

Snap!

There it was again. The sound grew louder, hidden in the blinding fog. Footsteps, unmistakable footsteps. Aidan spun in circles, trying to pinpoint any movement, but the fog was too thick. "Hello! Who's out there?" he hollered.

"You need to run," a woman's voice echoed from every direction. Aidan looked around the emptiness, but he couldn't see anyone. "*He's coming, you need to hurry!*"

Through the fog, he saw a faint whisper of yellow.

"Emily!" He went to run after her, but it was like his legs had sprouted roots, anchoring him to the forest floor. He tugged at them, trying to free himself, but it was no good.

"*Come to me,*" a dark, familiar voice whispered.

The voice didn't echo. It came from inside Aidan's head. The hold on his legs lifted, and he tried to run to where he had seen Emily. Instead, his entire body turned and started walking in the opposite direction. It was like his body was possessed and had a mind of its own, and Aidan was only there for the ride.

What the fuck are you doing?

His body trudged through the fog-covered forest with ease, knowing exactly where it was going, while Aidan watched in wide-eyed horror, unable to do anything about it.

"Who are you?" Aidan yelled, surprised he could still speak.

"You know who I am, Aidan," the dark voice whispered. "People call me the Bogeyman, the thing under the bed. I'm the chill that runs down your spine. The unseen thing in the shadows that follows you home. Your greatest fear and your worst nightmare. I am the emptiness. I am... the darkness."

"Don't listen to him!" Emily's voice rang out from the fog.

"You're special, Aidan. More special that you could ever imagine," the dark voice said.

"Special?" Aidan laughed. "There's nothing special about me."

"Oh, but there is. I've been inside your mind. I've seen and felt everything you have. In a single moment, I lived your entire life. You could be so much *more*, Aidan. You are more powerful than you could ever know."

"Powerful?" Aidan whispered, shaking his head, confused.

"Aidan, don't listen to him. You have to fight him and take back control."

Aidan looked around in the fog for Emily as his body marched on, but he couldn't see her.

"Give yourself to me and join us, Aidan," the dark voice hissed like a snake. Aidan could almost feel its breath on his neck.

"Don't listen to him, Aidan. It's all a lie!" Emily pleaded.

A faint droning sound bellowed through the forest. It sounded like a foghorn, far off in the distance. The thrumming grew louder and louder as Aidan passed through two arched trees into a large circular clearing cut out of the forest. From within the fog, a long black arm with lengthy fingers reached out and beckoned him to come closer, then faded away into the emptiness.

Aidan's body followed and took him to the middle of the

massive circle, before finally coming to a stop.

In front of him was a large, square stone. It looked like it was growing out of the ground, like an ancient tumour spreading from the earth. The fixed grip that had a hold of him eased back. Aidan crouched down and ran his fingers across the ice-cold surface of the stone. It had a wavy texture, like someone had carved something into the top of it.

The fog started to fade away.

Up ahead, beyond the stone, Aidan could see something coming through the lifting mist at the edge of the clearing.

Something red.

As Aidan crept closer, it came into focus. It was a door.

Aidan's ears rattled with the growing droning sound, but he moved it to the back of his mind, trying to ignore it as he approached the door. It stuck out like a sore thumb against the dark woods, standing unnaturally upright with no walls to hold it up. All the hairs on the back of his neck stood at attention. The fog had completely disappeared, as if it had never been there in the first place. Aidan reached out for the door's golden handle with a shaking hand.

"Aidan, no!" Emily screamed.

Something ran up behind him. Aidan spun around, but there was nothing there. When he turned back, the crimson door had vanished.

Now, he stood on a dark, empty stretch of road. He knew exactly where he was without needing to look around. The pounding rain thrashed off the road but made no sound. The only sound came from the wailing horn all around him.

"Emily?" Aidan called out as he turned to his car, covering his eyes from the glare of the headlights.

"There isn't much time," Emily's voice said from behind him.

Aidan turned to her.

Emily stood a few feet away from him, her yellow raincoat

shining like a beacon in the darkness, her hood up and hiding her face. "You need to get to Laura before it's too late."

"Where is she?" Aidan took a step towards her.

"They have her."

"Who does?" Aidan asked, his voice cracking.

"The Or–"

Emily jolted forward, gargling from deep within her throat. "Emily?"

Thick, black sludge dripped from her mouth, over her chin and onto her raincoat. She reached a trembling bone-white hand up and touched her face. Black crept over her fingers and spread across her hand. She looked up at Aidan. Her hood fell back, revealing her terrified, bulging eyes.

"Aidan, I..." She vomited more black sludge.

Emily fell to her knees. Her arms shot out at her sides like the crossbar of a crucifix, as if some invisible force had pulled them. Black sludge ran down from her nose. Aidan stepped towards her. Emily shook her head frantically from side to side as she groaned through gritted teeth for him to stay back. Her head shot backward, and she screamed into the night sky. Aidan didn't know what to do. It all happened so quick.

The symbol etched into Emily's forehead burst into black flames. The *V* overlaid with the cross. Aidan had seen it before, he knew he had; it was the same symbol he'd seen drawn in Nicolas' journal.

Black leaked from her eyes and dripped down her cheeks like bleeding mascara.

The drone of the horn was deafening now, drowning out Emily's screams.

A shadow grew up from behind Emily and towered over her. It was the dark shape. It reached out with its unnaturally long arm and slowly laid its fingers over Emily's head.

Emily's entire body erupted in black fire.

Aidan's eyes burst open. White pain shot through his head.

It felt like someone had ploughed him with a sledgehammer. The foghorn blared around him. He rubbed at his eyes, trying to clear his vision, but the cut on his head had reopened and bright red blood covered his face. His entire body ached. The shattered windscreen looked like an enormous spider's web and the front of the car was a mangled mess of metal wrapped around a tree.

"Laura... Laura, are you okay?" Aidan said groggily, wiping the blood from his eyes. He was in the car. In the driver's seat...

He glanced over at the passenger side. It was empty, the door wide open. Blood dripped from the deflated passenger-side airbag. Aidan fumbled with his seatbelt, unbuckled it, pushed opened the door and fell out of the car. The world was spinning all around him. He could feel the dark at the edges of his vision creeping closer as he pulled himself to his unsteady feet.

"Laura!" Aidan called, grabbing hold of the door to stop himself from falling. He shuffled himself around the back of the car towards the passenger side, in case she was unconscious at the side of the road.

"Laura!" Aidan yelled feebly.

There was no reply.

She wasn't there, but there was something.

A shoe.

Aidan spat a mouthful of blood onto the tarmac and stumbled towards it. His legs buckled under him and he dropped to the ground. His eyes felt heavy as he lay on the cold road. The dark was closing in again. He crawled along the tarmac, pulling himself over broken glass towards her shoe. He reached out and grabbed it, gripped it in his hands.

"I'll find you," Aidan said, so softly it was almost inaudible. It got harder and harder to keep his eyes open. He tried to fight it. *There isn't much time. You need to find Laura before it's too late.*

Emily's words repeated over and over in his head as the world around him turned black.

CHAPTER EIGHTEEN

"Mr. Crain, can you hear me?"

Aidan opened his eyes a crack.

"He's waking. Mr. Crain, can you hear me?"

Everything was a bright, blinding white when he finally managed to peel his eyes all the way open. The muffled voice sounded like someone talking in the next room. Coloured shapes moved around him in the white. The blinding light faded as his eyes adjusted with every crust-filled blink.

"Laura?" Aidan groaned. He sat up, but an arm forced him back down into the bed.

He was in a bed.

"Mr Crain, you shouldn't try to move," another voice said to his right.

"Laura," Aidan thrashed on the bed, his heart raced as panic sunk in. "Laura!" He screamed, the memory of the smashed car flashing in his mind. Alarms and beeping sounds wailed around him.

"Calm down, Mr Crain. You've been in an accident and you're in the hospital," a voice said to his left.

"Where is she? I need to find her!"

He ground the crust from his eyes. The blurred shapes he could see were two doctors. One stood at either side of him.

They had a hold of him, pinning him to the bed.

"Mr Crain, if you don't settle down we'll have to sedate you," the doctor to his left said. He was an older, balding man with a deeply wrinkled face. The other, to Aidan's right, must have been in his late forties and looked like he hadn't had a good night's sleep in over a month. Aidan took a deep breath and relaxed. The beeping machines quietened.

"That's good, breathe," the younger doctor said.

"We're going to let go of you now, all right?"

Aidan nodded, his jaw clenched. The two doctors let go and took a step back.

"Sir, you're in Elmwood General Hospital. I'm Doctor Carson, and this is Doctor Davidson," the older of the two said as he gestured to the younger man.

"Where's my wife?" Aidan said through his teeth. "Where is she?"

"Mr Crain, you've been in an accident. You've been in the hospital for a little under a week."

"A week?" Aidan snapped upright in the bed.

Doctor Davidson placed a firm hand on Aidan's shoulder. "Five days, to be exact. You weren't in a coma, Mr. Crain, but something like one. We're not entirely sure what, exactly, but we'll need to do some more tests."

"Is my wife here? Was she brought in with me?"

"I'm afraid you were brought in alone, Mr. Crain," Carson said. "You were involved in a car accident. A passer-by found you at the side of the road. You were in pretty terrible shape when you were brought in."

Aidan shook his head. "They took her. The person at the side of the road. They were wearing some kind of costume."

The two doctors looked at each other, concerned.

Aidan realised he must have sounded like a rambling madman. *Keep your mouth shut or they'll throw you in a padded cell*, he thought.

Doctor Davidson picked up Aidan's chart and started flicking through it.

"Mr Crain, there were high levels of alcohol in your system when you were brought in."

"Are you kidding me?" Aidan looked at the two men, stunned. "I had a couple of drinks, yes, but I wasn't drunk. And what about Laura? She was with me in the car when we left the bar, and now she's gone. Please explain that to me."

"Well, I don't know what to tell you, Mr. Crain. We have your results here and you were... *extremely* over the limit," Davidson said. Aidan rubbed his face and took a deep breath. He flinched as his hand grazed over the bandaged gash on his forehead. The wound thumped like it had its own heartbeat.

Doctor Carson took the chart from Doctor Davidson and flicked through a few pages.

"It says here you have prescribed medication for your anxiety and depression. Have you been taking your meds, Mr. Crain?" Carson asked.

"What? Yes... I mean..." Aidan stumbled, thrown by the question. "I was taking them, but I ran out. I haven't been able to get a new prescription."

Doctor Davidson wrote something on Aidan's chart.

"What are you writing?"

"Have you ever thought about or attempted to take your own life, Mr. Crain?" Carson asked.

"What? No, of course not!" Aidan shook his head. Red-hot heat started working its way up his neck. "Are you trying to say I did this on purpose?"

"No," Doctor Carson shook his head. "Not at all. We have to ask these questions when a patient is on medication for depression or anxiety. Just to make sure you weren't trying to hurt yourself or anyone else."

"None of this explains what's happened to my wife. She's

163

out there, hurt, and I'm stuck here when I should be out there looking for her."

"Well, that's for the police to figure out," Doctor Davidson said.

"Detective Walker wants to ask you some questions, so you can let him know about your wife and he'll take it further. He should be here shortly," Carson said as a nurse walked in with a bag full of clear fluid.

Shit, anyone but Walker, Aidan thought.

The nurse handed Doctor Carson the clear bag and left without a glance in Aidan's direction.

"This will help with the pain in the time being," Carson said, replacing the empty bag with the new one and attaching it to the tube jammed into Aidan's arm. "Try to get some rest, Mr. Crain. Everything will be okay. We'll be back to see you shortly."

Carson set the chart back down at the end of the bed. Both doctors stared at him for a moment, then left the room, closing the door behind them.

Aidan had always hated hospitals. They were like prisons, but cleaner. Told when to eat, when to sleep, confined to your room – or worse, in a shared ward with people sick and in pain – screaming and yelling throughout the night. Aidan shivered at the thought. Even the sterile smell made him feel sick. Luckily, he had a private room. It was quiet enough; the only sound came from the beeping of the machines hooked up to him and the chatter in the hallway.

The room was quite large; the upper portions of the walls were painted white and the lower half was a dark blue. There was a small flatscreen TV attached to the wall facing him and a single blue vinyl chair in the corner, upon which his clothes had been neatly folded.

Aidan closed his eyes and thought about Laura as the painkillers worked their way through his body. He replayed their night at the bar over and over in his head. The Sidney Thomas song echoed through his mind like it was playing in an empty arena. The images came to him. Slow-dancing in the bar, playing pool.

Then, as if someone hit the fast-forward button in his mind, he saw a crow watching him. Then he was driving. Laura sat next to him, smiling, then sheer panic took over her face. Aidan winced, but kept his eyes shut.

He saw a stag's skull, then blood on the passenger airbag. Aidan's stomach sank like a rock thrown into the ocean.

There was a knock at the door. Aidan grimaced, sitting up in bed. Detective Walker pushed the door open and came into the room. He was wearing the same suit from before, but his hair looked messier, like he had just climbed out of bed.

"Detective," Aidan said

"Mr. Crain," Walker sighed as he approached the foot of the bed. "I thought I told you I didn't want to hear from you again." He didn't look amused.

You're not exactly who I wanted to see either, asshole.

"Laura… my wife, she's missing," Aidan said.

"What's happened now?" Walker rolled his eyes as he pulled out his little black notepad and a pen from his jacket pocket and flipped it open. He looked at Aidan over the notepad, waiting for him to begin. Aidan took a deep breath to compose himself.

"Laura and I, we went out to the bar in town. We wanted to relax for a while after… well, you know. Everything. We went there for a couple of hours, played some pool, had a couple of drinks, and then last orders were called so we headed home."

"Did you drive or did your wife drive?"

"I drove. I wasn't drunk, I only had a couple."

Walked scribbled something in the notebook. "I checked with the doctors and they said you were over the legal limit."

"But –"

Walker held up a finger. Aidan stopped talking.

"Officer Young told me he saw you that night, that you were highly intoxicated."

"Are you serious? He was still in the bar when we left! Did he also tell you he was harassing the barmaid? Or that he was the one who was so drunk he could barely keep his head up?"

"Tell me about your wife," Walker continued, as if Aidan hadn't said a word.

Aidan clenched his jaw.

"When we were driving home, a person…" Aidan fiddled with his fingers as he contemplated what he should say next, then he continued. "A person walked out onto the road in front of the car. I swerved, but I lost control and hit a tree. I must have blacked out, but when I woke up… I noticed Laura was gone and the passenger side door was open."

"So you're saying some mysterious person just walked in front of your car, for no apparent reason in the middle of the night, and took your wife?"

"It's what happened!"

"I find that hard to believe. What I do believe is you had too much to drink and lost control of your car. That, to me, sounds plausible."

Aidan seethed.

"But let's just say I buy into your story of this… person, causing the crash. Why would they do that? And why would they take your wife and leave you?"

"I don't fucking know! I *wish* they'd have taken me instead of her." Aidan threw his arms into the air. "When I woke up, she was already gone. The passenger side door was wide open and there was blood on the airbag."

Walker wrote something else in his little notebook, then tucked it back into his pocket. He rubbed his hand over his grey, sandpaper stubble. "Look, Aidan. I have a blood test telling me you were over the legal limit. You even said yourself that you were drinking, and that *you* drove home. Now you're trying to spin some bullshit story about some third party making you crash. It seems a lot more plausible – and *likely* – to me that you were drunk when you drove home, and your impairment caused you to crash. I've already been down this road with you once and I'm not going down it again."

"That still doesn't explain what happened to Laura," Aidan snapped.

Walker took two steps towards him, his hand clenched tightly into a fist at his side. "Look, I don't even know if she was there with you. I have a witness telling me you were there alone. You don't have an outstanding track record where your memory is concerned. So I'm sorry if I don't jump the gun like the last time."

"What?" Aidan shook his head in disbelief. "Of *course* she was with me. I didn't go to the bar alone. You can even check with Officer Young. He saw her with me."

"Officer Young says he only saw you at the bar."

"This is bullshit!" Aidan couldn't even look at Walker. All he wanted was to get the hell out of this hellhole and go find Laura.

"Have you tried calling her? She could be at home."

"Are you serious?" Aidan laughed. "There's no service in this fucking town – and besides, the doc said I've been here for almost a week. I'm sure if she was at home and I'd made this whole thing up in my head, she would have noticed by now that I hadn't come home, don't you think? Have you been in touch with her to tell her I'm in the hospital?"

"No."

"And has she been in touch with *you*, to report me missing?"

"No."

"So, doesn't it strike you as strange that my wife could just be sitting at home? How about you do your fucking job and go find her!"

"Listen here," Walker snapped. "You're lucky I don't write you up for a DUI. You're *lucky*, Mr. Crain. You're lucky I don't just jump straight to worst-case scenario and arrest you on suspicion of murder. This car crash… hell of an alibi to concoct for yourself. If anyone had even seen *Laura* at the bar, I might reconsider."

Walker's face had turned a reddish pink colour. A thick vein bulged out from his neck. Looking at him, Aidan thought he might drop at any second.

Let the bastard fall.

Walker dabbed at the sweat on his forehead with his sleeve, then turned and stormed out of the ward, slamming the door behind him.

***

Walker thundered down the corridor, yanking at his tie to loosen its grip around his neck. Sweat dripped down his face, the dark patches under his arms growing by the second. His entire body trembled. He needed out of that room. If he stayed even a second longer, he knew he'd do something that he would regret. Up ahead, he could see Doctor Carson chatting to a nurse.

"Doctor!" Walker yelled.

A woman walking past stared at him with a disgusted look on her face.

"What are you looking at?" Walker spat. The woman tutted and glanced away.

Doctor Carson looked down the corridor in his direction. "I'm sorry, excuse me," he said to the nurse, starting towards

Walker. "What can I do for you, Detective?"

"Aidan Crain," Walker said, catching his breath.

"Yes, what about him?"

"I want him sedated. Shackle him to the bed. I don't give a fuck, but he can't leave this hospital."

"We can't just –"

"There's something not right with him, up here." Walker tapped frantically at his head. "He could be a risk to himself or others. I had a run-in with him last week and believe me, he isn't all there." Walker licked the salty sweat on his upper lip.

Doctor Carson frowned. "Maybe you should take a seat, detective." He gestured to a metal chair beside a large window overlooking a small, square garden. "You don't look too good."

"I'm fine! Just make sure Mr. Crain doesn't leave this hospital until I get back."

Walker pushed past Doctor Carson and headed for the exit.

Aidan bounced up from the bed. He ripped the IV cord from his arm and pulled off the other cables attached to him. The machines on the side of his bed screamed to life.

Shit!

Reaching around the back of the bank of machines, he found a switch and shut them off, hoping he'd gotten to them before anyone noticed. He stood still for a moment, holding his breath, listening for footsteps. None came. His tense muscles relaxed, and he hurried to the clothes piled on the chair. He ripped off his gown and started dressing himself. His shirt had gone stiff with dried blood, but he put it on anyway. He slipped his shoes on and headed to the small bathroom on the other side of the room. Aidan looked at himself in the mirror above the sink.

He was a little banged-up, to say the least.

Jesus Christ.

The bandage wrapped around his head had a small, dark bloodstain at the top corner. Quickly, he unwrapped it, revealing the gash on his head. Eighteen stitches in total. He threw the bandage into the bin and grabbed some blue paper from the dispenser on the wall, soaking it in cold water. He dabbed it over the stitches, washing off the dried blood, wincing every time the cool water touched the cut. The light in the bathroom flickered, but Aidan didn't take any notice. He threw the paper into the bin, grabbed his phone and his wallet, and went to the double doors of his room.

He placed his hand on the door and pushed it open a crack, hoping there was no one on the other side.

So far, so good.

He inched it open a little further, enough to poke his head through, and looked up and down the ward. It was empty. All he could hear were the sounds of beeping machines, people coughing in other rooms, and distant chatter.

Doctor Carson and Doctor Davidson walked around the corner. Aidan pulled his head back inside, closing the door, praying the two doctors hadn't decided to come check on him. Their footsteps reverberated down the corridor, getting closer and closer until they stopped outside his room.

Shit! Shit! Shit!

Aidan wrapped his hand over his mouth as he held his breath, trying to listen to the two doctors chatting.

"Detective Walker said he had an incident with him last week. Isn't all there in the head, apparently. The detective wants him sedated until he gets back," Carson said.

"Can we do that?"

"The detective must have his reasons – and you saw him earlier, he isn't stable. We'll keep a close eye on him. Give him forty milligrams of Chlorpromazine and fifty Fentanyl to start him off."

Aidan could hear the scratching sound of someone writing

something down.

"Okay, so who do we have next?" Doctor Davidson asked.

Their footsteps faded into ambient sound as they walked up the ward. Air burst from Aidan's lungs. He grabbed hold of his knees, catching his breath. When his lungs had settled, he slowly opened the door and looked up and down the corridor.

Now or never.

In a second, he was out of the room and hurrying down the hallway, hoping he was going the right way. Up ahead was another set of double doors. He reached out and pulled the handle.

Locked. There was a black keycard lock at the side of the door. A red LED stared back at him like an evil, beady eye.

"Sir, you shouldn't be here," a nurse said behind him.

Aidan squeezed his eyes shut. This was it. They'd caught him before he even started, and now they would pump him with all kinds of shit. He pictured himself sitting in a padded cell wearing a straitjacket, drool falling aimlessly from his mouth. He wondered how long he would have if he forced the key card from her. Would she scream? Would he be able to get out before they raised the alarm, or would he have to hurt her to get the key? He didn't want to hurt her, but Aidan knew deep inside that he would do whatever it took to get to Laura.

"Visiting ended an hour ago, sir."

His eyes sprung open; he turned to face her. "I'm sorry, I… lost track of time," Aidan said, wrapping his arms around his stomach to hide the bloodstains on his shirt.

"All right, but don't make it a habit." The nurse took the keycard lanyard from around her neck and scanned the little black box on the side of the door. The red light turned green, and the door clicked open.

"Thank you. And yes, sorry, it won't happen again," Aidan

said.

He hurried down a large hallway, looking over his shoulder, making sure the doctors weren't coming for him after finding his room empty. Finally, he saw the word *EXIT* on the wall ahead of him, above a green arrow pointing down towards an escalator.

He got onto the escalator and went down to the main foyer. The hospital was quiet; only a handful of people sat in the small waiting area. An old woman sat behind the reception desk, watching TV and chewing on the end of her pen. Aidan hurried past, hoping to not draw any attention to himself.

Shit, I don't have a car.

The thought hit him as he walked through the double doors to freedom.

***

Aidan walked down a long stretch of road that ran alongside the hospital. It was like every other road on the outskirts of town, cutting straight through the middle of the forest, towering trees on either side. He had been walking for a little over an hour and Aidan didn't have a clue where he was or if he was even going in the right direction. He just walked. The adrenaline and painkillers had faded a while ago, and now the aches and pains were working their way through his body.

He looked around the empty road, as if he expected to see someone.

"Emily?" he called.

Everything was still.

Is she really gone? He believed that she had truly been there with him, that she couldn't have been a figment of his imagination; after all, if it wasn't for her he would still be wondering around the forest – or worse, taken by the dark thing.

Aidan suddenly felt very alone.

He heard a vehicle coming up the road behind him. The first sign of life since he'd started along the road. Aidan stuck out his thumb.

A red pickup truck shot past him and pulled onto the side of the road with a skid, kicking dirt up in a cloud behind it. Aidan ran to the passenger side of the truck and pulled open the door.

"Thank you so much!" Aidan exclaimed as he climbed inside. He looked over at the driver.

"Jesus, what's happened to you?" Jack asked.

CHAPTER NINETEEN

The pickup's wheels screeched as Jack pulled out onto the road. Aidan was barely inside before he was thrown back into the seat. He fumbled with the seatbelt, pulling it across his bruised chest. There was a police scanner duct-taped to the dashboard of the truck; every so often, crackling voices murmured from it.

"Thanks for picking me up," Aidan said.

"You're welcome. Aidan, right?" Jack said, glancing across at him.

"Ah, yeah, and you are…"

"Jack. We met in the coffee shop."

"Yes, Jack, of course. Look, I need to get back to town. I need to find…" Aidan stopped himself, unsure if he should mention Laura to a complete stranger.

"You look like you've been through the wars," Jack said.

A feeble chuckle hopped from Aidan's chest. "Yeah, I guess you could say that."

"You went in, didn't you?" Jack asked.

"What do you mean?"

"You went into the woods. I told you not to go in." Jack shook his head.

"How… how did you know?" Aidan asked. *How could he?*

"You've got a look on your face that's all too familiar." Jack shook his head. "You don't know what you've done, do you?"

"My dog chased something into the woods. I couldn't just leave him, I had to get him back."

"You should have left him," Jack snapped. His intense stare burned into Aidan. "There's something dark, something evil in those woods – hell, maybe it's in every forest, I don't know. But now that it's seen you, felt you... had a *taste* of you... it won't stop now until it has you and everything you ever loved."

The dark thing's long, beckoning arm flashed through Aidan's mind.

"Elmwood isn't a normal town," Jack continued. "Ever since this place was founded, it's been cursed. Strange deaths, countless missing people... just outright *weird shit*. I don't know why or how to explain it, but the forest seems to be like... a beacon of dark energy, like some kind of vortex. Bad things happen in this town, horrible things."

Any other day, Aidan might have thought Jack was some crazy conspiracy theorist rambling about nonsense, but he'd been through his fair share of crazy lately, and for the first time he felt like this was someone he could talk to about it, someone who would understand what he'd been going through; someone onto whom he could unload all the madness he had experienced and who, maybe, could help him make sense of it all.

But more importantly, someone who would believe him.

"When I was in the woods, I found a ditch full of bodies, but –"

"When you went back, there was nothing there," Jack interrupted.

"Yes!" Aidan exclaimed.

"That's it. That's the forest fucking with your head. It's

what it does. It makes you feel like you're losing your shit, beats you down until it gets a hold of you. You aren't the only person I've seen with that same expression on their face."

"How many have there been?"

"Fuck! How long's a piece of string?"

Aidan pondered that for a moment. *How many others have seen what I've seen?*

How many others has the Darkness called out to?

"I've seen things in the house, unexplainable things – heard footsteps, seen doors open and close on their own – you name it. Laura even recorded a voice on her phone. Then there's the nightmares –"

The police scanner erupted with a deafening screech.

"Sorry, it does this sometimes," Jack yelled over the static, smacking the top of the scanner. The white noise stopped, and a voice came over the radio. It was Detective Walker.

"I've just been informed that Aidan Crain has left the hospital without being discharged. All officers, be on the lookout for a male in his thirties, probably on foot, heading towards town. He's an out-of-towner, so you should be able to spot him easily enough. Mr Crain isn't of a stable mind, so approach with caution."

Jack shut the radio off.

Aidan slammed his fists down onto the plastic dashboard. "Fuck!" he screamed, his arms shaking with anger. He stared blankly out of the windscreen, his hands squeezed into white-knuckled fists. They sat in silence for a short time. The only sound was the rattle of the pickup's engine.

"Don't take any notice of that fucker," Jack said finally.

"My wife's missing," Aidan mumbled, fidgeting with his fingers.

"What?"

"My wife's missing!" Aidan yelled. "And that," he pointed to the police scanner, his nose wrinkled in a snarl, "*worthless* excuse of a detective doesn't believe me. And better yet, he thinks I have something to do with it." Aidan laughed. "I guess, in a way, he's right. If I hadn't gone into the woods like you said, none of this would be happening."

"You're right, it is your fault," Jack said.

"What did you just say?"

"I said, it is your fault. But we will get her back."

Aidan glanced over to Jack, then looked away, nodding to himself. "Someone or something stepped out in front of me," Aidan said.

Jack glanced at him, puzzled.

"In the road. That's why I crashed the car. That's why I look like this," he gestured to his face. "They were wearing a black, hooded cloak and had a stag's skull for a head."

"A fucking stag's skull?"

"Yeah, well… at least, I think that's what it was. It all went so fast." Aidan shook his head.

"And you think it took your wife?" Jack asked.

"Yeah," Aidan stared out the window at the passing trees. "I passed out. But when I woke up, she was gone." Aidan's eyes welled up, but he wouldn't let himself cry.

"I'm telling you, it's the woods. Almost every person to ever go missing in Elmwood ventured out into the forest at some point."

"But Laura didn't go into the woods, I did. Why didn't it take me?"

"I don't know, maybe it has other plans for you."

Those words drove an icy chill down Aidan's spine. "How do you know so much about this?" he asked.

"Let's just say I've seen my fair share of crazy in Elmwood."

Jack said nothing else. They drove through the town and turned onto the road that led to the lake house. The sun had dipped behind the trees as the evening approached.

"Here, pull in here, this is where it happened!" Aidan

pointed to a lay-by. Jack pulled over and skidded to a stop. Tyre marks zigzagged across the road towards the tree that had totalled the car. Aidan jumped out of the pickup and hurried to the tree. There were pieces of broken glass and plastic at the edge of the road. The tree looked almost perfect, save for a few inches of missing bark. He hunkered down and touched the tyre marks burned onto the road. Just the sight of them made him feel dizzy. He jumped to his feet and rushed to the side of the road and vomited.

"You okay?" Jack asked as he got out of the pickup.

Aidan wiped his mouth and nodded.

A switch sparked to life in his head.

The shoe.

His eyes widened as he stared at Jack.

"What is it?"

"Her shoe." Aidan looked up the side of the road and between the trees, searching for it.

"A shoe?" Jack asked.

"Her shoe was on the road after I woke up."

"The police probably took it for evidence or something."

"Walker thinks I was in the car alone, even though there were bloodstains on the passenger airbag. If they've taken her shoe as evidence –"

"Then that proves she was with you at the time of the accident."

"Or it proves the police are trying to cover something up. Maybe it has something to do with the woods as well, I don't know, but this whole thing is so…"

"It makes sense. I've always thought the police have had something to do with what's been going on here from the start. You know how many of the missing people they have found?" Jack held his hand up, the thumb and forefinger touching, creating a zero.

"None?"

"Zilch," Jack nodded. "After a while they just stop looking for them, and the town goes on as if nothing ever happened. It's bullshit."

"How can they be linked to the woods, though?"

"I haven't been able to figure that part out, but something definitely stinks about the whole thing."

Aidan stared into the forest. "I need to find her, Jack."

"You will, and I'll help you." He looked up at the darkening sky. "But not tonight."

"What do you mean not tonight? We need to get out there and look for her. If you aren't coming, I'll go myself." Aidan took off up the road.

"Don't be stupid, Aidan," Jack called after him. "Where are you even going to start?"

Aidan stopped. Jack had a point. Where *would* he start?

"We need to come up with some kind of plan or we'll be chasing our tails." Aidan heard the pickup's door slam behind him, then the engine roared to life. Jack pulled up alongside him. "Come on, get in."

They headed up the road, but instead of turning left towards the lake house, Jack turned right.

"Where are we going?" Aidan asked.

"My place. I have things that'll come in handy. Maps, compass, torches. A gun. Things like that."

"A gun?"

Jack didn't answer, just smiled to himself. It was dusk now, but it was even darker under the cover of the towering trees.

"Thank you," Aidan said.

"What for?"

"For helping me. I feel like I've been losing my mind lately. Most other people would think I was crazy if I told them the things I've told you, but somehow you know what I'm going through."

"It's no problem. Believe me, I've been there. Hell, I'm still there."

Aidan decided not to ask him what he meant. They drove in silence down the winding road towards Jack's cottage.

A small white cottage lit up ahead of them, illuminated by the headlights of the truck. It was a small, one-storey building surrounded by a weathered picket fence. The garden was wild and overgrown, the grass almost as high as the fence.

Jack pulled up outside and turned off the ignition. "You coming?" he asked as he jumped out of the pickup and headed towards the cottage. Aidan got out and caught up with Jack as he unlocked the front door. He pushed it open and they stepped inside, disappearing into the darkness. Jack swung the door shut.

In the dark, Aidan could hear the clicking sound of multiple locks sliding into place. He couldn't see an inch in front of him, and for a second he thought he was back in the emptiness. With his arms stretched out like a zombie from a comic book, he tiptoed forward in the dark.

WHACK!

"Shit!" Aidan yelled, rubbing at his throbbing shin.

"Yeah, watch your step," Jack laughed. "Just a second, the switch is just over here."

With a flick, the cottage filled with light, blinding them both for a second before their eyes adjusted. "Make yourself at home," Jack said, taking off his black Puffa coat and hanging it over the top of a dusty green sofa that looked like something straight from the nineties.

The cottage was as small inside as it had looked from the outside. In the small living room was the vintage sofa and a metal and glass coffee table, which took up most of the floor space. There were two other doors; one that led to the kitchen, and the other to a hallway that led to the bedrooms.

Jack picked up empty food packets off the floor in a hurry,

gathering as many as he could into a massive bundle in his arms and taking them into the kitchen. There was no television, only a large metal locker secured with a deadbolt and padlock and a bookshelf filled with books. A far wall was covered in newspaper clippings and photos from floor to ceiling.

Intrigued, Aidan walked over to take a closer look. The old newspaper clippings dated back as far as the eighties. Some of the countless missing persons posters had yellowed with age.

He scanned the wall, looking over the dozens – *hundreds* – of faces smiling back at him. The people came from all walks of life: men, women, young, old, local, tourist, white, black, and everything in between.

One smiling face jumped out at him from the top left corner of the wall. The photograph was of a pretty girl with long, dark brown hair. He recognised her instantly.

"You've got to be kidding me," Aidan said out loud, without realising he'd spoken. He reached up and pulled the missing person poster off the wall, staring at the grinning woman in shock.

"Ah, Emily Pembrook," Jack said as he came back into the living room, looking at the poster in Aidan's trembling hand. "Pretty girl."

"Did you know her?"

"No, not personally, but she's one of only a handful of locals on that wall. I think she's been missing for a little over two years now."

"She… she's from Elmwood?" The colour drained from Aidan's face.

Jack stared at him, concerned. "You okay, buddy? You look like you've seen a ghost."

You have no idea, Aidan thought. "I know her," he said, finally prying his eyes away from the poster.

"You know her? How?"

"This is unbelievable." Aidan shook his head, feeling a little lightheaded.

"Aidan, how do you know her?"

"I'm the one who found her." He handed Jack the poster, unable to look at it anymore.

"You found her? Holy shit, that's amazing. Where is she?" Jack's wide, excited eyes quickly faded when he saw the sullen look on Aidan's face. "What, what is it?"

"She's dead, Jack. She's the reason Laura and I came to Elmwood."

"What?" Jack asked, somehow bleak and curious at once.

"I'm the one who found her body. I was having a hard time dealing with it, so Laura thought it would be a good idea to come out here. To get away and reset. But I just can't believe she's from here. What are the odds?" Aidan said dolefully.

"What are the odds, indeed? Do you know what happened to her?"

"You don't want to know, believe me."

"That bad?" Jack winced.

Aidan only nodded. He didn't want to go into the gory details. He considered telling Jack about seeing Emily in his dreams and how she'd somehow come back to guide him through the woods that night, but ultimately, he decided against it.

She was gone now, really gone. He knew it in his heart, and he thought it better to finally let her rest.

Another photo stood out to him. This one was in colour and pinned in the middle of the wall, surrounded by other photos and newspaper cutouts like the centrepiece of a shrine. It was a photo of Sophie Henderson. It was the same photo that had been used for her poster, only this looked to be the original.

One of the news clippings read: *local girl Sophie Henderson*

(9) still missing after weeks of intense searching. Another read: *Search for a local girl called off by Elmwood Police Department after dead end.* Aidan scanned over the other photos. One was Sophie with her parents; she was a lot younger in it. He pulled it off the wall and studied it.

"She was five when that was taken," Jack said, leaning against the wall.

"I… I had no idea, Jack," Aidan stuttered. Jack reached out and took the photo. Without taking his eyes from it, he went to the sofa and sat down.

"This was the first day of our vacation in Hawaii. She was so excited. She'd never left Elmwood before, and it was the first time she had been on a plane. It was incredible seeing her experience it all for the first time. She was always such a carefree kid; even when she was a baby, she was always smiling, always giggling." Jack held the photo tightly in his hands. His eyes welled up.

"I'm so sorry, Jack," Aidan said as he sat beside him.

"She's been missing now for over six months. I never stopped looking for her. Every day I'm out searching for her."

"Even in the woods?"

Jack nodded. "Even in the woods."

"You said not to go –"

"My life is already over, Aidan. Nothing could make it worse. My only goal in life now is to find her."

"What about the police?" Aidan asked.

"The police. Pfft," Jack snorted, shaking his head. "You've seen first-hand how useless the Elmwood P.D. is. They gave up searching three months ago. They made me out to be the town nutjob. An outcast. And all I wanted was my little girl back."

"What about your wife?" Aidan asked. Jack rubbed his finger. There was a pale mark where his wedding ring used to be. "Nancy. She left me about a month after Sophie went missing."

"Fuck," Aidan sighed. "Talk about a kick in the teeth."

"She said I was obsessed. That I should leave it and let the police do their job. But I couldn't, I couldn't just sit back and not look for my daughter. One day... I came home, and she was gone. Took everything with her as well, except this ugly sofa and the bed."

"Why did she leave?"

"She just couldn't deal with it anymore, I guess. She still lives in Elmwood, in a little apartment complex by the harbour."

"Do you ever see her?" Aidan asked, then immediately regretted it.

"Sometimes," he laughed. "It's a small town. But she just pretends I don't exist like everybody else in Elmwood. But I can't give up on my little girl. I will find her. And you will find your wife."

Jack had never given up; no matter how hard things got, he fought every day for his daughter, and Aidan admired him for it. Jack pulled himself to his feet with a groan and pinned the photo back up on the wall, wiping his tears away with the back of his hand. Aidan watched Jack from the sofa, then pointed to something on the wall.

"Where did you get that?" he asked.

Jack looked to where Aidan was pointing and pulled a card off the wall. It had the *V* and cross symbol printed on it.

"It was nailed to the front door the day Sophie went missing. I've no clue what it is or what it means. The police didn't think much of it either, but that doesn't surprise me. Why, do you know what it is?"

"I don't know what it is, but I've seen it somewhere else."

"Where?"

Aidan hesitated. He didn't want to say, but he knew he had to. Emily was connected to all this, somehow. How, he had no clue, but it was something they needed to find out.

"It was carved into Emily's forehead."

Jack's head shot up. A grave look took over his face. "Are you shitting me?"

Aidan shook his head.

"What the fuck is going on?"

"It was also drawn in a journal that Laura found in the house. The journal of Nicolas Wright."

"Nicolas Wright... *the* Nicolas Wright?"

"Yeah, I guess so. I don't know much about him, other than that he was a serial killer."

"The man was a monster, that's what he was." Jack sighed. "What in God's name does any of this have to do with Nicolas Wright?"

"Do you think it could be a copycat or something?" Aidan asked.

"Fuck, I hope not. I really, really hope not." Jack's hands were shaking noticeably now. He stuck the card back onto the wall. "We should go. We have a lot to figure out." He pointed to a backpack sitting beside the sofa. "Throw that over."

Aidan threw the backpack to Jack.

He took it to the metal locker. With his free hand, he reached into his back pocket and pulled out a small silver key. He stuck it into the padlock and clicked it open, slid the deadbolt across, and opened the doors. Inside was a collection of knives, a couple of flashlights, and a Glock 17 pistol. Four boxes of ammo were neatly laid out behind the gun, along with three or four extra magazines. Jack picked up a machete and a small knife and threw them into the backpack along with two flashlights. He picked up the pistol, checked it was loaded – it was – and stuffed it into the backpack along with one box of ammo and a spare magazine.

"All right, that's everything. Let's go," Jack said, zipping up the bag. He slipped on his coat and started unlocking the front door.

They headed out into the night. Jack threw the backpack into the back seat and turned the ignition. The truck sputtered and choked.

Jack turned the key again and pumped the gas pedal.

"Come on, not now!" he pleaded.

With a roar, the engine came to life.

"Yes! She never lets me down," Jack laughed, pulling a u-turn and taking off towards the Lake House. They were pretty close; maybe only five minutes away.

Up ahead, blue and red flashing lights bounced off the pine trees as a police cruiser turned off towards the town. Jack turned on the scanner. The static drowned the silence in the truck. A voice broke through.

"Detective Walker... we are..." The voice broke off into static.

Jack hit the scanner with a hard thump, and the voice became clear again.

"Officer Young?"

"Just letting you know I've left the Lake House."

Aidan's ears perked up; he leaned in towards to the scanner to get a better listen.

"There was no sign of Mr Crain. The house was empty."

"Did you do as I asked?"

"Yes sir, I'm on my way to the station now." Young laughed.

"All right. Over and out."

The scanner hissed down to white static again. Jack turned it down.

"What do you think he did?" Jack asked.

"I've no idea," Aidan said, perplexed.

They pulled into the driveway, leaves crunching under the truck's tyres. The house was in complete darkness.

They got out and Jack grabbed the backpack from the backseat, throwing it over his shoulder. Wooden boards creaked under their feet as they crept to the front door. It was leaning open just a crack.

Aidan pushed the door gently with his foot. It opened with an eerie creak. He stepped inside and turned on the light.

Young had trashed the entire living room. The sofa was tipped over on its back and the pictures on the walls were smashed to pieces. Books and board games were scattered across the floor like hundreds and thousands. The house rested in deadly silence. Aidan went into the kitchen.

"Fucking bastards," Jack said, looking at the chaos of the room.

In the kitchen, all the drawers had been pulled open and their contents thrown out. Broken plates and smashed glass littered the floor.

Jack set his backpack on the floor and flipped the sofa back onto its feet.

The fridge and freezer doors were wide open. Young had thrown food all over the place. Aidan checked the back door. Locked. He passed Jack and went upstairs to the bedroom. The mattress had been thrown against the window. Their suitcases were open, their clothes scattered around the room.

The bag filled with his bloody clothes was gone. His laptop lay on the floor, smashed to bits along with his camera. *Bastards!*

He checked the other bedrooms, but they were all untouched. The house looked like a bomb had gone off inside. Aidan went back downstairs; Jack had started putting things back into their place and was carrying the coffee table back to its usual spot.

Aidan spotted a packet of cigarettes on the floor and picked them up. "At least they left me a couple smokes." He put one in his mouth, took the lighter from the fireplace and lit it. "I needed this so bad," Aidan said, taking another draw.

He offered the pack to Jack, who waved him away. "I don't smoke."

"Fair enough." Aidan stuffed the packet and lighter into his pocket and went into the kitchen. A distant beeping noise came from somewhere in the room. He searched for the sound, then saw the landline hanging from the wall. He picked it up and put it back on its mount. The beeping stopped. One button flashed red and the LED screen read *One new voice message*. He pushed the button and a man's voice came through the speaker.

"Mr. And Mrs. Crain, It's Mr. Stine calling from Elmwood Veterinary Clinic. I'm just calling to let you know you can come and collect Max in the morning at your earliest convenience. Thank you."

The message ended with another loud beep. Aidan sighed.

"What's this?" Jack asked, standing in the doorway between the kitchen and living room.

"It's one of Nicolas Wright's journals," Aidan said. Jack stared wild-eyed at the book. "There should be more in here."

Aidan went into the living room. He searched for them but couldn't find any of the other books.

"They took them. They took the journals."

CHAPTER TWENTY

Aidan finished up putting the house back to normal – or, at least, as close to normal as he could manage.

Jack hunched over on the sofa, engrossed in Nicolas Wright's journal, basking in the heat from the fire. Aidan searched through the cupboards to see if anything had made it through the ransacking. Behind some food containers, he spied a bottle; a half-empty bottle of vodka, covered in dust. He pulled it out, blew on it, then cracked the lid open and took a deep sniff. *Yep, that'll do,* he thought as he choked on the fumes.

"I still can't believe you've got Nicolas Wright's Journal," Jack shouted from the living room.

"There was more than just the one, before Elmwood's finest stole them. I think Laura said there might be more up in the attic. If you want, we can go have a look," Aidan said as he set the bottle on the counter. He opened the cupboard that had been full of glasses, hoping some had made it. There were two still intact, a pint glass and a small tumbler. He lifted them out, picked up the bottle of vodka, and headed into the living room.

"Holy shit, listen to this," Jack said as Aidan clinked the glasses down on the coffee table and sat down next to him.

"'Fiona came back to me. I don't know how he did it, but he brought her back. In return, he's asked me to join him. He spoke about his plans for the creation of The Order."

"The Order?" Aidan asked, pouring them each two fingers of vodka. "Have you ever heard of that?"

Jack shook his head. "No, never. And who's this 'he' that he keeps mentioning?"

"In parts that I read, it says he could hear a voice in his head, that it told him to do things. I think that's the 'he'," Aidan said, conveniently leaving out the fact that the voice had also talked to him.

"Crazy fucker."

Aidan sunk his vodka and poured himself another. "Wait, did you say his wife came back?"

Jack scanned over the entry, then said, "Yeah, that's what it says here"

"But, she killed herself."

"She didn't kill herself, he murdered her. She was one of his victims."

"What?" Aidan said, shaking his head. "I read an entry where he said his wife killed herself. He said the voice told him it could bring her back." He paused for a moment. "You don't think…"

"No way, that's impossible. These…" Jack flicked through the pages of the book. "As fascinating as they are, they're just the ramblings of a crazy man."

"People would be quick to call us crazy too."

"No mixers?" Jack laughed, changing the subject. He picked up his glass of vodka and took a sip, grimacing. He flicked through a few more pages, then finally stopped on one and read it to himself. Aidan watched the smirk leave his face and turn into a focused frown.

Jack downed the rest of his vodka and stared grimly at Aidan.

"Listen to this," he said warily. "'The Order is growing. There will be five of us tomorrow night. We're preparing our offering for the initiation ritual. Just some drifter that rolled into town about a week ago, alone. He seems nice, when he isn't crying and blabbering. We have him tied up in the cave while we prepare the clearing.

"'Tomorrow, Al will give himself to the Darkness in a baptism of blood to become the fifth member of The Order.'"

They looked at each other in stunned horror.

"Who's Al?" Aidan asked.

"Al Stevenson. He was the principal of Elmwood High in the eighties and nineties." The journal shook in Jack's hand. Aidan reached out and took it from him.

Something fell out and fluttered down next to Aidan's foot. A black, rectangular slip of paper with a white border. He set the book on the table and picked the thing up off the floor. It was a Polaroid.

Aidan turned it over. A coppery taste filled his mouth as he stared at the picture. He couldn't believe what he was looking at.

"What is it?" Jack asked, seeing the haunted expression on Aidan's face. He snatched the photo from the other man's hand. "Holy shit!"

The black-and-white photo had bleached slightly over time, but the image was still clear. The photograph was of the thing Aidan had seen at the side of the road, standing in the forest and clenching a long blade in its hand, pointed to the sky. Something was on fire behind it. The bottom of the photo was signed: *Nicolas, 1982*.

"That's him," Aidan said, his voice trembling. "That's who I saw that night."

"How's that even possible?" Jack asked, bewildered.

"I don't know, I –"

The house went pitch black. Aidan and Jack bounced to

their feet, hearts racing in their chests. Aidan's mouth was as dry as a desert. The faint, flickering glow of the fire was the only light in the house.

Reaching over the edge of the sofa, Jack pulled up the backpack and took out the two flashlights, handing one to Aidan.

"Hello?" Aidan called to the empty house, slicing the beam of light across the room.

The basement door creaked open.

Both beams fixed on the door as it came to a stop. A strange humming sound drifted up the stairs from the basement. Like someone humming a tune they couldn't get from their head.

"You can hear that, right?" Jack croaked.

"Yeah," Aidan whispered. "This is what I've been dealing with."

"Jesus Christ."

"We need to go down there."

"What? Are you mad?" Jack said.

"Laura thinks whatever's in this house needs our help, so that's what I'm going to do."

Jack pressed his eyes shut, then sighed. "Fine, lead the way."

Aidan inched towards the basement door, pulled it the rest of the way open with his foot, and shone the light down the stairs. The low humming sound drifted up towards them.

"You ready?" Aidan asked, starting down the stairs before Jack could reply. Everything in his body screamed at him to turn around, but he kept pushing forward. Jack followed closely behind. Every groaning step increased the agonising fear building up inside of them.

It was noticeably colder in the basement. Plumes of breath billowed out into the beams of light.

The basement door slammed behind them with a

deafening *bang*. Aidan almost jumped right out of his skin.

Jack rushed to the door, pulling at the handle to get it open. He rammed his shoulder against the door, but it didn't budge.

"I don't think it's giving us a choice," Aidan said.

The humming stopped. Somehow, Aidan thought, the deafening silence was worse.

They made it to the bottom of the stairs and scanned the room with their flashlights. There was nothing down here.

"Why did you bring us down here?" Aidan asked, surprised by the strength in his voice.

In the corner of the room, a kind of mist swirled around like a breath of white smoke. Aidan pointed his light at it.

"Do you see that?" Aidan asked.

"See what? I don't see anything."

"The mist, or smoke, or whatever it is. You really don't see that?"

The swirling mist took on a shape. It contorted until it was in the shape of a person. Aidan's jaw trembled. He couldn't believe what he was seeing. The mist had turned into a little girl.

It was Sophie.

The light from his torch shone right through her. Her skin was porcelain white; she stared directly at him with her dead, colourless eyes. "Jack," Aidan whispered without taking his eyes off her.

"What? What is it?"

"Can't you see her? She's right there."

"Who's there? I can't see anything." Sweat dripped down Jack's forehead and stung his eyes. He shone his light to where Aidan's was pointed, but all he saw was an empty room.

"It's Sophie."

"What?" Jack hissed, turning to Aidan, who was still

focused on the corner of the room. Jack's light wavered. He looked back into the corner.

Still nothing.

"Sophie?"

"Daddy?" Sophie said, turning towards Jack. Her voice sounded distant.

"She can see you," Aidan said.

"Sophie?" Jack's voice broke. "I can hear you, but you sound far away." Tears streamed down his face. "Why can't I see you?" Jack hurried to the corner and fell to his knees.

"I have an idea," Aidan said, going to him. "Don't ask me how or why, because I have no idea what I'm doing. I just have a feeling that it'll work."

Jack didn't answer him; he just stared into the corner.

Aidan hunkered down beside him, took a deep breath, and laid his hand on Jack's shoulder.

Jack blinked hard, like there was something in his eye. A tingling sensation crawled over his body from Aidan's hand. In the torch's light he saw something, fading in and out of visibility.

"Sophie, is it really you?"

Tears ran down his cheeks. He lifted a hand to stroke her face, but it passed straight through her like she was nothing but smoke.

"My baby girl," Jack cried. She leaned in towards him and kissed his cheek. He felt nothing – there was no pressure, just ice-cold static against his face.

"I missed you, Daddy."

"I missed you too, sweetie," Jack moaned. "Where have you been? I've been looking all over for you."

"I've been here."

"Why are you here, Sophie? Why didn't you come home?"

"I wanted to, Daddy, I tried, but… I can't leave this place… the woman, she keeps us all here."

"The woman? What woman?" Jack clenched his teeth. All he wanted to do was wrap his arms around his little girl and take her home, where she would be safe.

"The woman with no eyes. This is her house," Sophie said. "She brings us here, but she doesn't let us leave."

"Who else is here?" Aidan said, looking around the room. "Is my wife here?"

"No, my friends are here. They've been looking after me and keeping me safe."

Aidan felt something as the words left Sophie's translucent lips, something he hadn't felt in a while. Hope. Hope that he would find Laura. Hope that they would get out of this nightmare.

"But there's no one else here, sweetie," Jack said.

"Sure there is, they're all around us."

Jack and Aidan looked nervously around the room. It was empty.

"I can't see anyone else," Aidan said.

"That's because they're hiding, silly," Sophie giggled.

Aidan smiled at her.

"Sophie?"

She looked at Jack. "Yes, Daddy?"

"Who took you from me?" he asked, his gaze intense.

Sophie's face turned sombre. She held a hand out to her dad. He placed his hand on hers, but he couldn't feel anything except the cold air between his fingers. She glanced over at Aidan and held out her other hand. His hand tingled as he took hers.

Sophie closed her eyes.

Everything went white and in a blink, Aidan was outside.

***

The sun burned brilliantly in the sky, and not a single cloud stained the perfect blue. It was warm and birds sang from the telephone cables overhead.

Aidan walked along a country road, the forest at either side of him. He recognised this place; it was close to Jack's cottage. Aidan tried to turn his head to look around, but couldn't. He tried to move his arms and nothing happened. A familiar song hummed in his head, only he wasn't the one humming it. It was a little girl; it was Sophie. A car drove past and a woman in the driver's seat waved at her. Sophie waved back.

Aidan could feel everything she could feel, every emotion, every thought. He felt the wind blowing through her hair, the road beneath her feet, even the sting of the scrape on her knee. She was happy, not a single care in the world. Just walking home from school like any other day.

There was a strange sound from behind the trees to her left, a shuffling sound. She stopped and looked into the forest. A small, grey rabbit hopped out from behind a tree.

Sophie smiled.

Her dad had always told her to come straight home after school, that the forest was a dangerous place for little girls to play, but she really wanted a closer look at the bunny. Just a look, just a *second*, then she would go straight home. He would never know.

She climbed over the metal barrier into woods. Crawling between the trees, she edged closer and closer to get a better look, hoping she wouldn't scare it away. She held her breath, watching the bunny hop along the mossy forest floor.

There was another sound.

This time it came from behind her. The rabbit stood up on its hind legs, looked at her, then took off running into the forest.

"Aww," Sophie groaned, disappointed.

Something dark snuffed out the sun and tightened around

her neck.

Gasping for air, she clawed at the sack over her face. Tiny glimmers of light shone through the fabric. She kicked, punched, screamed, but it was no use. Jagged branches cut her legs as someone dragged her through the forest by the neck.

Aidan could feel the panic, the terror that she felt. She screamed as hard as she could, trying to get the attention of somebody – anybody – to come save her, but every time she did, the person pulled harder, choking her more. Sophie cried and thought of her mum and dad, cursing herself for looking at the stupid bunny.

Not willing to give up without a fight, she dug her heels into the soft forest floor.

She hit the ground with a thump, the air bursting out of her lungs. Choking and gasping, she pulled and tugged at the sack, prying it from her head. Bright light dazzled her as she guzzled as much air as she could. She tried to scream, but nothing came out except for a harsh rasp.

Something shuffled behind her; Sophie scurried across the forest floor on all fours. The smell of the raw earth stung her nostrils.

Something solid and heavy came down on the back of her head, and everything went black.

***

Sophie groaned as she opened her eyes, the sack still blotting out the world around her. She tried to move but couldn't. Something constricted her. A rope was bound around her chest, pinned her to what felt like a tree. It was so tight she could only take quick breaths. Her arms, tied behind her back, throbbed painfully. She couldn't move her legs. Small glimmers of light flickered through the sack. The smell of burning wood made her feel sick.

Aidan could feel the panic racing through her. She wriggled and thrashed, trying to free herself from the grip of the ropes. Her throat was raw from all the screaming.

Footsteps approached her. Through the fabric, she could make out the black silhouette of a person. They pulled the sack from her head and the world came alive. She was deep inside the forest in a place that Aidan recognised.

He had been there before in his dreams.

Sophie's eyes bulged from their sockets. The thing in the stag's skull stood in front of her. The black holes of its eyes pierced through her. It took a step back and four more masked things came from behind Sophie and stood side by side, all with different animal skulls for heads.

Wooden torches hung from the surrounding trees, lighting the clearing with bright orange, flickering flames. They had tied Sophie to a large, debarked tree in the middle of clearing. Chopped wood was bundled in a circle under her feet.

It smelled like gasoline.

Sophie's breathing became erratic. The robed things stood in silence, watching Sophie squirm and cry. Three of them took a step to the left, the other two to the right, in perfect synchronicity. Behind them, a square rock grew out from the forest floor.

An old human skull sat proudly on top, beside with a long, curved bronze knife. There were strange markings on the blade.

In one perfect movement, the shadowy figures turned to face each other, lifting their arms into the air. They began chanting, words that Sophie didn't recognise. The chanting grew louder and louder until they were yelling the words into the night sky. A long gust of wind blew through the forest, making the torches flicker.

Abruptly, the chanting stopped.

Everything was silent.

Tears streamed down little Sophie's face; all she wanted was for her mum and dad to come and save her.

The things lowered their arms. One, with a bear's skull for a head, stepped forward and knelt behind the square stone, staring directly at Sophie through the sockets of the skull. It reached out and lifted the top of the skull like a lid, placing it on the stone.

It picked up the bronze knife. A pale white arm reached up to the sky.

They're people, Sophie realised.

The figure lifted the blade to the sky and slowly brought it down, slicing their palm. Sophie winced. Bright red blood poured down their arm like a red river.

They squeezed their hand into a fist, pouring the blood into the top of the skull and sliding the knife into a holster at their waist. Blood dripped from their hand as they carefully picked up the skull and rose to their feet. Sophie screamed and struggled against the ropes as the person walked towards her.

"Daddy!" Sophie called out, pleading.

The others lined up, single file, behind the one wearing the bear skull. Stopping just short of Sophie, the figure lowered the human skull and gently placed it on the floor.

They took a step closer and pulled their hood down. Fiery red hair swirled around the bear skull. They grabbed the skull mask and lifted it over their head.

It was a woman. Aidan could feel Sophie's heart beat harder.

"Mummy?" Sophie whispered.

Aidan's heart sank.

Sophie stared at her mother, confused. Why would her mother do this to her? She was meant to be trying to find her, trying to save her. Not doing this.

"Mummy, what's going on? I'm scared," Sophie gasped, trying to wiggle her way out of the ropes.

Her mother reached out and held the girl's head still, smearing blood across her cheek. Nancy leaned in and kissed her daughter on the lips.

"Mummy, help me, please!" Sophie pleaded.

"I love you," Nancy said with an emotionless stare.

She pulled the knife from her waist and in one smooth motion, sliced Sophie's throat open from ear to ear. A cold grin stretched across her blood-spattered face as she watched her daughter drown in her own blood.

Her white dress turned red.

Sophie choked as she tried to breathe, unable to grab hold of the air that her lungs so desperately needed. She started flailing, trying to break free.

Her mother calmly picked up the skull and pushed Sophie's head back against the tree, opening the wound further. She held the skull under Sophie's throat, filling it with her blood.

Sophie had grown weak; she felt tired. Blood gargled in her throat as she tried to breathe; her mouth tasted like a hundred pennies. When the skull was full, Nancy walked back to the others, then turned to face Sophie. She held the crimson skull in the air, said something in that strange language, and drank the blood from the skull.

Blood spilled over the edges of her mouth and ran down her chin. She didn't stop until every last drop was gone.

The person in the stag's skull took it from her and set it back on the square rock. Nancy wiped the blood from her chin with her sleeve and fell to her knees.

A nightmarish scream roared from her.

A thick black swirling smoke came from the darkness of the forest, weaving its way through the trees and into the clearing. Nancy arched her back and tilted her head. The smoke danced around her before flying down her throat.

Everything was silent again.

Nancy fell forward, catching herself at the last minute. She lifted her head to look at Sophie, bright red hair covering her face. Sophie watched in numbed horror as she clung to the remnants of her life.

Her mother's eyes were completely black.

Nancy floated to her feet, turned to the person wearing the stag's skull, and smiled. The cracks between her teeth were stained red with blood.

A person wearing a fox skull took a torch from a tree and handed it to Nancy. The woman walked towards her daughter with a devilish smile across her face, her eyes as dark as night. Sophie barely had enough strength left to look at the evil that was her mother.

Nancy leaned in and whispered to Sophie, "Thank you for your sacrifice."

She threw the burning torch into the chopped wood under Sophie's feet and stood back, laughing hysterically. Sophie could feel the heat rising from under her. The smoke stung her eyes. She wanted to scream but she couldn't; she felt her skin begin to burn and blister as the flames reached her legs.

She wanted it all to be over.

Nancy watched as Sophie burned to death, choking on her own blood.

Finally, Sophie let go.

Aidan was in the basement again, gasping for breath.

Sophie was gone.

Jack hunkered down with his hands covering his face, sobbing. Aidan wiped away his tears as he caught his breath and sat down at the base of the stairs. He couldn't believe what he'd seen. True evil was the only way he could describe it. The thought of someone doing that to a child – to their own *daughter* – made him feel sick.

Jack screamed a muffled cry into his hands and jumped to his feet. Anger and rage engulfed him.

"Jack, I…"

Jack took one last look around the empty basement, then pushed past Aidan and took off up the stairs.

Aidan bounced up and chased after him. "Jack! Where are you going?"

By the time Aidan got to the top of the basement stairs, Jack was already slamming the front door behind him. He took a couple of steps towards the door and stopped. Outside, Jack's truck roared to life.

Wheels spun on the gravel as he sped off down the driveway.

The house filled with amber as all the lights in the house turned back on.

"Sophie," Aidan called to the empty room.

The house was silent.

Aidan went back down to the basement, collected the flashlights, and put them back into Jack's backpack. The photo of a masked Nicolas Wright stared up at him from the coffee table. Aidan couldn't bear to look at it, so he stuffed it into the journal and went to bed. He lay there staring at the ceiling, his mind racing as he tried to process everything that had happened.

A dark, haunting voice whispered to him.

"I can give you what you want. But first, you have to do something for me…"

CHAPTER TWENTY-ONE

Jack burst out of the house and into the pickup. He heard Aidan calling him, but he couldn't stop; he needed out.

The pickup skidded down the driveway and out onto the road without stopping. Jack got to the junction at Hawthorne Road before he had to pull over. He couldn't hold it in anymore. The pickup's door swung open and Jack threw up onto the side of the road. Coughing and spluttering, he rubbed the tears from his face and the vomit from his mouth with trembling hands.

He slammed the door shut and stared blankly out of the windscreen, his eyes welling up again already. He gripped the steering wheel tightly in his hands, then lost it. Jack screamed and punched the steering wheel, over and over again. Blasts of the horn echoed down the empty road.

"Fuck!" Jack screamed through clenched teeth.

His head fell into his hands as he sobbed.

How could she do that to our little girl?

The porch light of a nearby house turned on and a man in a blue bathrobe and matching bedroom slippers stepped out. Jack hadn't noticed the man approaching the pickup, his head still buried in his hands.

Knock, knock, knock.

"Jesus fucking Christ!" Jack exclaimed, startled by the sudden burst of noise. The man in the bathrobe was right by the car door, unaware he was standing in Jack's vomit.

"Is everything okay, mister?" the man's muffled voice came through the window. "I didn't mean to scare you... I heard your horn and thought there might be something wrong."

"I'm alright," Jack said, sniffing.

"You sure? You don't look alright."

"I said I'm fine, now fuck off!"

The man took a step back, his palms up in surrender. "All right, I was only trying to help. No need to be an asshole about it." The man turned and went back to his house, muttering under his breath.

Jack wiped the snot from his nose, shifted the pickup into first and took off down the road towards town. The tyres screeched in protest as he sped around the corners. A million thoughts raced through his mind at once, making him dizzy. His stomach growled at him. *When was the last time I ate?* He couldn't remember. He checked the time on the dash; it was 1.30 a.m.

There was only one place in Elmwood that would be open.

Jack pulled up outside *Harald's Diner*. A bright red and blue neon sign flashed, *Best burgers in town!* Truckers and passers-through made up for most of the clientele, but since Sophie had gone missing, Jack had become part of the furniture. It was somewhere he could always rely on for a decent meal and a comforting cup of coffee on a sleepless night. The bell above the door jingled as he went inside and took a seat at his usual red-and-white striped booth. There were only a handful of other people in the diner, all keeping to themselves. The smell of old grease and lard filled the diner. A small radio on the counter was playing EFM, the local radio station. The smooth, deep voice of Dan Waterman, the late-night presenter, announced the next song; a guitar strummed, snuffing out the quiet in the diner.

"What can I get for you, Jack?" a waitress asked, standing at the side of the booth in her grease-stained uniform, small notebook in hand.

"Just the usual please, Jane."

"Double cheeseburger, fries, and a large coke?"

"Actually, can I get a coffee, black, please?"

"Sure thing, sweetie."

She scribbled the order down in her little notebook and strutted off towards the kitchen. Jack watched her swaying hips as she walked away. Jane was only a couple of years younger than him, a beautiful woman who always had a spring in her step and a smile in her eyes, and during the last few months the pair had become close. Jack had confided in her and she was always there to lend him a sympathetic ear, never judging him like everyone else in Elmwood.

Jane came back with a jug of filter coffee in her hand.

"I haven't seen you in here for a little while. Is everything okay?" Jane said as she filled his mug. Jack didn't know what to say; there was no way he could tell her about what he'd just seen. Even Jane would think he was losing it. He wished he could tell her everything, to release some of the pressure that was building up inside him, but he couldn't.

"Yeah, I'm fine," he lied. "Just been busy, that's all."

Jane studied his puffy face and bloodshot eyes. "Are you sure? You know you can talk to me."

Jack stared blankly at his reflection in the coffee and nodded. "I'm fine, don't worry."

"Okay, I'll be right back with your food," Jane said, the chirpiness gone from her voice. She went back to the kitchen, topping up the other guests' coffees on the way. A few minutes later she was back, burger and fries in hand, and set them down in front of him.

"Thank you," he said without looking up. If he had, he would have seen the hurt in Jane's eyes. She huffed and hurried away.

Jack sighed and took a bite of his burger.

The food helped a little, and Jane came back at least three times to top up his coffee without saying a word. The visions of Sophie choking on her own blood, engulfed in flames, haunted his mind, and he thought they probably would for the rest of his life. Seeing her like that had broken him. There was no coming back.

Why her, why Sophie?

Jack knew exactly where to get the answers he wanted. The only thing that had been stopping him was the knowledge of how far he'd go to get them, and that scared him a little. He knew there was no coming back from that.

Fuck it. My life's over, anyway. Jack threw a twenty on the table and left.

The pickup roared down the empty road into town and pulled into a car park opposite an apartment building by the marina. Jack parked under a broken streetlight, hidden by the dark.

Nancy lived on the third floor.

Jack could see the main entrance to the building and the yellow light spilling out from her apartment window. He reached down and picked up the tyre iron sitting in the passenger footwell. Gripping the cold metal in his hands, Jack watched the window intently and got out of the pickup.

Nancy appeared at the window, staring out at the sea. Jack retreated into the cover of the pickup and slouched down in his seat. Someone was with her. A man. He wrapped his arms around her and pulled her in for a kiss. Nancy rubbed her hand lovingly over the man's face. Jack's stomach knotted.

Walker smiled back at her and pulled the curtain closed.

"Are you fucking kidding me?" Jack said out loud,

throwing the tyre iron into the back seat.

All this time, instead of looking for my daughter, he's been fucking my wife.

Jack clenched his fists, feeling the rage building up inside him like a volcano ready to blow.

He sat out there all night, watching, waiting, until the early morning light filled the sky. Never taking his gaze from the window. Nancy opened the door to let Walker out. She kissed him goodbye and went back inside. Walker sauntered across the road, a cheesy grin spread across his face, to a blue Hyundai parked up about five spaces away from Jack.

He crouched down to make sure Walker didn't spot him. Walker started his car and drove away.

Now's my chance, Jack thought, grabbing the tyre iron from the back seat.

CHAPTER TWENTY-TWO

The new day was a grey one; the low morning haze spilled into the bedroom, banishing the shadows of the night. Aidan rolled stiffly onto his side, looking out the window. He stroked the quilt on the empty side of the bed, wishing Laura was there next to him.

I can give you what you want. But first, you have to do something for me, the voice had said during the night.

He's using her to get to me, Aidan thought. *But do I really have any other choice?* He'd been thinking about it all night, unable to sleep even for an hour. Aidan scrunched up his face and sighed.

"Okay," Aidan said to the empty room. "What do you need me to do?"

A crow landed on the windowsill and stared in at him. As if it had been waiting right outside.

"Bring him to me," the voice said.

"Bring who?"

"Jack Henderson. Bring him to me and I will give you what you want."

"Why Jack?"

The voice didn't answer.

"What are you going to do to him?" Aidan asked, sitting

up in bed. Silence. "What if I refuse?"

"If you refuse, then I will have no choice."

"No choice? What do you mean, no choice?" Aidan yelled. Silence.

Resigned, Aidan said, "How do I find you?"

"I will guide you when the time is right."

The crow flew away. Aidan fell back onto the bed, staring up at the ceiling.

What do I do? There has to be another way.

Aidan jumped out of bed and ran up the stairs to the attic. The secret door that Laura had told him about was ajar. He pulled it open.

Inside, he grabbed the first box he saw and rummaged through it.

"Come on, come on, please be here…"

The box was full of random nick-knacks. No books. He threw it to the floor, scattering its contents everywhere, then grabbed another. Nothing. He reached for a third. This one was more promising; he knew just by the weight of it. He emptied it out onto the floor.

Books tumbled out in a stampede of literature.

Aidan flicked through the pile, tossing the discarded books over his shoulder until finally he found what he was looking for. Another Journal.

Aidan already knew about the cave from the entry Jack had read to him. He guessed that must have been where Laura was too – and if not, it was at least a starting point. The only problem was that he didn't know where the cave or the clearing were – but maybe, just maybe, there was something written in one of Wright's journals that would help. He thought about Sophie and the other souls trapped in the house.

Maybe they knew where the clearing was. It was a long shot, but one worth taking.

They'd knocked Sophie out and knotted a sack over her head, and Aidan imagined a similar fate for the others too.

"Hello, Sophie? Anybody? I need your help," Aidan called out from the dusty attic. There was no response, not even the creak of a settling pipe. "Please!"

Nothing.

Aidan groaned and went downstairs to the living room, opening the journal to the first page.

September 13th 1984

Today I became a father to a beautiful baby boy. Fiona gave birth to Noah in the basement. We could feel his presence there with us, welcoming our son into the world.

To make today even more special, Fiona has decided she wants to be the next offering to induct our son into The Order.

October 31st 1984

Tonight's a special night.

Not only is it All Hallow's Eve, but tonight my beautiful wife will offer herself to him for eternity in a baptism of blood, initiating little Noah Wright into The Order.

What better way than with the sacrifice of his mother? It's going to be a special night indeed. I'm so proud of them both.

Aidan finished reading the journal and slammed it shut, tossing it to the other side of the room. *Fucking useless.* There was nothing useful, just the horrible thoughts and actions of a monster, and now Aidan was right back to square one. There might have been something useful in the others, but they were locked away somewhere at the Elmwood P.D. He rubbed at his temples, wracking his brain, trying to figure out what to do next.

Just give him Jack and it will all be over. Jack will be with Sophie, he'll be happy. It's what he would want.

"No," Aidan murmured. He went into the kitchen and drank cold water from the tap.

The library. Aidan snapped up from the tap. *They'll have maps, hunting trails, all kinds of stuff that could point me in the right direction.*

He took a much-needed shower, pulled on some clothes and hurried out the door.

It was a blustery, grey day that suited Aidan's mood. Leaves scattered up the footpath, swirling like tiny tornados. He had the same feeling he'd often gotten when going to the airport; that constant anxiety of running late, nothing ever moving quite fast enough. The fear that he wasn't prepared.

Wishing he had his car, Aidan hurried through an empty Gray's Park, the heavy, dark clouds threatening to burst at any second. He pulled the collar of his coat up around his neck. On Main Street, he passed the coffee shop and spied the bookstore across the road.

Bex. Maybe she could help.

Aidan's phone buzzed in his pocket. The feeling had become alien to him since he'd arrived in town. He pulled it out. The phone had automatically signed on to the coffee shop's WiFi. Emails and Facebook messages flooded his phone. He opened the last email from his brother, Will.

Aidan, call me. I haven't heard from you in over a week. Is everything okay? I'm getting worried.

Aidan locked his phone and slid it back into his pocket. "If only you knew, brother. If only you knew."

The door of the bookstore squeaked as Aidan pushed it open. The man he'd seen in the store on his first day in Elmwood was there again, stacking books on a shelf. He turned and looked at Aidan.

"Sorry, one second and I'll be right with you," the man said in a pleasantly soft voice. He set the books down on the floor and headed to the counter where Aidan waited. "What can I do for you?" he asked, clapping his hands together.

"Hey, is Bex working today?"

"You haven't heard?" the man frowned. "I assumed everyone in town had heard already... She's gone missing."

"What?" Aidan exclaimed.

"Yeah, she never showed up for her shift last week and no one's seen her since."

"Jesus..." Aidan brushed a hand through his hair as the world spun around him. "I need to go." He stumbled out of the bookstore in a daze.

The man picked up a telephone from beside the till, keying in a number as he watched Aidan walk up the street through the window.

Aidan walked towards the library, lost in his mind, not paying attention to the world around him. *I'm a black hole, that's what it is. I'm a black hole, destroying everyone and everything around me.*

"Hey, watch it!" a muffled voice yelled, snapping Aidan back into the now. He felt like he just woken from a deep sleep. A guy rolling down the street on a skateboard gave Aidan the finger.

And then he was standing outside the library, dazed, with no memory of walking there. There was something on the door.

"No, no, no!" Aidan murmured, running up the steps. A sign on the front door read, *Closed.* Aidan grabbed hold of the handles and rattled the doors. "Fuck!" he screamed.

A police cruiser pulled up alongside him and beeped its horn. Aidan turned; his stomach dropped at the sight of the cruiser. The dark, tinted window lowered.

Officer Cross. He gestured with his head for Aidan to come over.

"What now?" Aidan jabbed.

"Just come here."

Aidan squeezed his lips together and went to the cruiser.

"Detective Walker would like to speak with you."

"Why? I've got shit to do."

"It's about your wife," Cross said, and Aidan's eyes widened, suddenly alert.

"What do you mean, it's about my wife?"

"Look, I don't know. I'm just the messenger. Detective Walker has all the information, so jump in."

Aidan got into the back of the cruiser. His mind was a tangled mess.

"I've been to the Lake House and driven around town looking for you all morning," Cross said, looking at Aidan through the rearview mirror. Aidan said nothing; he just stared out the window at the passing town, fighting the storm rattling inside his head.

***

The interview room was a small, dingy, square box. Grey walls, black-tiled floor, and a single table in the middle of the room with two of the world's most uncomfortable metal chairs at either side.

Aidan sat on the chair facing towards the door. The buzzing fluorescent lights were giving him a headache. A clock ticked loudly on the wall while a camera up in the corner blinked its little red light at him. Aidan had been waiting for almost an hour now, and Walker still hadn't shown his face. His legs fidgeted under the meal table as he bit his nails, glancing back up at the clock every couple of seconds.

From the other side of the door, the sound of footsteps grew closer. Aidan sat up straight. The doorknob turned and, finally, Walker entered the room, closing the door behind him, locking it.

"Where's Laura? What's this all about?" Aidan said as Walker sat down opposite him. He set a brown folder on the table and shuffled in the seat. Aidan glared at him.

"Thanks for coming in," Walker said, opening the folder.

"Where is she?"

"Did I ever mention my father was a police officer?" Walker interrupted.

"What? No," Aidan said, shaking his head, confused by the remark. "What's that got to do with –"

"He was a detective here. Retired in '92," Walker continued as if Aidan hadn't said a word. "He passed away only two years later. Lung cancer, isn't that a bitch. He's the reason I wanted to be a police officer."

Walker cleared his throat.

"Did you know Elmwood was once home to notorious serial killer Nicolas Wright?"

"I did, actually, but what's that –"

"I thought you might," Walker cut him off again. Aidan dug his fingernails into his palm. "My father was the one working the Wright case. I used to drive him crazy, asking him if they had any leads or new clues. Of course, he would never tell me. I was only a rookie then, but I just found the whole thing *fascinating*. They arrested him one time, you know? Nicolas. Brought him in for questioning, the whole nine yards. He sat in this exact interview room, actually." Walker stared around the room. "It wasn't long after his wife went missing, actually. There were rumours around town that she was pregnant before she disappeared. Then people did what they always do in small towns. They talked. They said he *murdered* them both. Her and the unborn baby."

Walker glared at Aidan.

"He was a special kind of crazy. Everyone in town knew it,

but he never gave us anything. He just rambled on and on about *the darkness...* whatever the fuck *that* was. There was talk that he and a few others from town would meet up in the woods and do God-knows-what. But no one else was ever brought in." Walker shook his head in disbelief.

"What's this got to do with Laura?" Aidan spat.

"When Nicolas left here," Walker continued, completely ignoring Aidan's question, "he went straight back to the Lake House and hanged himself. You know, from the big oak at the front of the property? Well, my father got the call about an hour later, when a passer-by saw him swaying there like an old rag and called it in. He and a few officers went to the scene and searched the property.

"My father said he would never forget what he saw that day. Jars with body parts stuffed inside. *Countless* skulls, animal and human. There was even some strange symbol carved into the floor of the basement. Seeing all of that – and the stuff he didn't share with me – well, it ruined him. He could never get the people he couldn't save out of his mind. He felt like a failure even though the monster was gone."

"I don't see what this has to do with me or Laura, detective."

"As I said, Nicolas was a special kind of crazy... and I think *you* might be too, Aidan," Walker said, pulling a piece of paper from the folder and sliding it across the table towards Aidan.

"I... what..." Aidan stuttered.

"Officer Young found this at the Lake House yesterday when you took your little stroll out of the hospital."

"You mean when he broke in and trashed the place?" Aidan snapped.

"I don't know what you're talking about." Walker leaned back in the metal chair, grinning. He gestured to the piece of paper in front of Aidan with a flick of his wrist.

Aidan turned the page. It was a photograph of a black, high-heeled shoe. Laura's shoe. The same one Aidan had found at the side of the road when he woke up after the crash.

"What is it?" Walker asked.

"It's one of Laura's shoes," Aidan said, staring at the page. "The ones she was wearing the night of the crash."

"And can you tell me why your blood would be on that shoe?"

"I found it at the side of the road after the accident. I held it in my hand. Blood was pissing from my head, of course it would be on it."

"All right," Walker nodded. "Then why did Officer Young find it at the house?"

"What? That isn't possible."

"What can I tell you? That's where it was."

"This is bullshit," Aidan jumped up, sending the metal chair skidding across the small room. "I'm telling you, the shoe was not in the house. You've planted it, or Young's done it for you."

Walker laughed. "Such an imagination, Aidan. You know what I think... I think you killed your wife. And I think you have something to do with those murders in Fallbridge, too."

"I would never hurt Laura, or anyone else for that matter!" Aidan slammed his fists down on the table.

"You look pretty capable to me. Given the right push, anybody is capable of murder."

"Am I under arrest?" Aidan snapped.

Walker paused. "No."

"Then I want to leave," Aidan said.

"That's fine," Walker said, rising to his feet. He unlocked the door, pulled it open and stood to the side, gesturing to the open door.

"What about the journals?"

"What journals?"

"The journals Young took from the Lake House."

"I don't know anything about any journals, Aidan," Walker answered with a sly grin. "Are you leaving or not?"

Aidan went to Walker, stopping inches from his face. Both men glared at each other. Aidan's balled fists grew clammy. All he wanted to do was wipe that smug look off the bastard's face.

After a long second, Aidan left. Walker stepped into the hallway and yelled, "You're running out of time, Mr. Crain. I'm coming for you!"

***

Aidan marched down Main Street, legs carrying him on autopilot.

"Aidan," a voice called out, but he didn't hear it, too engrossed in his own thoughts. "Aidan!"

He looked up to find the source of the voice. It was Jack, driving slowly alongside him. Aidan stopped; the pickup's brakes squealed as it came to a halt. Jack looked grim, and Aidan could see the purple hue of a black eye blossoming.

"Get in."

"What happened to you?" Aidan asked.

"Just get in the fucking truck," Jack snapped. Aidan climbed in. The pickup roared down Main Street, leaving a plume of white smoke in its wake.

CHAPTER TWENTY-THREE

Jack gripped the wheel with white knuckles, clenching his jaw as he stared blankly out through the windscreen.

"Where are we going?" Aidan asked.

"My place."

Jack took a corner without slowing down. Aidan's shoulder slammed into the door. "Fucking hell, Jack. I've already been in one crash, I don't want to be in another."

Jack didn't answer. They turned right onto Hawthorne Road and rumbled down the road. Jack slammed on the brakes. Aidan shot forward, the seatbelt snapped across his chest. They were outside Jack's cottage.

"Jesus, Jack. What the hell's going on?"

"You'll see," Jack said. A thin smile crept in from the side of his mouth. They got out of the pickup and Jack went to unlock the front door of the cottage. He pushed it open and gestured for Aidan to go inside. Uncertain, Aidan stepped into the dark. Jack followed, locking the door behind him. There was a strange smell in the air, a mixture of body odour and piss.

"Ugh, what's that smell?" Aidan asked, disgusted. He breathed through his mouth, but it didn't help much.

"Are you ready for the big reveal?" Jack said, excitement in his voice.

Before Aidan could reply, the lights flicked on.

Nancy was unconscious, tied to a wooden chair in the middle of the living room. Jack had covered the windows with black bin bags and pushed the sofa up against the wall with the newspaper clippings. The coffee table sat off to Nancy's right, covered with an array of knives, pliers, and all kinds of tools. Aidan spied a taser in the mix. There was a rope tied around Nancy's chest; her arms were bound behind her back, her ankles tied to the legs of the chair. It was like some crude reproduction of the way Sophie had been bound to the tree. Her head hung heavily in front of her, her face covered by bright red hair. Aidan stopped where he was, his eyes as big as marbles. He thought of her evil smirk blaring out from behind her fiery hair as she ended her daughter's life. His blood ran cold.

"Is she dead?"

Jack eagerly went and stood next to Aidan, marvelling at his handy work. "No, but she should be. I went to her apartment last night. Guess who I saw leaving her place, around five this morning?"

Aidan dragged his stare from Nancy and looked at Jack, who was nodding to himself, still admiring his achievement.

"None other than Elmwood's finest, Detective Walker."

"Are you –"

"Yep," Jack cut him off. "She's been fucking him. My guess, ever since Sophie went missing. Hell, maybe even before all this happened. Fucking murdering *slut*." Aidan heard the crack of Jack's teeth as he clenched his jaw.

"I knew it! I fucking *knew* Walker had something to do with all of this. He makes the missing cases disappear. Excuse the pun. He's a part of that Order that was written in those journals, he has to be." Aidan turned away, raking his hands through his hair.

Nancy groaned and stirred, in-between states of consciousness.

"Looks like it's time to have some fun." Jack slapped Aidan's shoulder and walked to the coffee table, picking up the taser.

Aidan watched grimly; fingers interlinked on top of his head.

Crack! Crack! Crack!

Nancy screamed. Her body stiffened as the electricity jolted her awake.

"Wakey-wakey, Nancy," Jack sneered, then shocked her again. Her screams erupted through the house. Aidan was thankful Jack didn't have any neighbours. Nancy's body slumped over as she tried to catch her breath.

"What... where... where am I?" Nancy mumbled, disoriented. She sat up in the chair, blinking rapidly as she realised where she was and what was going on. She tugged at her arms and tried thrashing in the chair, but she didn't budge.

"You're home, Nancy. Don't you recognise the place?" Jack teased.

"What's going on? Who is he?" she said, staring at Aidan.

"I think you already know who he is, Nancy," Jack said. "We just want to have a little chat with you, that's all. Isn't that right?" Jack turned and looked at Aidan.

"That's right," Aidan nodded.

"What are you talking about? I don't know him," Nancy shook her head. "If you wanted to talk, why do all this? Why not just come and talk to me?"

"Come on Nancy, we're not stupid."

Aidan knew what they were doing was wrong, but he didn't care. He'd been treading water for far too long, and now he wanted answers. But seeing her small frame tied to the chair, blood and snot running down her face, he couldn't help but feel sorry for her. His sympathy quickly faded. That was no innocent woman; Nancy was as evil as they came and would kill them both without a second glance, given the chance.

"I don't have a clue what you're talking about. Please, just let me go," Nancy pleaded.

She played the part well. Aidan thought. *She deserves much worse than this.*

"I know about you and the detective," Jack spat. "How could you? While I was out day and night looking for our little girl, you were fucking the man standing in my way."

Jack pulled the wedding ring off his finger and threw it at her; it hit her in the chest and fell to the floor with a *ting.*

"Jack, I can explain –"

"I don't want to hear it, Nancy," Jack stopped her. "It's time to cut the bullshit." He turned away from her for a second and took a deep breath.

"We were drifting apart, Jack," Nancy continued. "You can't say you didn't notice. We hadn't been happy together for years, then when Sophie went missing…"

"Don't you say her name!" Jack yelled, rushing at her, grabbing her by the neck. Her eyes bulged as her lungs pleaded for air. "I've brought you here for answers and you aren't leaving until we get them." He threw her head back, almost toppling the chair. Nancy coughed, sucking in air, the redness on her face fading.

"Jack, I don't know what you are talking about," she said, her voice raspy. "So what if I screwed someone else?" A single tear fell down her face.

"Sophie! Our little girl. I was never going to find her, all that time spent searching and it was all for nothing, but I guess you and Walker already knew that."

"What about Sophie? She's still out there – we will find her, Jack, please… this is crazy. You're scaring me."

"I'm scaring you? Ha, that's a laugh. Cut the waterworks, Nancy. We know what you did. We know what you are."

"What do you think you know?" Nancy glowered.

Aidan took a step towards her and said, "We know what you did to Sophie. How could you do that to your own daughter?"

The tears stopped. The fear-filled expression dropped like a falling mask. A sickening grin crept across her face.

Rage poured into Jack at the sight of her smile. He snatched the machete up from the table and pointed it at her. Nancy laughed, not phased in the slightest by the blade.

"Just tell us why you did it. Why did you murder our little girl?"

Nancy spat in Jack's face and laughed.

Jack calmly wiped the spit from his face and flicked it to the floor. He went behind her and crouched down to the small gap in the chair where her hands were.

"If you don't tell me, I'm going to start with your fingers. And then – see those pliers over there?"

Nancy glanced at the coffee table.

"I'll pull each of your teeth out, one by one. But one way or another, you will tell me why."

"You don't have the balls," Nancy sneered.

Jack grabbed hold of her pinky finger and placed it against the chair. Nancy squirmed. Jack laid the blade over the base of her finger. "Tell me."

"Go fuck yourself!"

Jack tightened his jaw and pushed down on the blade. Nancy screamed. There was a snapping sound. Aidan thought it sounded like a twig snapping.

The finger fell to the floor. Nancy cried out in pain, flailing around on the chair.

"What's The Order?" Jack asked. Sweat dripped down his face.

"Why were you such a shitty father?" Nancy yelled back. Another twig snapped. Another finger fell to the floor.

"How could you do that to our little girl? How could you tie her up and cut her throat? She was terrified and confused... she didn't know why her own mother would do such a thing to her."

"How do you know that?" she cried out. *Snap*. Another finger hit the ground. Tears ran down her face as she howled. This time, they were genuine.

"She showed me," Jack whispered into her ear. He went back around and faced her. Blood dripped down the blade of the machete. Nancy's bloodshot eyes widened as the sickening grin returned.

"How?"

Jack glanced at Aidan, then back to Nancy.

"So you're the seer." Nancy stared Aidan up and down.

Jack squeezed her face, forcing her to look back at him. "Tell me why you did it. Why did you sacrifice our daughter?"

Nancy laughed. "I can always have another child. Mother bears in the wild, Jack... they eat their own to survive. But to sacrifice a child, *my* child, showed him I am loyal, I am his forever. And now so is Sophie. There could be no greater gift."

"Who is he?" Jack demanded, tightening his grip on the machete.

"He's the night, and the shadows, the thing you see at the corner of your eye. He's what makes your heart race when you hear a sound in the middle of the night. He is the Darkness, and he chose me, called out to me, the same way he calls to you." Nancy looked at Aidan.

Aidan frowned.

"What's she talking about?" Jack asked, turning to Aidan.

"I've no idea." Aidan shook his head.

"He's lying," Nancy said. "I know you can hear him, that he calls out to you."

"You lying bitch!" Aidan lunged forward and swung a fist at Nancy. It connected with her nose. Aidan felt it break. Crimson poured down her face, but Nancy just laughed, snarling in defiance with blood-stained teeth, almost oblivious to the pain. Jack pulled Aidan back. His hands trembled. He squeezed them into fists to stop the shaking.

Nancy spat out a mouthful of blood. "You couldn't save her, Jack, you never could. Just like *he* can't save his wife. She is his now. They both belong to him."

"What about my wife?" Aidan snapped. "Where is she?"

"He wants you, Aidan. If you want her back, you must go to him."

"Tell me where she is!"

"You already know. You just have to remember."

"Remember what?" Aidan frowned. "If I knew where she was, I wouldn't be standing here."

"Join him, Aidan. Join us."

"Go fuck yourself."

Nancy's bloodied face snapped towards Jack. "Sophie tasted incredible. Her youth pulsed through my veins when I drank her blood."

"Stop this," Jack snapped.

"She cried for her daddy to come and save her." Something swirled around in Nancy's eyes, like black ink in water. It spread out until both her eyes looked like two pieces of coal. She leaned forward in the chair towards Aidan and Jack. The devilish, blood-stained grin stretched wider across her face. The lights in the cottage flickered and sparked. Aidan looked around the room, heart hammering in his chest. Jack never wavered, never took his eyes off Nancy. "She cried out for you. But you let her down, you let her die!"

"No!" Jack hissed. Tears filled his eyes. "You murdered

her!"

"It's your fault she —"

Jack swung the machete and drove it deep into Nancy's skull. Blood sprayed out of her head and splattered up the wall. The lights stopped flickering.

Nancy's body went limp, held up only by the ropes holding her to the chair. Aidan couldn't move. He tried to speak, but the words wouldn't come. Jack's breathing was shallow and fast.

Nancy's sprayed blood dripped down his face. His eyes were still locked on her when he yanked the blade out from her skull and dropped it on the floor.

Jack walked out into the cool night air, closing the door behind him. Dark red blood poured from the trench in Nancy's head and pooled at her feet. Aidan's mouth filled with coppery saliva. He swallowed it, but more kept coming. A mighty heave groaned inside him; he retched, his stomach in ropes, but nothing came up.

"*It's time. Bring him to me,*" the dark voice said. Aidan squeezed his eyes shut and punched at his temples.

"Get out of my head!" he screamed through his teeth.

"*Go to the Lake House and wait for the sign.*"

"Where is she?" Aidan said, looking around the room. "Where's my wife?"

Silence.

Fuck! Aidan punched the wall. *What am I supposed to do?*

After calming himself as best he could, Aidan went outside to find Jack. He quickly glanced around to make sure no one was there. The light hurt his eyes. Jack wasn't in the front garden. There was a rustling sound coming from the back of the cottage; Aidan followed the sound and found Jack pulling a large blue tarp off some dead bushes.

"Come on, give me a hand. We need to wrap her up and find somewhere to bury her."

They were words Aidan had never thought he would hear in his life, except maybe in movies. He helped pull the rest of the tarp from the bushes; it was soaking wet and smelt fusty and old. Jack laid it on the grass and began folding it up to make it easier to carry. "Grab that corner and fold it in towards me." Aidan did as he asked. "Were you talking or something, a minute ago? I thought I could hear something."

"Oh... I was just composing myself," Aidan lied.

"Look, I'm sorry I did that," Jack said.

"Don't be sorry. She wasn't a person, she was a monster," Aidan sighed.

Jack nodded as he lifted the tarp. They headed back towards the cottage.

Aidan twisted the handle of the door and pushed it open. "What the..."

"What? What is it?" Jack pushed past Aidan into the cottage. Nancy was gone. The empty wooden chair stood in the middle of the room, the loose rope looped around its legs and soaking in her blood. There were no footprints, no trail of blood, and the machete was still lying on the floor where it had fallen. She was just gone.

Jack threw the tarp to the floor and ran outside. Aidan continued to stare at the empty chair. Jack burst back in and for the first time there was panic in his voice.

"What do we do?"

"We need to get away from here."

CHAPTER TWENTY-FOUR

Aidan and Jack burst through the door into the Lake House. "What the hell just happened?" Aidan asked. "People don't just up and disappear after a machete to the head. She was dead, Jack, stone cold dead." Aidan tried to light a cigarette, but his shaking hands made it difficult. Eventually, he got it lit. The nicotine hit him in just the right spot.

"Sophie?" Jack called. "Can you see her?"

Aidan looked around the room, but she wasn't there. "No, sorry," he shook his head. "Is anybody else here?"

The house was silent.

"How did Nancy know you could do that *seer* stuff?"

"Fuck if I know! I didn't even know I could do it until last night."

"How did you know that grabbing my hand would let me see what you could see?"

"I don't know," Aidan shook his head. "I just had this... feeling, that it would work."

"Well, I'm glad it did," Jack said as he sat on the sofa, lifting the journal Aidan had found. "New one?" Jack asked.

Aidan nodded as he took a draw. "Found it in the attic. It's super fucked up, I wouldn't read it if I was you," he said, grimacing. "I need to make a phone call."

Aidan went into the kitchen. He picked up the landline and dialled his brother's number.

"William Crain. Sorry, I can't come to the phone right now. Leave a message and I'll get back to you as soon as I can. Thanks."

"Will, it's Aidan. Sorry I haven't been able to get back to you. The service out here is non-existent, and the house doesn't have any WiFi. Everything's fine, so you don't need to keep worrying or come racing out here. We're all good... I love you, bro."

Aidan hung up, took another drag off his cigarette, and leaned against the wall. *Please, please don't come out here, Will,* Aidan thought. Through the kitchen window, he saw something moving.

"What is that?" he murmured, going to the window for a better look. He cupped his hands around his eyes to see through the glare of the window. An orange glow flickered from within the blackness of the woods, disappearing between the trees like a dancing ghost.

The sign.

"It's time. Bring him to me," the dark voice said. Aidan took one last draw off his cigarette and flicked it into the sink.

Fuck!

He took a deep breath, squeezing his eyes shut. "Jack, come here and see this!" Aidan said, hating himself the moment the words left his lips.

It's the only way, It's the only way, It's the only way, he tried to convince himself, over and over in his head.

"What is it?" Jack asked, hurrying into the kitchen.

"Look, there's a light." Aidan pointed out of the window towards the forest.

Jack rushed to the window and looked outside. "Holy shit!"

"That's gotta be them, right?"

Without saying a word, Jack hurried into the living room

and grabbed the backpack of supplies. Aidan sighed, then followed him. "We have to be quick, or we might lose them." Jack pulled the two flashlights from the bag and threw one to Aidan. He pulled out the gun, checked the magazine, and stuffed it into his jeans. "Ready?"

Aidan nodded.

They hurried out into the cold. Thunder rumbled in the dusky sky like an angry god. A low-lying mist crept from the lake and drifted into the woods, covering the ground with a blanket of translucent white. The full moon shone above them like a watchful eye.

Aidan yanked the axe from the stump where he'd left it, clenching it tightly in his hand. The orange light was still visible, disappearing and reappearing through the trees. Aidan and Jack looked at each other, both with an expression of bone-rattling fear, then together they stepped into the darkness of the woods.

CHAPTER TWENTY-FIVE

They had been trudging through the misty forest for half an hour. The hiss of the trees in the wind hid the crunch of their footsteps as they followed the light. Paranoia had begun to edge its way into Aidan's mind. The constant feeling of being watched from the shadows was almost more than he could bear. Especially now, knowing what was lurking in the dark.

The flickering orange light danced between the trees. Aidan guessed it must be one of the wooden torches that he had seen in Sophie's vision. They followed it like moths to a flame.

"Closer," the voice said. Aidan looked over his shoulder, back into the blackness they'd left behind. His grip on the axe tightened.

Jack grabbed his arm and pulled him to a halt. "Quick, turn the flashlights off," he said in a frantic, hushed voice.

"What is it?" Aidan whispered, clicking the power button on his flashlight and plunging them into complete darkness. He looked around the forest, but he couldn't see a thing. "Where did it go?"

"I don't know. It was there just a second ago. I blinked, and it was gone." Jack shook his head, but Aidan couldn't see him. "Let's keep going, but slowly. And keep the flashlights off."

"All right, let's go," Aidan whispered, then took an uneasy step forward. They pushed forward slowly, in the direction they had last seen the light. Aidan's eyes slowly adjusted to the dark, but he could still only see a couple of feet in front of him, illuminated by the faint moonlight that snuck through the gaps between the trees.

Bright light erupted behind some trees a few yards up ahead. Both Aidan and Jack instinctively dropped to their knees. Aidan leaned against a tree beside him. The light was growing, spreading from tree to tree.

They're lighting the torches.

The flickering lights grew and grew until a huge, circular clearing was visible through the trees. Aidan and Jack crawled along the floor to get a closer look. They stopped a couple feet from the edge of the clearing, hidden under the cover of the shadows, not daring to get any closer, not yet.

Aidan recognised the place. He had been here before, just like Nancy said, only it had been in his dream. In the middle of the circle stood the large, perfectly square stone. Beyond it, on the other side of the circle, huge moss-covered rocks had been stacked on top of one another to create a doorway. It looked like the yawning mouth of a giant leading underground into its gut. Aidan tapped Jack on the shoulder and pointed towards it.

"The cave."

Jack nodded. Someone in a black robe walked through the mouth with a burning torch, disappearing into the cave. Aidan took a step forward, but Jack grabbed hold of him.

"Wait. What's that?" Jack said, pointing to a wooden structure to the right of the square stone. They crawled closer to get a better look. It was an enormous tree trunk, staked into the ground – with another laid across its top to form a *T* shape. The trunks resembled a crucifix, but there was something different about it; they had stripped the bark from the trunks down to the cream wood underneath. Ropes hung from top to bottom in some kind of crude, medieval pulley system.

Sitting at the base of the structure was a bronze bathtub.

"I've no idea, and I'd rather not find out." Aidan said.

Screams for help echoed out from inside the cave.

"Laura," Aidan whispered. His heart leapt into his throat. He started towards the clearing. Jack grabbed his ankle. "What the hell are you doing?" Aidan snapped.

"We need to be smart about this. We can't just barge in guns blazing," Jack said. "Let's get a closer look and see what's happening."

Aidan was reluctant, but he knew Jack was right. They crept forward to the very edge of the clearing. The orange light of the flames glinted off their faces.

The thing in the stag's skull walked out from the cave, cupping the human skull protectively against their chest. They gently placed the skull on top of the rock, then raised their arms into the air, chanting in that unrecognisable language. A crack of lightning lit up the clearing, followed by the roar of thunder.

"Please someone, help me!" the woman screamed as two more masked people came from the mouth of the cave, walking her naked into the clearing. They had bound her arms behind her back and a black sack that muffled her voice covered her head.

Aidan dropped the flashlight and tightened his grip on the axe. His teeth almost cracked under the pressure of his clenched jaw. He watched as they forced her to the ground beside the bronze bath. "No! Let go of me!" Laura cried. Aidan jumped to his feet.

"Not yet," Jack whispered.

Rage blazed in Aidan's eyes.

"No, please... please don't do this," Laura pleaded.

Aidan's heart hammered in his chest. For a second he was light-headed, feeling like he was floating.

Those fuckers are going to die for this.

In the clearing, a person wearing a wolf skull tied a rope around Laura's ankles. The flickering light from the fire glinted off the skull's sharp canines. They nodded to another in a ram skull with horns curling out from behind their hood, who was standing next to the rope hanging from the huge wooden structure. They grabbed hold of the rope and heaved. Laura fell on her back, screaming. The rope dragged her across the forest floor and then into the air as they hoisted her upside down onto the structure. She swung from side to side as they lifted the bronze bath and placed it under her dangling body. "Please!" she begged.

Anger boiled inside Aidan, the pressure building and building. He didn't know how much longer he could hold it in.

The two masked figures went and stood beside the stag at the square stone and began chanting. Another – wearing the skull of a pig – emerged from the cave, arms bent at the elbows and palms upright, holding the bronze blade like a dinner tray. They went to the square stone, held the blade towards the night sky, then laid it down beside the skull and lined up with the others.

All four lifted their arms to the air in perfect synchronicity and started chanting in that strange language. They sounded almost choir-like.

Laura pleaded and begged as they chanted. The chanting stopped suddenly and the one in the stag's skull picked up the bronze knife and held it to the sky. Their sleeve dropped. It was the arm of a man. The bronze blade glowed.

Aidan rubbed at his eyes and stared, unable to believe what he was seeing. The man's free hand lifted to the air and with a smooth, unflinching flick, he sliced his palm open. Bright red blood streamed out from the slice and ran down his arm.

The one in the wolf mask picked up the skull and took off the top, holding it out towards the man in the stag's skull. He squeezed his hand into a fist, dripping his blood into the skull. He laid the blade back onto the stone and took the bony receptacle.

The dark figures stood back in line as their leader bowed his head and held the skull over the stone with outstretched arms. The trees hissed and groaned as a sudden gust blew up and around the clearing. The flames of the torches flickered, but stayed lit. A fifth person walked from the mouth of the cave and entered the clearing.

Bright red hair spilled out from under their bear's skull and hood.

"Nancy?" Jack whispered in disbelief.

The bear stopped in front of the stag, bowed, then took the skull from him.

"*It's almost time,*" the voice said in Aidan's head.

"Shut up, shut up, shut up." Aidan said, scrunching up his face.

"Who are you talking to?" Jack asked.

Aidan ignored him. Laura's scream forced his eyes open. Nancy lifted the skull into the air.

"We offer this sacrifice to the dark one!" she yelled into the night, then she lowered the skull and drank the blood. When she'd drained it, she laid it back onto the stone, pulling her hood down to peel the bear's skull off her face. Nancy looked exactly as she had before; there were no marks or scars on her face, no sign at all that she once had a machete embedded into her skull.

"Let us begin," the one in the stag's skull said.

Nancy took the blade from the stone, grasped it in her

hands, and stabbed it into the night sky. She leaned her head back, her hair billowing around her in the wind. Another flash of lightning lit up the sky like a strobe light, chased by a roaring thunderclap. Nancy chanted. Laura screamed.

In the darkness of the trees on the other side of the clearing, Aidan saw something lingering in the shadows, watching. The others walked towards Laura as Nancy chanted. Everything was done with purpose and reason.

The axe trembled in Aidan's hand. *It's now or never.*

Jack tried to grab him, but he was too slow. "Shit," he said, as Aidan rushed into the clearing –

"No!" he screamed.

The masked figures turned to stare.

"Help! Help me!" Laura cried.

"Laura, I'm here. You're safe."

Nancy and the others walked towards him, stopping short of the stone. "I'm here. I've done what he asked. Now let her go." Aidan pointed at them with the axe.

"You're just in time for the offering," the man in the stag's skull said.

"No!" Aidan hissed. "He told me I could have what I wanted. I want my wife, let her go!"

Nancy cackled.

Jack watched from the shadows. "What the fuck is he doing?" he rasped.

"I think you're forgetting something. Where's Jack?" Nancy said.

"What?" Jack whispered to himself, stunned, his face full of hurt.

"I didn't forget him." Aidan turned and looked into the forest.

"Aidan, what have you done?" Jack said. He reached behind him, pulling out the gun as he stepped into the clearing.

"Ah, welcome," the man in the stag's skull said, gesturing towards him. Jack lifted the gun and pointed it at him. His face curled up in a snarl. The man in the stag's skull threw back his head and let out a loud, humourless laugh.

"What the fuck is happening?" Jack demanded.

"I'm sorry, Jack. I didn't have a choice," Aidan said.

"Of course you fucking did!" Jack turned and pointed the gun at Aidan. Tears welled up in Jack's eyes. "I'm the only person who believed you, the only person who was willing to help you, and this is my thanks. You're no better than *her*," Jack spat, glaring at Nancy.

"Now, now," the man in the stag's skull intervened. "He has given your life purpose –"

"My life had a purpose until you sick fucks took her away from me!" Jack pointed the gun back to the man in the stag's skull. The gun trembled in his hand; beads of sweat dripped from his forehead.

"Ah, yes. Your daughter, Sophie."

"Don't you fucking say her name! Don't you dare!"

The man fixed his unwavering gaze on Jack through the dark, hollow eyes of the skull.

"Jack," Aidan took a step towards him. Jack swung the gun back onto Aidan, his finger on the trigger.

"Shut your fucking mouth!" Jack hissed.

"I didn't have a choice." He took another step closer.

"Don't come any closer." Jack steadied himself and took aim.

"I had to get Laura back. It was the only way –"

BANG!

The man in the stag's skull clicked his fingers.

Aidan snapped his eyes shut.

Laura screamed.

The bullet dissolved into black smoke inches away from Aidan's face. Aidan cracked his eyes open. Jack stared at him in amazement, the flickering of the burning torches reflecting in his bloodshot eyes. Smoke drifted lazily from the barrel of the gun.

The man in the stag's skull flicked his wrist and Jack fell to his knees, grunting through his teeth. Spit dripped down his chin. He tried to move, but he couldn't. Red hot panic rumbled inside him. Jack tried to move his arms, but they wouldn't budge. "What... what's happening?" he called out. The hand holding the gun lifted. He tried to fight it, but it was no use. He felt like a puppet being manipulated by its master.

The gun came up and rested against his temple. His finger squeezed gently against the trigger. "Do it! Come on, fucking do it!" Jack screamed.

The man in the stag's skull walked to Jack and knelt down in front of him. He stared deep into Jack's eyes and said, "Sleep."

Jack's eyes rolled into the back of his head. He fell headfirst onto the moss-covered floor, unconscious.

"Don't worry, he's not dead," the stag said.

"I should be dead."

"He wouldn't let that happen to you, you're too important to him."

"I did what he asked," Aidan said, pointing to Jack. "So let my wife go."

"Who? This?" Nancy said, strolling over to Laura.

"Let her go. I've done what he asked. Now please, let her go."

"What a fine specimen," Nancy said as she ran the tip of the blade over Laura's naked body. She didn't press it in hard enough to cut her, but Laura felt the sharpness of the blade against her skin and flinched at the icy touch of the metal.

"Please, please let me go..." Laura's muffled voice pleaded.

Nancy squeezed her breast. Laura yelped.

"Don't you fucking touch her!" Aidan charged towards them, axe raised over his head, ready for a skull-crushing blow. The man in the stag's skull flicked his wrist as if he was swatting away a fly. Aidan skidded along the forest floor, his axe skittering across the clearing. Aidan felt a pressure around his throat. He grabbed at it, but there was nothing there. It felt like someone had their hands around this neck, strangling him. Aidan slapped and clawed at his neck, the blood vessels in his face and eyes ready to burst.

Air flooded his lungs as he gasped for a breath, the hold on his neck now gone. He tried to get up but couldn't move.

Nancy lifted the blade and carved the *V* and cross symbol into Laura's stomach. She cried and flailed in the air. Dark red blood dripped down her body and into the bronze tub.

With the grace of a ballerina, Nancy stepped out of her robe. Pale, white skin shone like moonlight against the dark backdrop of the forest. She stepped into the tub and wrapped an arm around Laura. The blood from Laura's stomach smeared across Nancy's face. Aidan pulled and fought the invisible shackles, but they didn't budge. He had never felt more powerless in his life. Nancy grinned at Aidan with that devilish look in her eye.

"Don't you hurt her!" Aidan rasped, his throat on fire.

"Or what? You'll kill me?" Nancy laughed.

The blade sliced through Laura's neck like butter, showering Nancy in her blood.

"No!" Aidan screamed. He grunted as he tried to free himself. Laura's body flailed and thrashed as her blood showered over Nancy's pale skin. She gasped for air, but she was like a fish out of water. Lightning cracked in the sky above them.

Nancy rubbed blood over her naked body, bathing in it. She kneeled down in the tub, pouring handfuls of blood over herself. She rubbed it over her face and over her breasts. The whites of her eyes and teeth stood out in contrast to the crimson. She licked the blood slowly off her fingers, enjoying every drop. Laura's body swayed limply from the rope, her blood still dribbling into the tub. Tears streamed down Aidan's face. He choked, trying to get a breath.

She's gone.

"Just fucking kill me!" Aidan screamed at them.

"Join us, Aidan," Nancy said.

"Fuck you!"

Nancy grabbed the sack over Laura's head and yanked it off.

It wasn't her.

As soon as Nancy pulled the sack from her head, the illusion clouding Aidan's mind was broken. He would have sworn on his life that the woman was Laura. It was her body; it was *her* voice. He was sure of it. But his ears and eyes had lied to him. The woman swinging lifelessly in front of him wasn't Laura.

It was Bex.

"What the fuck is going on?" Aidan cried. The man in the deer mask knelt down and stared at Aidan.

"Do you really think he was going to show you the truth?" the man laughed. "He needed to know how far you would go. He was testing you, Aidan." The man in the stag mask rose to his feet. Aidan's mind was scrambled. A moment ago, he had thought he'd witnessed his wife being slaughtered. He didn't know what to believe. What was reality anymore? *Is any of this real?* he thought, looking at his dirt-covered hands.

"Where is she?" Aidan demanded, snarling up at the stag.

"All in good time."

"You sadistic fuck! I know it's you, Walker. You don't need to hide behind that mask," Aidan spat.

The man laughed. Thunder rumbled overhead as if the world was laughing along with him. Like Aidan was nothing but a big joke. He reached up and slid the skull from his head.

"Cross," Aidan whispered.

"That's right," he said, dropping the stag's skull to the ground. "Well, that's what they call me now, anyway. You look shocked, Aidan." Cross grinned.

"Why are you doing this to me?"

"It's written in the stars, Aidan, can't you feel it?"

Aidan stared up at the sky; there were no stars, not tonight. Only endless dark.

"I was just continuing the family tradition. My father... he started all of this..." Cross flung his arms out wide, gesturing all around him, spinning in circles before finally stopping to face Aidan again.

"You're Noah Wright," Aidan said breathlessly.

"In the flesh. I see you've been reading my father's journals. That's good, it'll move the process along quicker."

"What process?"

"Your initiation, of course."

"I'm not joining you!"

"Oh, but you will." Cross snarled at him, baring his teeth like a wild animal. "The Darkness, he's had his eye on you for some time now. You're powerful, Aidan, and he needs that power in The Order. You can do things that none of us can do, not even I. All it took was a little nudge in the right direction and you brought yourself right to him." Aidan's eyes flicked back and forth, his mind racing. "Come on, Aidan, have you still not worked it out?"

He stared up at Noah.

"Sister Emily," Noah hissed.

"Emily?" Aidan said, his voice sounding far away.

His heart broke.

"Emily is one of you?" Aidan said, dismayed.

"Well, she was. Emily thought she could run away, start a new life, but when you give yourself to him, there is no running away. There is no *start over*. You are his until he decides that you're not. Then you will join him in the emptiness for eternity."

"You killed her?"

Noah nodded. A sombre expression took over his face. "Not me personally, no. But she had made her choice, and she knew the consequences."

Emily had tried to warn him. Tried to make him listen, but he was too ignorant to what was going on in front of him and now, he was here.

"How did you know I would come here?"

"Oh, just little whispers here and there to your lovely wife, Laura. Planting the seed in her head without her even knowing it."

"You've manipulated this whole thing. Like some kind of fucked up chess game."

"He gets what he wants, Aidan."

"And what about her?" Aidan looked to Bex's lifeless, hanging body.

Noah glanced over his shoulder at her, then back to Aidan. "Her? She was just an offering. Even gods need to be fed."

Aidan saw something moving in the shadows of the forest, watching, listening. "What makes you think I'd ever join you?"

"He's already inside you, Aidan. He will take you, willing or not. He's made sure of that. But it'll be better for you if you give yourself willingly to him."

"He told me I could have what I want if I brought him Jack." Aidan pointed to Jack, unconscious on the forest floor. "I want my wife. Where is she?"

"Oh, Aidan. You really need to catch up," Noah said,

kneeling down in front of him.

Aidan stared deeply into Noah's eyes and found only darkness.

A long, slimy grin spread across Noah's face as he placed his hand on top of Aidan's head. "Remember," he whispered.

CHAPTER TWENTY-SIX

The car horn blared. Laura's head thumped as she leaned back in the passenger seat. Her vision was blurry and the crick in her neck ached. She was groggy, like she had just awoken from a deep sleep.

What's that sound? Laura thought, covering her ears, still dazed. She turned to Aidan. He was slumped over, head against the steering wheel, resting on the horn. Blood dripped down his face from the reopened gash on his forehead. The windscreen was a mess of cracks and steam billowed out from the destroyed hood.

"Aidan," Laura said in a small voice. She reached over and nudged his shoulder. "Wake up."

He didn't move. Laura touched her forehead. Her hands were red with blood. She blinked heavily and her vision began to clear. So did her thoughts, the fog in her mind finally lifting. She stared at her deflated airbag, a blood-stain smeared over the white nylon.

What happened? she thought, trying to piece together the events that lead to the crash. The horn sounded like it was getting louder and louder. Her eardrums rattled inside her head. "Aidan, wake up!"

She turned and looked out the passenger window. All the

air left her body at once. It was there, the thing in the stag's skull, standing right beside the car, pointing straight at her. She gasped, her mouth open wide in a silent scream. The wailing horn stopped. She turned around.

Aidan was sitting upright, staring right at her. His face was red, covered in blood. "Aidan, quick, there's something out there." She grabbed hold of his arm as she turned and looked out the window.

The thing had vanished.

Laura twisted herself, looking out of every window, but there was no sight of it; it was like it had disappeared into thin air. "Aidan, we have to get out of here," Laura said as she turned to him.

Aidan stared at her with a strange smirk on his face. It startled her, made her pull away from him.

"Are you okay?"

There was a look in his eyes that she had never seen before, and it made the hairs on the back of her neck stand on end.

Aidan licked the blood from his lips. The coppery zing made his tongue tingle like he had licked a battery. Laura reached behind her, fumbling for the door handle, not daring to take her eyes off him. Finally, she felt it and clicked it open. She turned and looked up –

Aidan stood outside the car.

She managed a raspy scream before Aidan reached down and grabbed her by the throat, snuffing out her screams, and yanked her out of the car and onto the cold tarmac. Laura coughed and tried to get up, but Aidan kicked her back to the ground. "Aidan, what are you doing?" she cried out. Tears streamed down her face.

Aidan knelt down and rolled her onto her back. Laura glared up at him, illuminated in the orange glow of the streetlight, wide-eyed and full of terror. They weren't his eyes staring back at her. They were evil eyes, as black as night.

"Aidan?" she whimpered.

"Aidan's gone, for now," he said, with a dark voice that wasn't his own. "But I will make him mine, and you're going to help me."

Laura punched Aidan in the face.

He just laughed as he wiped the blood from his mouth. In a blink, he was on top of her, pinning her to the ground. Laura struggled and slapped and pushed him, but it had no effect.

"Help!" she screamed into the empty night. Aidan looked up at the sky, taking a deep breath through his nose, smelling the fear that radiated off her. It was like a drug to him, a drug that would never quench his thirst. He stared at Laura with his wicked grin and wrapped his hands tightly around her neck. Her bloodshot eyes bulged from her head; her face turned purple. His grip was vice-like and there was no weaving it. Laura choked and gagged, her legs kicking out onto the road as she struggled to fight him off. She slapped and punched at his face, but her arms grew heavy and tired. Her head throbbed with her slowing heartbeat. Darkness crept in around her. She managed one last thump against his chest before her arms dropped limply to her sides. Laura looked up at Aidan with a glazed, eternal stare as she drifted away. The throbbing in her head grew quieter and quieter until there was only silence.

When Aidan saw the life in Laura's eyes fade away, he got up off her and fixed his clothes. Something hissed in the forest surrounding the road. Aidan smiled at the trees like they were old friends. There wasn't much time left. The real Aidan would be back any minute; he could already feel the pull.

He grabbed a handful of Laura's hair and dragged her lifeless body towards the woods. Her shoe slid off her foot and rested at the side of the road. He heaved her between the trees and over roots that spread out into the forest floor like veins. The pull grew stronger. He wasn't as far into the woods as he would have liked, but he knew he was out of time. There was a shallow ditch beside a row of trees. He dumped her body and hurried back to the car. The pull screamed inside his head; he stared at himself in the rearview mirror and smiled.

"See you soon."

The blackness in his eyes faded, creeping back inside his head like retreating tentacles.

Aidan slammed his head down onto the steering wheel, sending the horn screaming into the night.

CHAPTER TWENTY-SEVEN

Aidan jolted upright with a gasp. The chilly damp of the forest floor had crept into his clothes, making his teeth rattle. The howling wind rustled the trees as tears streamed down his face. "No, no, no, no," Aidan muttered as he stared, petrified, at his trembling hands.

Lightning cracked overhead.

He looked up. Noah, Nancy and the others stood side-by-side in front of him, watching. His stomach heaved; waves of nausea washed over him. Saliva flooded his mouth, and he vomited. He wiped his mouth and pulled himself to his unsteady feet. It felt like his bones were rattling under his weight. Noah stepped forward from the line and came to Aidan. "Get the fuck away from me!" Aidan spat, taking an unsteady step back.

"There's a way," Noah said.

"What?"

"There's a way you can have her again."

"What the fuck are you talking about? She's dead. He killed her... he used *me* to kill her."

"He can bring her back, Aidan. Like he did my mother. All you have to do is join us."

Nancy and the others chanted simultaneously. "Join us.

Join us. Join us..."

Aidan's mind whirled with a million thoughts. Noah pulled the bronze blade from under his robe and held it out towards him. "The amount of blood spilled from its edge would fill oceans. It's a thing of beauty, don't you think?" Noah stared at the blade, wide-eyed, dazzled by it. "Join us and you can have Laura back, but you must give yourself to him totally and completely. There's no going back once you are part of The Order. You must learn our ways and do as we do. There are no exceptions."

He looked over his shoulder towards Jack. Aidan followed his gaze. Thunder roared in the distance. He thought of Laura. The terror on her face as her life ended at the hands of that thing wearing him like a meat suit. *Do I even have a choice?* he thought.

Reluctantly, Aidan took the blade. The weight of it in his hands suddenly made everything real. He studied it for a moment, taking in the intricate symbols carved into the metal, wondering what they all meant.

"What do I do?" Aidan whispered.

"You must sacrifice him to the Darkness."

Aidan's heart pounded like a jackhammer. *Can I really do this? Can I kill an innocent man?* he thought.

Nancy and the others split down the middle and sidestepped, creating a pathway for him. They had tied Jack to the wooden structure that only minutes ago held Bex. They hadn't strung Jack up from the ankles like they had with her. He simply had his arms tied behind his back and a rope around his chest, binding him to the wooden post. The bronze tub lay a few yards away; a pale hand hung limp over the edge, never to touch or feel again.

They discarded her like a piece of trash, Aidan thought as he dragged himself towards Jack.

Jack gazed intently as Aidan approached. The line of his

mouth tightened a little more.

Snot ran down Aidan's face, his eyes pink and puffy from the tears. He came to a stop in front of the man who had helped him, the man he had betrayed. It was just the two of them. The others were standing back at the square stone, watching, waiting.

"She's dead, isn't she?" Jack asked.

Aidan nodded.

Jack sighed. "Then you don't have a choice. You have to do it."

"But –"

"But nothing. If I was in your shoes... if I could bring Sophie back, you better believe I would do it."

Aidan smiled sadly. "If I do this, you get to be with Sophie, forever. But you'll be trapped in that house with the rest of them."

"I don't care," Jack said. He was smiling. A single tear rolled down his face. He looked up and stared at the night sky. "As long as I get to be with my Sophie again, that's all that matters to me."

Aidan leaned into his ear and whispered. "I'm sorry, Jack. I'm so sorry I brought you here. And I'm sorry that I can't... I want to give you what you need, Jack, I want to give you Sophie, but... I don't know if I can do it. I don't know if I can kill you."

"Yes, you can. It's better this way. If you don't we will both be miserable... at least this way we get what we want," Jack said, still smiling. Jack looked down at the bronze blade trembling in his hand. "Just do me one thing."

Aidan tilted his head towards him.

"Can you make it quick?"

Aidan nodded, unable to speak. Tears welled up in his eyes again. Noah came and stood beside him, holding the human skull. Blood dripped from his gory palm. He lifted the skull into the air and began chanting in that strange, dark language.

Jack closed his eyes, waiting for death.

Aidan steadied himself and gripped the blade tightly in his hands against the howling wind. His entire body felt electrified. Black smoke came from the darkness of the forest, twisting and weaving around the clearing like a huge tornado. The trees groaned and protested in their rhythmic dance.

"Thank you for your sacrifice," Aidan whispered, and with one fluid swipe Jack's throat opened up, showering Aidan in blood. Jack's eyes bulged from their sockets. Aidan couldn't look away.

Nancy danced and laughed hysterically in the background, throwing her arms in the air and spinning in circles, her hair billowing in the wind like a raging fire.

Blood poured from Jack's mouth and down his chin. His throat made horrible choking, gargling sounds as he tried to breathe. He thrashed against the ropes as he drowned in his own blood. His face grew pale and after only ten or fifteen never-ending seconds, his head dropped to his chest. Lightning crackled, scolding Nancy to silence.

Noah held the skull under Jack's open throat, filling the rest of the skull. "Drink," he said, holding the skull out to Aidan.

He took the skull and looked into the dark crimson liquid floating inside. For the first time, he wondered who the skull had belonged to. He lifted the skull towards Jack.

"Cheers," he whispered as his heart broke again.

He drank. The blood was still warm; its consistency reminded him of syrup, but it tasted like liquid copper. Aidan grimaced, wiping away the dribble that ran down his chin and smearing blood across his face. He handed Noah the skull.

Jack stood next to his body, staring at the thing hanging limp from the wooden post. He looked down at his hands and saw the forest floor through them. "Wow," he said. The trees danced in the wind, but he couldn't feel the icy breeze against his skin.

"What's it like?" Aidan asked, noticing the pain and suffering that had become ingrained in Jack's face had finally gone. Jack turned to him.

"I don't know how to explain it," he said, studying his arms and body. "You know when someone rubs a balloon on your hair and you get that... static? Well, it kind of feels like that."

From out of the twisting darkness, a woman in a long linen dress walked gracefully into the clearing. Long, blonde hair lay perfectly over her shoulders, not a strand out of place in the blistering wind. Both Aidan and Jack turned to her, unable to take their eyes off her. Noah and the others could only see Aidan turn and look at the space in the clearing. Her footsteps were soundless as she walked towards them.

The woman was beautiful, almost perfect. She looked like a goddess that someone had carved from marble, but as she got closer Aidan noticed something about her, a slip of the chisel in the masterpiece. She didn't have any eyes. Only two hollow sockets where they should have been.

"Who are you?" Jack said.

"My name is Fiona," she smiled as she stopped a couple of feet away from them. "I've come to take you to your daughter."

"You're Fiona? Fiona Wright, Nicolas's wife?"

Noah took a step towards Aidan, then stopped himself.

She turned to Aidan and lowered her head, answering his question. "You are the seer."

She turned back to Jack before Aidan could answer her. She held her hand out towards Jack. "It's time, Jack," she said.

Jack hesitated for a moment, then placed his hand in hers. He could feel her, feel the grooves of her fingers, feel the coldness of her skin. It was like touching electricity. He smiled in wonder and went to her side.

"I'll be seeing you," Jack said to Aidan. Hand in hand, Jack and Fiona walked towards the forest, fading into the darkness.

"Even in death, she serves him," Noah said, then he turned to the others. "Brother James, please step forward." He gestured to the one in the ram skull. The howling wind grew stronger. The smoke groaned and screamed as it went around the clearing. Aidan held his hand over his eyes, squinting against the wind.

The man in the ram skull stepped forward and went to the square stone. He bowed at Noah and took off his mask, placing it on top of the stone and lowered his hood. Aidan couldn't believe his eyes. It was the man from the bookstore. He lifted his arms towards the sky and began yelling something in that unknown language, then dropped to his knees, a grin stretching from ear to ear.

"I give myself to you, o Dark One!"

As soon as the words had left his lips, black, burning arms pounced from the smoke like snakes going in for the kill. The arms grabbed hold of him, covering him in shadows until his whole body was engulfed in black fire. He didn't scream or yell, he just knelt, smiling as the Darkness took him away. Ash drifted into the night air like forgotten embers until the black fire finally burned itself out, leaving no evidence that James had ever been there at all. As soon as the last piece drifted off into the dark, the wind died and the circling smoke faded away like a thin mist in a summer morning. An eerie quiet took over the clearing.

"What just happened?" Aidan asked, bewildered.

"There must always be five in The Order. He wanted you,

so he took *him*."

Knock, knock, knock.

Aidan startled and turned towards the sound.

Stood at the edge of the clearing was the crimson door. The door he'd seen in his dream. Three more ominous knocks echoed through the forest.

Noah gestured towards the door. Aidan could feel himself being pulled toward it, like a planet being pulled to a black hole.

As Aidan walked towards the crimson door, it slowly creaked open. On the other side, waiting for him, was nothing but darkness and emptiness.

Noah and the others chanted.

"We are the children of the night. The brothers and sisters of darkness. We are eternal. We are the children of the night. The brothers and sisters of darkness. We are eternal. We are the children of the night. The brothers and sisters of darkness. We are eternal." They repeated the chant over and over again. Aidan stopped at the foot of the door and stared into the abyss. He thought of Laura and, as he stepped inside the emptiness, he felt at home.

***

When Aidan came out the other side, he was standing in the living room of the Lake House. The handle of the basement door was in his hand. The fire crackled as music played from the record player in the corner.

There was someone sitting on the sofa facing away from him. Aidan's heart leapt into his throat as Laura turned and faced him.

She smiled.

CHAPTER TWENTY-EIGHT

A full moon shone brightly in the night sky like a silver coin, shining its comforting glow onto a long stretch of pitch-black road. Tall pine trees hugged it at either side so that it looked like someone had cut the road straight through the middle of the forest.

A lone car cruised along the empty road, beaming like a shooting star. There hadn't been a single streetlight for miles – or another car on the road, for that matter. A man sat behind the wheel, yawning. He couldn't remember how long he'd been on the road, but his aching buttocks told him it had been too long. He picked up the cold coffee that he had bought at least two hours ago and downed the dregs with a grimace. *Nothing worse than cold coffee,* he thought to himself. The man sat in silence in the car. The radio signal had cut out about an hour ago and there wasn't any service to play music from his phone. With a groan, he leaned forward and gazed up at the bright moon floating in the sky, basking him in its silvery glow.

Something vibrated, and dazzling blue light filled the car. The man squinted in the sudden light. It was his phone. There was a new notification.

ONE NEW VOICEMAIL.

The man slammed on the brakes, sending the tyres screeching down the tarmac. He looked at the top corner of the phone screen. Two bars. Snatching the phone from the holder suction-cupped to the windscreen, he clicked play, hoping he didn't lose signal. Static erupted through the car's speakers, followed by a man's voice.

"Will, it's Aidan. Sorry I haven't been able to get back to you. The service out here is non-existent, and the house doesn't have any WiFi. Everything's fine, so you don't need to keep worrying or come racing out here. We're all good… I love you, bro."

Will played the message again, then once more. There was something about the way Aidan sounded that didn't sit right with him. Will could hear it in his voice, in the hurried way Aidan spoke when he was anxious.

He clicked redial and Aidan's phone went straight to voicemail without even ringing. He tried Laura, but she was the same.

"Jesus Christ," Will sighed, his cheeks flushed. He locked the phone, plunging the car into darkness, and threw it onto the passenger seat. He stuck the car into first and set off down the long road.

Up ahead, the headlights lit up a road sign that read: *Elmwood 20 miles*.

"I'm coming for you, brother," Will said to himself as he roared past the sign.

He didn't notice the crow perched on top of it, watching as the red rear lights of the car faded towards town.

www.ntmorris.com